The Parliament House

The Parliament House

EDWARD MARSTON

First published in Great Britain in 2006 by
Allison & Busby Limited
13 Charlotte Mews
London W1T 4EJ
www.allisonandbusby.com

Copyright © 2006 by EDWARD MARSTON

The moral right of the author has been asserted.

A catalogue record for this book is available from
the British Library.

10 9 8 7 6 5 4 3 2 1

ISBN 0 7490 8285 2

Printed and bound in Wales by
Creative Print and Design, Ebbw Vale

Also by Edward Marston

The Christopher Redmayne Mysteries
The King's Evil
The Amorous Nightingale
The Repentant Rake
The Frost Fair

Inspector Robert Colbeck series
The Railway Detective
The Excursion Train

The Nicholas Bracewell series
The Queen's Head
The Merry Devils
The Trip to Jerusalem
The Nine Giants
The Mad Courtesan
The Silent Woman
The Roaring Boy
The Laughing Hangman

The shot came out of nowhere. He had removed his helmet to wipe away the perspiration dribbling down his face when he heard the sound of gunfire. The musket ball missed his right eye and ploughed a searing furrow along his unprotected temple. He felt as if someone had just used a hot chisel to gouge out skin and bone from the side of his head. Agony blended with fear. Blood mingled with sweat. Dropping his helmet, he tried to maintain his balance but his legs began to buckle under him. His mind was racing, his vision blurred. Sliced wide open, his right ear seemed to have trebled in size and turned into solid lead, weighing him down so hard that he keeled over and hit the ground with a thud. It was only then that he was able to let out a long, loud cry of despair.

It had all happened many years before, but Bernard Everett had never forgotten that fateful moment in September 1651, when he thought, mistakenly, that the battle was all over. He still carried the livid scar along the side of his head. Other men would have grown their hair over it or worn a periwig to hide the wound completely, but Everett bore it as a mark of honour. The ugly slit and the shattered ear were testimony to his role in a great military triumph. At the battle of Worcester, the Royalist army had been emphatically routed.

'What a day that was!' recalled Sir Julius Cheever.

'One of the proudest of my life,' said Everett.

'Even though it was very nearly your last.'

'God was there to save me, Sir Julius.'

'Had you kept it on, your helmet would have done that. And it would have left you looking a trifle prettier.'

'Who cares what I look like? We won the battle.'

'Yes,' said Sir Julius. 'That's what really mattered.'

Bernard Everett was a stocky man of middle years and medium height. His short grey hair surmounted a bulbous forehead. A pleasant face had been given a sinister quality by the hideous battle scar. Everett had served under Sir Julius Cheever in the army, and he was glad to be reunited with his old colonel. He was even more delighted by his recent election as Member of Parliament for Cambridge, a city that Oliver Cromwell, a man he revered, had represented in parliament.

Military service was not the only link between the two men. Sir Julius, too, was a Member of Parliament, representing his native county of Northamptonshire, and bringing a bold and uncompromising voice to any debate. Big, bulky, opinionated and forthright, he was sixty years old but he had lost very little of his vigour and he remembered, in precise detail, the experiences that he and Bernard Everett had shared on various battlefields during the Civil War.

'They fought well at Worcester,' he conceded, 'but we had the beating of them from the start. We had thirty thousand soldiers in the field.'

'Our army and militia were out in force,' recalled Everett.

'The Royalists were hopelessly outnumbered.'

'How many prisoners did we take, Sir Julius?'

'The best part of ten thousand,' said the other, 'in addition to the three thousand that were killed in action. Of course, we did have casualties on our side.'

Everett chuckled. 'I know – I was one of them.'

'Are you two still talking about the war?' asked Hester Polegate, clicking her tongue in disapproval. 'That's all in the past. It's time to look to the future, Bernard. Now come and see the rest of the house.'

'Gladly, Hester.'

'You, too, Sir Julius.'

Everett gave her a conciliatory kiss on the cheek. Hester Polegate was his sister, a plump woman in her late forties with a round, rosy-cheeked face and a genial manner. She took her duties as hostess very seriously. Along with others, her brother had been invited to celebrate the opening of the new business in Knightrider Street. Hester's husband, Francis Polegate, a lean, angular man, was a successful wine merchant who had been looking for new premises. He had purchased a corner site then searched for someone to design the building.

Sir Julius Cheever was a good friend of Polegate's and he had recommended a name to him. As a result, Christopher Redmayne, the young architect who had designed Sir Julius's own house in London, was given the commission. He, too, was present on the day that the merchant and his family took over their new quarters. It was a happy occasion. Christopher was not only pleased to receive endless praise from satisfied clients. He had an opportunity to spend time with the other guest, Susan Cheever, daughter of Sir Julius, the lovely young woman with whom the architect had an understanding that was slowly moving towards a formal betrothal. While everyone else was being shown around the building, he preferred to stay in the hall with Susan.

'It's a lovely house, Christopher,' she said. 'You worked hard on the plans. I'm so grateful that I'm able to see the final result. You have every right to be proud of your achievement.'

'Thank you.'

'Mr and Mrs Polegate are thrilled.'

'Yours is the only opinion I really value, Susan.'

'Then you have my unstinting approval.'

'But you haven't seen the house properly yet.'

'I don't need to,' she said. 'Everything that Christopher Redmayne designs has the hallmark of excellence.'

He laughed. Christopher was tall, lithe and handsome with long, curly hair that had a reddish tinge. Though conspicuously well-dressed, he wore none of the garish apparel that was so popular among younger men. There was an air of restraint about him that appealed to Susan. For his part, Christopher had been drawn to her from the moment they had first met. Slim and shapely, Susan had a bewitching face and the most beautiful skin he had ever seen. Sir Julius was a wealthy farmer and, for all his eminence, there was a distinctly rustic air about him. His daughter had not inherited it. She could have passed for a court beauty.

'This is the finest room in the house,' he explained, glancing around the hall. 'As you've seen, the living quarters are all on the first floor and I included a gallery that leads to further rooms over the back kitchen. The shop is at the front of the property, of course, with merchandise housed in the cellars and the warehouse. Mr Polegate imports wine from other countries so he needs plenty of space to store it. His counting house is over the main kitchen. The bedrooms are on the floor above us,' he went on, pointing upwards, 'with dormer windows in the roof – tiled, naturally. Since the Great Fire, nobody uses thatch.'

'The whole building is so compact,' she observed.

'When you have a limited area, you have to create extra height.'

'There's even a yard with its own well.'

'That's a valuable feature of the house, Susan. If it were not raining so hard,' he added, looking through the windows at the storm raging outside, 'I'd show you the yard. It's beautifully cobbled.'

'Clearly, no expense has been spared.'

'More to the point, my clients have paid both architect and builder. That's not always the case, believe me. With some projects, I've waited up to a year for my fee.'

'You should ask for more money in advance.'

'People are not always in a position to pay it.' He heard footsteps in the room above his head and moved closer to her. 'Before the others come back, I wanted to ask you about your father. Why does he seem so uncommonly contented?'

'Contented?'

'Sir Julius is truculent as a rule.'

'That's just his way, Christopher. Father is always rather blunt.'

'He's positively joyful today.'

'I think he's pleased to meet Mr Everett again.'

'It goes deeper than that,' said Christopher. 'There was a moment earlier on when I caught him standing at the window, staring out with a broad smile on his face. He was completely lost in thought. Something has obviously brought happiness into his life.'

Susan was almost brusque. 'It's not happiness,' she said with a dismissive wave of her hand. 'Father hates idleness. Now that parliament has been recalled, he'll be employed again and that's what he enjoys most. He thrives on the rough and tumble of debate.'

Christopher had a feeling that the mellowing of Sir Julius Cheever had nothing to do with parliament, an institution whose activities, more often than not, tended to enrage him beyond measure. Nor could his reunion with Bernard Everett explain his uncharacteristic mildness. It had another source. In trying to find out what it was, Christopher had unwittingly thrown Susan on the defensive. He regretted that. Not wishing to upset her any further, he abandoned the subject altogether.

Having inspected the upper rooms, the others rejoined them in the hall. Food and wine had been set out on the long oak table and a servant handed the refreshments out to the guests. Everyone was very complimentary about the house and shop. Christopher basked in their approbation. Since it was a purely functional property, it had not been the most exciting commission of his career but it had won him new admirers and would act as a clear advertisement for his talents. Sir Julius had passed on his name to Francis Polegate. Christopher hoped that Polegate would, in turn, speak up on his behalf to others.

Calling for silence, the wine merchant raised his glass.

'I think that we should toast the architect,' he said.

'The architect,' responded the others in unison. 'Mr Redmayne!'

'Thank you,' said Christopher, modestly, 'but we must not forget the builder. Without him, an architect would be lost.'

'Without you,' Polegate noted, 'a builder would be unemployed.'

'Yes,' said Sir Julius. 'You are an artist whereas he is a mere labourer, skilled enough, in his own way, but lacking the ability to conceive the house in his mind's eye. We are fortunate to get this young man, Francis,' he continued, indicating Christopher. 'He is destined for great things. In a few years, he may be well beyond our price.'

'I doubt that, Sir Julius,' said Christopher.

'You have ambitions to prosper, surely?'

'Of course.'

'And a desire to work on a grander scale?'

'In time, perhaps.'

'Then you will soon be emulating Mr Wren.'

'Emulating and surpassing him,' said Susan, loyally. 'There

will soon be only one Christopher they speak of in London and it will not be Mr Wren. He will have been eclipsed.'

'You are too kind,' said Christopher, touched by her comments. 'I like to think that I have artistic gifts but they will never compare with those of a genius. Who, in years to come, will feast his eyes on Mr Polegate's house when St Paul's cathedral has been rebuilt?'

'Hester and I will do so,' attested Polegate.

'Yes,' said his wife. 'It will always come first in our affections. Let us ask an outsider for his opinion. What do you think, Bernard?'

Everett grinned. 'This house has something that a cathedral will never have,' he pointed out. 'A wonderful wine cellar. Mr Redmayne is to be congratulated on his design.'

'Wait until you see our home,' said Sir Julius. 'It's an example of Christopher at his most inventive.'

'I thought you were taking me to the Parliament House first.'

'Ha!' Sir Julius was derisive. 'It's a den of iniquity.'

'Nevertheless, I have to take my seat there.'

'You shall take it beside me, Bernard. We could do with some more commonsense in there. Most of the members are charlatans, sycophants or ranting lunatics. The Parliament House is a species of Bedlam.'

'Yet it exercises so much power.'

'And does so very irresponsibly. My view is this, you see...'

'Why not discuss it later on?' suggested Susan, interrupting her father before he started on a diatribe. 'We are not here to talk politics.'

'No,' agreed Hester Polegate. 'We're here to celebrate.'

'Eat, drink and enjoy yourselves,' urged her husband, slipping an arm around her shoulders. 'The Polegates are at home to their friends. Have everything that you wish.'

Everett drained his glass. 'I'll have a spare key to the wine cellar.'

'Behave yourself,' chided his sister, good-naturedly.

'If I'm to lodge here when I'm in London, I can help Francis by acting as his taster. I have a most discerning palate.'

'You're not here to drink away our profits, Bernard.'

'You'll be amply repaid,' Everett joked. 'When I take my seat in parliament, I'll introduce a bill for the abolition of all import duties on wine. Sir Julius will support me – won't you?'

But the other man did not even hear him. He had drifted off into a reverie and there was a faraway smile on his lips. Christopher noticed it at once. His gaze shifted to Susan, plainly discomfited by her father's behaviour. The normally belligerent Sir Julius Cheever was acting very strangely. Christopher wondered why.

It was hours before the jollity came to an end. While the party was being held in the hall, Polegate's assistant was serving the first customers in the shop below. Both the house and business had been duly launched. Christopher Redmayne took the opportunity to conduct Susan around the property and she marvelled at some of its finer points. In designing the place for work and occupation, the architect had not wasted a single inch of space. Susan was impressed. When they returned to the hall, her father was getting ready to leave. Bernard Everett was going to share his coach so that they could call at the Parliament House together.

Christopher was sorry that the time had come to depart. He had been enjoying Susan's company so much. While she accompanied her father in the coach, the architect would have to ride home to his house in Fetter Lane. There was one consolation. The rain had eased off. Though it was still drizzling, the earlier downpour had spent its force. They would get wet but not thoroughly soaked. After a flurry of farewells, they descended to the ground floor in their coats and hats.

The coach was waiting in the street outside. Christopher escorted Susan to it and opened the door for her so that he could steal a kiss as she got in. Her smile was all the gratitude he required. Their eyes locked affectionately. Behind them, Sir Julius and Bernard Everett came into the street side by side. A voice suddenly rang out.

'Up here!'

The two men instinctively looked upwards. There was a loud report and Bernard Everett was knocked backwards as a musket ball went under the brim of his hat and burrowed deep into his skull. He was out of luck this time. There was no hope of survival. With blood gushing down his face, he landed in a puddle and splashed water everywhere.

One thing was immediately apparent.

He would never sit in the Parliament House now.

Chapter Two

Everything was suddenly thrown into confusion. Startled by the sound of the gunfire, the two horses bucked madly between the shafts and the coachman had difficulty controlling them. Christopher Redmayne, meanwhile, fearing that a second shot might be fired, dived into the lurching coach to protect Susan Cheever. Shocked by what she had just seen, Hester Polegate put her hands to her mouth to stifle a scream. Her husband rushed forward to bend over his fallen brother-in-law and Sir Julius Cheever, lacking a weapon, waved an angry fist up at a window opposite. People emerged from houses to see what had caused the commotion. A small crowd soon gathered around the dead body.

Christopher was the first to recover. Realising that Susan was not in any danger, he released her from his arms and peered through the window. Then he leapt out of the coach and went over to Sir Julius.

'What happened?' he asked.

'Some villain shot Bernard,' replied the other, purple with rage.

'From where?'

'Up there.'

Sir Julius pointed to the upstairs window of the tavern on the opposite side of the street. It was wide open but there was no sign of the killer. Christopher needed only a glance to see that Bernard Everett was dead. Curiosity was bringing more people out of their dwellings. They began to converge on the shop.

'Take him inside,' advised Christopher. 'I'll fetch a constable.'

Before doing so, however, he hoped that he might be able to apprehend the murderer. Dashing across the road, Christopher pushed through the knot of customers around the door and entered the tavern. He went into the taproom and saw the staircase against the far wall. He darted past bemused drinkers before going up the stairs to the first floor, running along a narrow passageway until he came to the last door on the right. Christopher flung it open, only to find that the room was now completely empty. Drizzle was blowing in through the open window. He went quickly across to it and gazed down at the scene below. The corpse was now being carried into the shop, away from the prying eyes of the neighbours. Hester Polegate was patently in great distress at the death of her brother. Susan Cheever had an arm around her as she helped the grieving woman inside.

Christopher went back into the passageway and saw that there was another staircase nearby. It corkscrewed its way to the floor below. Pounding down it, he came into a kitchen where an old woman was stirring something in a pot over the fire. When he popped up in front of her without warning, she turned to him with open-mouthed wonder.

'Did anyone else come through here?' he demanded.

'Yes, sir,' she croaked. 'A gentleman rushed in.'

'When?'

'Not a minute ago.'

'Which way did he leave?'

She pointed a stubby finger. 'That way, sir.'

Christopher opened a door and found himself looking at a row of stables on the other side of a cobbled yard. Nobody was there. One of the stable doors had been left ajar. He ran through a stone archway and into the street beyond, arriving just in time to hear the distant clatter of hooves as a horse galloped down Bennet's Hill towards Thames Street. Christopher caught the merest glimpse of the rider before he turned a corner and vanished from sight. Pursuit was out of the question. The killer had been calculating. He had planned his escape in advance.

Jonathan Bale had just returned home after patrolling the streets of Baynard's Castle Ward and his wife helped him off with his sodden coat. When she hung it on the back of the door, it began to drip on to the kitchen flagstones. Sarah was sympathetic.

'You must be soaked to the skin,' she said.

'A spot of rain never hurt anybody.'

'It was more than a spot, Jonathan. The storm lasted for hours.'

'We hardly noticed it,' said Bale with a shrug. 'One good thing about weather like this – it keeps villains off the streets.'

'It ought to keep *you* off the streets as well.'

'Don't fret, Sarah.'

He gave her an affectionate squeeze. Bale was a hefty man in his late thirties with a facial ugliness that his loving wife had somehow failed to notice. As one of the constables in the ward, he guarded his territory with paternal care as if its entire population belonged to his own family. His wife, Sarah, was shorter, stouter and had a bustling energy that never seemed to flag. She wished that her husband's devotion to duty were tempered with more caution. Sarah thought him too fearless for his own good. Bale lowered himself heavily on to a chair. Before he could give her an account of his day, however, there was a loud knock at the front door. He started to rise.

'Stay there,' she said, touching his shoulder. 'I'll see who it is.' When she opened the door, Sarah was pleasantly surprised. 'Why, Mr Redmayne!' she cried. 'Whatever are you doing here?'

'I'm hoping to find your husband at home,' said Christopher.

'Yes, I'm here,' called Bale, getting to his feet and coming to the door. 'What can I do for you, Mr Redmayne?'

'At least step in out of the rain,' urged Sarah.

'This is not a social visit, I fear,' explained Christopher. 'I've come to report a serious crime.' He turned to Bale. 'A murder has just been committed in Knightrider Street. You must come at once, Jonathan. I'll give you the details on the way.'

Bale did not hesitate. Going back into the kitchen, he grabbed his coat and put it on again. He thrust his hat on his head then promptly left the house. As he and Christopher walked briskly up Addle Hill, his companion told him what had happened. Bale was alarmed by the news. He and Christopher were old friends. Thrown together in an earlier murder investigation, they had solved more than one crime together and had the highest respect for each other. They were unlikely soul mates. While the architect was a man of Cavalier inclinations, the constable was a dour and implacable Puritan, who firmly believed that the restoration of the monarchy was a grotesque mistake. In the normal course of events, their paths would never even have crossed. Yet whenever they worked together, their essential differences somehow vanished.

Bale listened with interest to all that he was told.

'And you went into the tavern?' he asked.

'Yes, Jonathan. I thought that the man might still be there. But the bird had flown. He obviously had a horse, saddled and waiting.'

'Did you speak to Mrs McCoy?'

'Who?'

'Bridget McCoy. She owns the Saracen's Head.'

'I didn't have time for conversation,' said Christopher. 'As soon as I saw that the killer had fled, I came running to you.'

'I'm glad that I lived so close.'

'So am I. It meant that I knew where to find you.'

They turned into Knightrider Street and saw that a crowd was lingering outside the shop. Bale recognised a number of them. Calling him by name, he sent a boy to summon another constable. He and Christopher then went into the shop. Bernard Everett had been carried into the warehouse at the rear of the building and was laid out on a table. The women had gone upstairs but Sir Julius Cheever and Francis Polegate were standing beside the corpse, still shaken by the incident. An hour before, Everett had been a welcome guest in the house, a happy man on the brink of entering parliament. He was now a murder victim.

There was no need to introduce Bale to Sir Julius. They had met before in similar circumstances when the constable had been involved in the search for another killer, the man responsible for the death of Gabriel Cheever, the estranged son of Sir Julius. They had soon discovered a bond between them. Like Sir Julius – or, for that matter, the deceased – Jonathan Bale had borne arms at the battle of Worcester. Unlike the unfortunate Bernard Everett, he had come through it all unscathed.

'Good to see you again, Bale,' said Sir Julius, gruffly. 'We need your help. This is Mr Polegate,' he added, indicating the vintner. 'The victim is his brother-in-law.'

'So I hear,' said Bale.

'This is an appalling crime,' said Polegate, wringing his hands. 'My wife is distraught. Bernard was her only brother.' He shook his head.

'Perhaps you could describe exactly what occurred, sir.'

'I'm the best witness,' insisted Sir Julius. 'I was standing beside him when he was shot down. I actually saw the rogue at the window.'

'What else did you see?'

Sir Julius went on to give a highly emotional account of the crime and it was supplemented by a few comments from Polegate. Bale weighed all the facts at his disposal before speaking.

'You say that the weapon was a musket, Sir Julius?'

'True,' confirmed the other.

'Did you actually *see* it?'

'No – it all happened so quickly.'

'Then how can you be certain it was a musket?'

'By the sound, of course,' said Sir Julius, testily. 'I know the difference between a pistol shot and musket fire. I hear the latter far too often on my estate,' he grumbled. 'I'm plagued by poachers.'

'The shot seems to have been very accurate,' noted Bale, glancing down at the wound in Everett's forehead. 'To hit his target from that distance, he must have been something of a marksman.'

'A trained soldier, perhaps?' Christopher wondered.

'A hired killer with a black heart,' said Sir Julius.

'But why should he have shot Mr Everett?' asked Bale, raising an inquisitive eyebrow. 'And something else puzzles me. How could he be certain that the gentleman would be here?'

'I can answer that,' said Polegate. 'It was no secret that the shop was to open for business today. There's been a sign in the window for weeks. We had a party to celebrate.'

'But how did the killer know that Mr Everett would be present?'

'He's my brother-in-law. Bernard was going to stay with us.'

'That information was private,' argued Christopher. 'Nobody

outside the family could possibly have been aware of it.'

'Someone was.'

'Yes,' agreed Sir Julius, 'and he lay in wait at that window until Bernard finally made his appearance. Speak to the landlord, Bale. He'll be able to tell you who rented that room.'

'The Saracen's Head is run by a woman,' said Bale, 'and I'll talk to Mrs McCoy in due course. But I'd like to establish a motive first. Can you think of anyone with a grudge against Mr Everett?'

'No,' replied Polegate. 'Bernard had no enemies that I know of.'

'What about you, Mr Polegate?'

'Me?'

'Do you have any serious rivals?'

'Naturally. I face the heaviest competition in my trade.'

'Would any of your competitors stoop to this kind of thing?' asked Bale. 'It does seem an odd coincidence that it happened on the day that you opened your new premises. What better way to hamper your business than to leave a dead body on your doorstep? It's a bad omen.'

'I never thought of it that way,' confessed Polegate.

'The notion is certainly worth considering,' said Christopher.

Sir Julius was impatient. 'It's a mere distraction,' he asserted. 'I know why Bernard Everett was shot, and it has nothing whatsoever to do with the opening of the shop. Bernard was a man of strong convictions and he was about to bring them to bear on the Parliament House. The moment one enters politics – as I learned myself – one makes a host of vicious, merciless, unseen enemies. That's why a decent man was murdered in the street today. He was a victim of political intrigue.'

There was a tap on the door and Tom Warburton, the constable who had been sent for, entered with his dog trotting at his heels. Tall, stringy and weasel-faced, he was much older than Bale but had nothing of his authority. Whisking off his hat, he nodded to everyone present then stared wide-eyed at the corpse.

'Who's that, Jonathan?' he said.

'Mr Everett,' returned the other. 'We need to take him to the coroner, then we must seek a grant of hue and cry. A heinous crime has been committed under our noses, Tom, and we must solve it quickly.'

'There'll be a reward if you do that,' volunteered Polegate.

'I'll double it,' promised Sir Julius. 'As for the body, it can be conveyed in my coach. But, first, disperse that collection of ghouls outside. Respect for the dead is the least that we can ask.'

Christopher watched while the constables did as they were told. He then helped to carry the body out and lay it gently on the floor of the coach. Before clambering into the vehicle himself, Sir Julius ordered his coachman to drive very slowly to their destination. Bale and Warburton plodded side by side in its wake but the dog scampered irreverently between the wheels, blithely unconcerned with the solemnity of the procession. The rain had finally stopped. It was scant consolation.

Anxious to see Susan again, Christopher reasoned that she would be preoccupied with comforting Hester Polegate over the loss of her brother. It would be wrong to intrude. In any case, Christopher wanted to assist the murder inquiry and he could think of one obvious way that he might do that. Retrieving his horse, he hauled himself up into the saddle and trotted away. The crime had cast a dark shadow over the house he had designed. Until it was solved, he would never be able to look at the building with real satisfaction again.

Henry Redmayne was in a bad mood. His superior at the Navy Office had chastised him at length that morning. His physician had told him to drink far less and exercise far more. His tailor had failed to deliver his new suit on time. And – compounding his misery – the young lady whom Henry had been courting so sedulously for weeks had succumbed to an attack of marital fidelity, spurning his advances in the most hurtful way before returning to the arms of her undeserving husband. Henry was thoroughly piqued. The servants at his house in Bedford Street had the sense to keep well out of his way.

He was still nursing his wounds when his brother arrived. Draped across a couch, Henry did not even get up when Christopher was shown into the room. A sigh of discontent was all that he could rise to by way of a welcome. Christopher identified the telltale signs at once.

'Who is the lady *this* time, Henry?' he asked, wearily.

'I would not soil my tongue by naming her.'

'Yet you pursued her with your usual tenacity, I daresay.'

'Sheer folly on my part,' said Henry. 'I should have known better than to choose such an unworthy creature. She was utterly beneath me. And since she refuses to *be* beneath me in a bedchamber, I am liberated from an attachment that could only have tarnished my reputation.'

'It's tarnished enough already by now.'

Henry sat up. 'I expect sympathy from my brother, not mockery.'

'Then leave off this show of self-pity,' said Christopher.

'Is that all you have to say to me?'

'No, I've come in search of a favour.'

'Then search elsewhere!'

Arms folded, the elder brother turned petulantly away. Only a few years separated them but Henry looked much older. Dissipation had added untold years to his age, hollowing his cheeks and leaving dark pouches beneath his eyes. His face had a deathly pallor and, since he had cast his periwig aside, his balding pate completed the destruction of what had once been handsome features. Ostentatious by nature, Henry could still cut a dash when dressed in his finery and puffed up with an aristocratic arrogance. Now, however, he looked like a rag doll cast aside by an indifferent child. Christopher sat beside him and gave him a compassionate pat on the knee. All that he got in return was a glare of hostility.

'Come now, Henry,' he encouraged. 'Whatever your tribulations, you must rise above them. Display the true Redmayne spirit.'

'I've forgotten what that is, Christopher.'

'Perseverance is our watchword.'

'Bah!'

'Imagine what our father would do in the same circumstances.'

Henry let out a wild laugh. 'Our father?' he exclaimed. 'I don't think that the old gentleman could ever have been in such a position as I find myself. The Church of England would be rocked to its foundations if it learned that one of its holiest prelates had been pursuing a married woman with the ardour that I've shown this past month. The kind of impassioned language that I've been using to her would not be found in the Book of Common Prayer, I assure you. Father is a saint. He would never dare to stray from the strait and narrow. I – thank heaven – have never been in the slightest danger of finding it.'

'Perhaps the time has come for you to mend your ways.'

'Unthinkable!'

Henry was defiant. Blessed with a sinecure at the Navy Office, he also enjoyed a handsome allowance from their father. The pious dean of Gloucester cathedral, a man of private wealth and high moral principle, did not realise that he was supporting an existence that was freely dedicated to every vice in the city. Christopher Redmayne was a conscientious architect, striving to make his mark. Henry, by contrast, was a confirmed rake. Yet he could sometimes be useful to his younger brother. Moving in court circles, and befriended by those sharing his decadent tastes, Henry knew almost everyone of consequence in London.

'What's this about help, Christopher?' he asked. 'If you've come in search of money, I've none to lend you. As a matter of fact, I'd like to borrow some from you – just enough to keep penury at bay.'

'You've not repaid the last loan I gave you.'

'Brothers are brothers. Let's have no talk of "loans". We share and share alike. My purse is ever open to you.'

'Only so that I can fill it yet again,' said Christopher, wryly. 'But enough of that – I'm here on more serious business. A foul murder occurred earlier on. I was there at the time.'

As he listened to the description of events in Knightrider Street, Henry was torn between interest and derision. When the name of Sir Julius Cheever was mentioned, he curled his lip.

'*Sir* Julius!' he said with a sneer. 'The fellow is nothing but an ignorant farmer who got his knighthood from that vile monster, Oliver Cromwell. If it were left to me, such freaks would be stripped of their titles forthwith. They were illegally bestowed.'

Christopher did not rise to the argument. There was no point in antagonising Henry by challenging his opinions. To get any assistance from him, his brother had to be wooed, and that meant showing tolerance in the face of his many prejudices. Christopher was patient.

'How is Sir Julius viewed in the Parliament House?' he asked.

'With appropriate disgust.'

'I'm told that he is a forceful speaker.'

'Empty vessels make the most noise.'

'What of Bernard Everett?'

'The name is new to me,' said Henry, disdainfully, 'but, if he is another renegade from Cambridgeshire, I'll not shed a tear for him. We've had trouble enough from that part of England.'

'Others in the Parliament House might think the same.'

'They'd not have welcomed a friend of Sir Julius Cheever.'

'Why not?'

'Because he'd have shared the same damnable republican views. Parliament is a jungle,' said Henry, warming to his theme. 'It's full of conniving groups, factions, clubs and temporary alliances. There's a party that supports the King, another that favours his brother, the Duke of York, and a third from the country that opposes both with equal vehemence.'

'Sir Julius will belong to the country party, then.'

'It is not as simple as that, Christopher. Within each party are many smaller groups whose loyalties are constantly shifting. Look what happened to our once-revered Chancellor,' he went on. 'The Earl of Clarendon wielded enormous power until the Members of Parliament joined together in a ravenous wolf pack and tore him to shreds. By God – he's the Duke of York's father-in-law but even that did not save him.'

'I know,' said Christopher. 'Clarendon was not only impeached, he was exiled from the kingdom. His fall from grace was absolute.'

'Sir Julius Cheever was one of the wolves who brought it about.'

'He could never admire such a staunch Royalist.'

'There are still plenty of those to be found,' affirmed Henry, moved by patriotic impulse, 'and I am one of them. So, I trust, are you.'

'Of course,' said Christopher, readily. 'At the Restoration, I threw my hat as high in the air as anyone. I owe full obedience to the Crown.'

'Then why do you consort with those who would overthrow it?'

'Oh, I think that Sir Julius is reconciled to the idea of monarchy.'

'That's not what I hear.'

'Indeed?'

'He and his confederates are plotting rebellion.'

'Surely not.'

'Sir Julius has gathered other firebrands around him.'

'Bernard Everett was no firebrand – I met him, Henry. I took him to be a most amenable gentleman.'

'What you met was his public face, the one he wore to beguile and deceive. In private, I venture to suggest,' said Henry, raising a finger, 'he was a fellow of a very different stripe. Everett was another skulking Roundhead and it cost him his life. Look no further for an explanation of his murder, Christopher. I can tell you exactly why he was killed.'

'Can you?'

'He had been recruited by Sir Julius Cheever to depose the King.'

Jonathan Bale was familiar with all the taverns and ordinaries in his ward. Much of the petty crime with which he had to deal came from such places. Peaceful citizens turned into roaring demons when too much drink was taken. Law-abiding men could be seized with the desire to wreak havoc. Bale had lost count of the number of tavern brawls he had broken up over the years, or the number of violent drunkards, male and female, he had arrested. The Saracen's Head in Knightrider Street caused less trouble than most. It permitted none of the games of chance that bedevilled other establishments, and prostitutes were not allowed to ply their trade there.

Bridget McCoy kept a very watchful eye on her premises.

'When did he arrive here, Mrs McCoy?'

'This morning.'

'What did he say?' asked Bale.

'He wanted a room for one night that overlooked the street.'

'Knightrider Street, you mean?'

'Yes, Mr Bale, even though our best room is on Bennet's Hill.'

'Did you tell him that?'

'Of course.'

'But he still chose the other room. Did he say why?'

'I didn't ask,' said Bridget. 'When someone wishes to lodge here, I try to give them what they want. It's a small room but I keep it very clean. He said that it would be ideal for him and he paid me there and then.' She bit her lip. 'I hate to think that I was helping him to commit a murder. He seemed such a quiet man.'

Bridget McCoy had been outraged that her tavern had been used as a vantage point by a ruthless killer. There were occasional scuffles among her customers and pickpockets had been known to drift in from time to time, but the Saracen's Head had never been tainted by a serious crime before. It upset her. She was a short, compact Irishwoman with a surging bosom that made her seem much bigger than she really was, and a tongue sharp enough to cut through timber. Talking to the constable, she had a soft, melodious, Irish lilt. Raised in anger, however, the voice of Bridget McCoy, hardened by years in the trade and seasoned with the ripest language, could quell any affray.

'Did he tell you his name, Mrs McCoy?'

'Field. His name was Mr Field.'

'No Christian name?'

'He gave none.'

'How would you describe him?'

'He was a big man, Mr Bale, with something of your build. Older than you, I'd say, and with a broken nose. But it was a pleasant face,' she added, 'or so I thought. And I spend every day looking into the faces of strangers. Mr Field had a kind smile.'

'He showed his victim no kindness,' remarked Bale, sharply.

'How much did you see of him?'

'Very little. Once I showed him to his room, he stayed there.'

'Biding his time.'

'How was I to know that?' she said, defensively. 'If I'd understood what business he was about – God help me – I'd never have let him set foot over the threshold. The Saracen's Head has high standards.'

'You were not to blame, Mrs McCoy.'

'I feel that I was.'

'How?'

'By letting that devil take a room here.'

'That's your livelihood. Customers rent accommodation. Once they hire a room, you are not responsible for what they do in it.'

'I am, if they break the law,' she said with a grimace. 'I should have sensed that something was amiss, Mr Bale. I should have sounded him out a little more. My dear husband would have smelled a rat.'

'Patrick, alas, is no longer with us.'

'More's the pity. He'd have been first to join the hue and cry.'

'You are still a valuable witness,' Bale told her. 'You met the man face to face. You weighed him up.'

'Not well enough, it seems.'

'Did anyone else here set eyes on him?'

'Only Nan, my cook. He ran past her in the kitchen when he made his escape. It gave her quite a start.'

'I'm not surprised,' said Bale. 'We may need to call on both of you at a later stage to help to identify him. Do you think that you'd be able to recognise Mr Field again?'

'I'd pick that face out of a thousand.'

'Good.'

'Recognise him?' she howled, quivering with fury. 'Recognise that broken-nosed rogue? I'll never forget the slimy, stinking, turd-faced, double-dealing son of a diseased whore. May the rotten bastard roast in Hell for all eternity!'

'He will, Mrs McCoy,' said Bale, calmly. 'He will.'

Chapter Three

Christopher Redmayne waited until the next day before calling on them. In the interim, he had spoken with a couple of people to whom his brother, Henry, had introduced him, veteran politicians who had sat in the House of Commons long enough to become familiar with its deadly currents and treacherous eddies. Neither of them had spoken kindly of Sir Julius Cheever and Christopher had, of necessity, to conceal the fact that they were talking about the man whom he hoped would one day be his father-in-law. His brief researches into the murky world of politics had been chastening. When he rode towards Westminster in bright sunshine that morning, Christopher was unusually subdued.

His spirits revived as soon as the house came into view. It had been built for Sir Julius so that he could have a base in the city during periods when parliament was sitting, or when he wished to spend time with his other daughter, Brilliana, who lived in Richmond. The property was neither large nor particularly striking but it had a double significance for the architect. It had been the first substantial commission he had gained without the aid of his brother and, as such, marked the beginning of his independence. Previous work had always come his way because Henry had used his influence with various friends. By no stretch of the imagination could Sir Julius be looked upon as a friend – or even a nodding acquaintance – of Henry Redmayne.

But the house had a much more powerful claim to a place in Christopher's heart. It was the catalyst for the meeting between him and Susan Cheever, a relationship that had begun with casual interest before developing into a firm friendship, then gradually evolving into something far deeper. The promise of seeing her again made him sit up in the saddle and straighten his shoulders. He just wished that he could be bringing happier tidings on his visit.

Arriving at the house, he met with disappointment. Sir Julius was not there. It gave him a welcome opportunity to speak alone with Susan but it was her father whom he had really come to see.

'What time will Sir Julius return?' he asked.

'Not until late this afternoon.'

'In that case, I may have to call back.'

'Why?' said Susan. 'Do you have a message for him?'

'Yes, I do.'

'Can you not trust me to pass it on?'

'I'd prefer to speak to him myself,' said Christopher, not wishing to alarm her by confiding what he had discovered. 'Meanwhile, I can have the pleasure of spending a little time with you.'

She gave a wan smile. 'It's hardly an occasion for pleasure.'

'Quite so. What happened yesterday was appalling.'

'I still cannot believe it, Christopher.'

'No more can I. It had been such a joyous occasion for all of us. Then, in a flash, it turned into tragedy. How is Mrs Polegate bearing up?'

'Indifferently well. Mr Everett was very dear to her.'

'It was kind of you to offer some comfort, Susan.'

'I stayed there for hours but I could not ease the pain of her bereavement. Mrs Polegate was inconsolable. The only thing that might take the edge off her grief is the arrest of the man who killed her brother.'

'Jonathan Bale and I will do all we can to find him.'

They were in the parlour of the house, a room that reflected the taste of the client rather than that of the architect. Sir Julius had been the most decisive employer that Christopher had ever had, knowing exactly what he wanted from the start. That brought advantages and disadvantages. The main benefit was that valuable time had been saved because there had been none of the endless prevarication that made other clients so frustrating. On the debit side, however, was the fact that Christopher had to agree to an interior design that was serviceable while also being totally out of fashion. Even when seated beside the woman he loved, he was aware of how much more intrinsically appealing the room could have been had he been given his head.

Gazing fondly into her eyes, he forgot all other problems.

'These past couple of months have been wonderful,' he said.

'Have they?'

'Of course, Susan. I've been able to see so much of you.'

'That's been the saving grace of our visits,' she confessed.

'Don't you *enjoy* coming to London?'

'Only if I can see you, Christopher. As you know, I'm a country girl at heart. We may have St James's Park on our doorstep, but it's not the same as being surrounded by thousands of acres of land.'

'There are plenty of fine estates on the outskirts of the city.'

'But none that I'd exchange for the one we already own.'

'What about your father?' asked Christopher. 'He used to describe the capital as a veritable cesspool. His exact words, if I recall them aright, were that London is a swamp of crime and corruption.'

'He still holds to that view.'

'Then why has he spent so much time here recently?'

'Commitments of a political nature.'

'But the House of Commons has not been sitting.'

'Father doesn't confine his activities to the Parliament House,' she said. 'He claims that the most fruitful debates take place outside it. He's gathered a small group of like-minded men around him.'

'Men like Bernard Everett, for example?'

'Yes, Christopher. As soon as he was elected, he paid us a visit in Northamptonshire. He and father discussed political affairs all night.'

'That must have been very tiresome for you, Susan.'

'It's worse when we come here.'

'Is it?'

'Far worse,' she complained. 'There are evenings when the whole house seems to echo with political gossip. They talk about who's rising in power, who's likely to fall, how this objective can be best achieved and that one cunningly blocked, how the King exercises too much sway over the House of Commons and how his brother is an even more dangerous threat to civil liberty.'

Christopher laughed. 'Someone has been eavesdropping, I see.'

'What else can I do when the place has been invaded like that?'

'How many people attend these meetings?'

'Five or six, as a rule.'

'And your father is the acknowledged leader?'

'The habit of command is a difficult thing to break. Father likes to be in charge. Oh, I'm sure that they have worthy aims and pursue them with due sincerity,' she conceded, 'but it makes for some dull evenings from my point of view. I foolishly assumed that you had designed a London home for us.'

'That's precisely what I did do.'

'No, Christopher. This is merely another Parliament House.'

'Then we'll have to devise more ways to get you out of it.'

'I'd be so grateful.'

'I hadn't realised that it was matters of government that had drawn your father back here so much. It crossed my mind that the city held some other attraction for him.'

Susan bridled slightly. 'What can you mean?'

'Nothing, nothing,' he said, seeing her reaction and regretting his comment. 'I was obviously mistaken.'

'You were, I assure you. Father is eager for political advancement. He will not get that by languishing on his estate in Northamptonshire. Friends have to be seen, ideas discussed, plans agreed. There's never a day when he's not engaged in some aspect of parliamentary work.'

'Is that where he is now, Susan?'

'Of course,' she said with an unaccustomed edge to her voice. 'Father is dining with a close political ally.'

'I thank the Lord that you have no interest whatsoever in affairs of state,' said Sir Julius Cheever, beaming at her. 'That would have been disastrous.'

'Why?'

'Because, dear lady, we would never have agreed.'

'I cannot imagine our disagreeing about anything, Sir Julius,' she said, sweetly, 'for you are the most agreeable man I've ever met.'

He chortled. 'Nobody has ever described me as agreeable before.'

'Nobody else has ever divined your true nature.'

Dorothy Kitson was a handsome woman in her early forties with the kind of sculptured features that only improved with age. Twice widowed, she had inherited considerable wealth on each occasion but it had made her neither extravagant nor overbearing. She had remained the quiet, intelligent, unassuming woman she had always been and, while she had had many suitors, none had been treated as serious contenders for her hand. That, at least, was the situation until Sir Julius had come into her life. He was so unlike anybody she had ever met before that she found him intriguing.

They were dining together at his favourite establishment in Covent Garden, a place that combined excellent food with a degree of privacy not usually found elsewhere. Clearly enchanted with her, Sir Julius wanted Dorothy Kitson entirely to himself. Having started with oysters, they had a hash of rabbits and lamb before moving on to a chine of beef, all of it accompanied by a plentiful supply of wine. Since his guest ate and drank in moderation, Sir Julius reined in his own appetite as well.

'I bless the man who organised the races at Newmarket that day,' he said, raising his glass. 'He made it possible for me to meet you.'

'It was only by accident that I was present, Sir Julius. I had planned to spend the day in the city but my brother insisted that I go with him to Newmarket as he had a horse running there.'

'Then my blessing on your brother as well.'

'As it happened, his filly won the race.'

'It was not the only winner that day,' he said, gallantly.

'Thank you.'

'Once I'd seen you, Dorothy, I lost all interest in horses.'

She smiled. 'I'm not sure that I appreciate the way that you put that,' she said, touching his hand, 'but the thought is a kind one.'

'I meant no offence,' he insisted.

'None was taken.'

'Then you'll agree to come to Newmarket with me again one day?'

'Only if you consent to watch the horses this time.'

They shared a laugh then sipped their wine. The change that had come over Sir Julius was remarkable. In place of his blunt demeanour and combative manner was a tenderness that seemed wholly out of character. He never once raised his voice, never once lost his temper. In the company of Dorothy Kitson, he was restrained and gentlemanly. His battered face was permanently wreathed in smiles. She, too, was plainly relishing every moment of their time together but not without a trace of guilt. Dorothy waited until the plates had been cleared away before leaning in closer to him.

'You've been very considerate, Sir Julius,' she said, quietly, 'but you do not have to hold back on my account.'

'I've not held back, dear lady. I've eaten my fill.'

'I was not talking about the meal. You came here today with a heavy heart, and I know the cause. My brother is a magistrate, remember. Whenever a serious crime is committed, news of it soon reaches Orlando's ears.'

His face clouded. 'He's told you about it, then?'

'Yes. I'm so terribly sorry.'

'Thank you.'

'An innocent man, shot down in broad daylight – it's frightening. It must have been a dreadful shock for you to lose a friend in such hideous circumstances. The wonder is that you did not postpone a meeting with me so that you could mourn him properly.'

'I'd never dream of doing that, Dorothy.'

'I could have waited for a more appropriate time.'

'Every second spent with you is appropriate,' he said with clumsy affection. 'In dining with you, I show no disrespect to Bernard. He will ever be in my thoughts.'

'Did he have a family?'

'A wife and three children.'

'This will be a fearful blow to them.'

'I advised Francis Polegate not to send word by letter. Such bad tidings ought to be delivered in person so that he can soften their impact and offer condolences. He rode off to Cambridge this morning.'

'Where will the funeral be held?' she asked.

'At Bernard's parish church,' he replied. 'I've taken it upon myself to arrange the transfer of the body when the coroner releases it.'

'That's very considerate of you.'

'He was a good friend, Dorothy. He'd have done the same for me.'

'Heaven forbid!'

The arrival of the next course prompted them to change the subject. They talked about their first meeting at Newmarket races and noted how many happy times they had spent together since. Sir Julius was eager to see even more of her but Dorothy was cautious. Feeling that their friendship was moving at a comfortable pace, she was content to leave things as they were. At the same time, however, she did believe that one important step could now be taken.

'When will I be able meet your family, Sir Julius?' she said.

'As soon as you wish,' he told her, delighted at what he perceived as a real advance. 'My younger daughter, Susan, lives with me and is in our London abode even as we speak.'

'She has not yet married, then?'

'No, Dorothy.'

'Does she have prospects?'

'Yes, she is being courted by the young man who designed our house here. The problem is that Susan will not commit herself wholly to him while she has to look after her aged and infirm father.'

'You're neither aged nor infirm, Sir Julius.'

'My daughter treats me as if I were.'

'How will she respond when she is introduced to me?'

'Susan will be unfailingly polite,' he said, 'but you will still need to win her over. She's rather possessive, you see. Though I may be her father, she sometimes treats me like an errant child. I mean that as no criticism,' he added, quickly. 'Susan is very dutiful. When my dear wife died, it was she who took on the task of caring for me.'

'What about your other daughter?'

'Brilliana?'

'Was it not her place to look after you?'

'It never even crossed her mind.'

'Why not?'

'Because she had other imperatives in her life,' he explained. 'My daughters are like chalk and cheese, so unlike every particular. Susan is selfless and tender-hearted – Brilliana has inherited my defects.'

'I refuse to believe that you have any.'

'Oh, I do, alas. I can be headstrong and stubborn at times. Outspoken, too. Above all else, I like to have my own way. In those regards, Brilliana takes after her father.'

'How will she look upon me?'

'With utter amazement.'

She stifled a laugh. 'Am I such a freak, then?'

'No, Dorothy,' he said, taking her hand, 'you are the most remarkable woman in London and, therefore, Brilliana will refuse to accept that her gnarled old oak tree of a father could hold the slightest attraction for you.'

'Then I will have to convince her otherwise,' she resolved. 'I look forward to meeting your daughters, Sir Julius. The younger one sounds like a paragon of virtue, and, in spite of what you say, I'm sure that the elder has many fine qualities. I like them both already.'

'And they are certain to like *you* – in time.'

Brilliana Serle looked at herself in the mirror as she tied her hat in place, tilting it at a slight angle to give her a more roguish look. Now in her early thirties, she was a woman of startling beauty enhanced by clothing of the very highest price and quality. Her husband, Lancelot, came into the hall and stood behind her.

'Do we really need to go to London today?' he asked.

'We do.'

'But I have business in hand here, Brilliana.'

'Then it can wait,' she said with a peremptory wave of her hand. 'You read that letter from my sister. She and Father had a distressing experience yesterday. They saw a friend murdered before their eyes in the street. They require solace. I'd be failing in my duty if I did not instantly repair to the city to provide it.'

'Can you not go without me?'

'No, Lancelot.'

There was a note of finality in her voice that he did not dare to challenge. Lancelot Serle was a tall, spare, nervous individual with features that could have been accounted handsome but for the blemish on his cheek. The little birthmark was all the more visible against the whiteness of his skin, and looked, at first glance, like a blob of raspberry preserve that he had forgotten to wipe away. There was, however, no blemish on his financial situation. He was a man of substance with a palatial house set in the middle of a vast estate. His combination of wealth, social position and readiness to obey Brilliana's every whim had made him an irresistible choice as a husband.

'We do not want to be in the way, my love,' he said.

'What a nonsensical idea!' she exclaimed, rounding on him. 'We are family, Lancelot. We could never be in the way.'

'I do not recall that Susan actually solicited your help.'

'Then why else did she write to me?'

'Merely to keep you informed.'

'I know when I am being summoned, so let's have no more evasion. The chest is packed, the coach is ready and we are going to drive to London. After all,' she said, leading the way to the front door, 'it will not only be a case of offering our commiserations.'

'Oh?'

'We can satisfy our curiosity at the same time.'

'About what?'

She stamped a foot. 'Really! Do you listen to nothing I say?'

'I do little else, Brilliana.'

'Then you must surely recall that father has befriended a lady, a certain Mrs Dorothy Kitson.'

'I recall mention of her,' he said, following her out of the house, 'but I assumed that the relationship would have expired by now. With respect to my father-in-law, he's a most unlikely suitor.

The roughness of his tongue would put any woman to flight within a week.'

'He seems to have curbed that roughness. I want to know why.'

The footman was waiting by the door of the coach and she took his hand so that he could help her into the vehicle. While she settled down and adjusted the folds of her dress, her husband took the seat opposite her so that he would travel backwards. Serle wore exquisite apparel but he could not compete with her finery or with the array of jewellery that set it off. A whip cracked above them and the horses pulled the carriage in a semicircle. They were soon rolling steadily up a long drive through an arcade of poplars.

'How much do we know about Mrs Kitson?' he asked.

'Precious little.'

'Has your sister actually met the lady?'

'Not yet – but Susan has grave reservations about her.'

'Why?'

'Because she has led Father to tell so many lies.'

'Lies!' He was astonished. 'That's quite unlike him. Sir Julius is the most honest man alive. Far too honest, in my opinion, for he blurts out things that should best be left unsaid in civilised company.' Serle was rueful. 'I've suffered a great deal at the hands of your father's famous honesty.'

'Then you should not annoy him so much.'

'My very existence is a source of annoyance to him.'

'You were my choice as a husband,' she said, briskly, 'and not his. You have merits that are not visible to the naked eye and I cherish each one of them.'

He was pleased. 'Do you, Brilliana?'

'You're a man of hidden qualities, Lancelot.'

'Thank you,' he said, basking in a rare compliment from her.

She did not allow him to savour the moment for long.

'By the same token,' she resumed, 'you have shortcomings that are imperceptible at first sight but that slowly emerge on closer acquaintance. I see it as my task in life to remedy those shortcomings.'

'I study to improve myself, Brilliana.'

'Then assert yourself more. Do not be so easily cowed into silence. Whenever you meet your father-in-law, you hardly ever say a word.'

'He gives me no opportunity to do so.'

'*Make* an opportunity, Lancelot,' she urged. 'You bear the name of a noble knight. Display some knightly heroism. When we are in Father's company, seize the conversation with both hands.'

'That's easier said than done.'

'You'll earn his respect, if you do. And in time, I trust, you'll have enough confidence to follow in his footsteps.'

'What do you mean?'

'You must go into politics,' she decreed. 'You have money and position enough but you lack even a semblance of power. I want a husband of mine to guide the fate of the nation. If my father can become a Member of Parliament, so can you.'

'But I disagree with everything that he stands for, Brilliana.'

'Then oppose him vigorously in the House of Commons. Stand up for your principles. Proclaim them with a full voice.'

Serle lapsed into a brooding silence. Since he first became involved with the Cheever family, the one thing he had never been allowed to do was to express his opinions with any degree of freedom. His wife muffled him and his father-in-law terrified him. As an unswerving Royalist, he had learned to button his lip whenever Sir Julius sounded off about the depravity of the court and the blatant unfitness of the King to reign. The thought of crossing verbal swords with the old man in the Parliament House made him shudder inwardly.

'Coming back to your earlier remark,' he said, finding the strength to speak again, 'what's this about your father telling lies?'

'He would probably call them excuses.'

'For what?'

'Concealing the fact that he is seeing so much of Mrs Kitson,' she pointed out. 'Whenever he leaves the house, he tells Susan that he is to meet other politicians but she knows that it is simply not true. Father has arranged clandestine meetings with his new friend.'

'Is he so ashamed of the lady?'

'On the contrary, Lancelot. He is inordinately proud of her. Susan can see it in his face and hear it in his voice. Yet he pretends that nothing is amiss. I'd not stand for such subterfuge,' she said, smacking his knee for effect. 'That's why I intend to do what Susan has so far been unable to do herself.'

'And what's that, Brilliana?'

'Confront him. Tax him. Bully the truth out of him, if need be.'

'Sir Julius will not be easily bullied.'

'That's why I may need to call on you.'

Serle winced. 'Me?'

'Father will see me as an interfering daughter, but you can speak to him man to man. You can probe for information, Lancelot. You can catch him unawares.'

'I've never managed to do so before.'

'Then see this as a test of your mettle,' she said, firmly. 'Susan and I need to know what is going on and you are the person to find out. If we cannot wrest anything out of him, you must use your wiles.'

'But I *have* no wiles, Brilliana.'

'Exactly. When you speak to him, Father will be completely off guard. He will not suspect you for a moment. Take advantage of that, Lancelot. Beat him at his own game and use political wiles against him. Prove yourself to me,' she exhorted with sudden passion. 'Will you become the husband that I know you can be?'

He nodded willingly but his heart was a giant butterfly.

Sir Julius Cheever returned to his house in Westminster in buoyant mood. As soon as he came in through the door, Susan knew that he had dined with Dorothy Kitson. She gave him a token kiss of welcome then she pointed in the direction of the parlour.

'Christopher is waiting to see you.'

'Christopher Redmayne?' he asked.

'Yes, Father. He called this morning after you had left. I suggested that he came back later this afternoon.' She shot him a reproving look. 'Though I did not expect it to be quite this late.'

'I'd better go and speak to him.'

He opened the door of the parlour and went in. Christopher rose from his seat but was immediately waved back into it. Sir Julius lowered himself into a chair opposite him.

'I take it that you've come about yesterday's sad event,' he said.

'Yes, Sir Julius.'

'Has any progress been made?'

'Not as yet,' replied Christopher, 'but it will be.'

'Bale is a good man. He'll not let us down. And I know that you have the instincts of a bloodhound as well, Christopher.'

'We'll find the villain between us.'

'I'm counting on it.'

Sir Julius's voice was stern yet he had not altogether shed his air of contentment. A smile still hovered around his mouth and his eyes sparkled. Christopher was puzzled. Whenever the older man had returned from a heady political discussion before, he had always been roused to a pitch of excitement. If he had dined with a parliamentary colleague, he should be highly animated. Instead, he was curiously happy and relaxed. Christopher had never seen him so tranquil before. He was sorry that he would have to disturb that tranquillity.

'I've been talking with my brother,' he began.

'There's nothing unusual in that, surely?'

'We spoke about you, Sir Julius.'

'Oh? To what end?'

'Henry has a wide circle of friends, not all of them entirely suitable, as it happens. But he's well-known at court and numbers several politicians among his intimates.'

Sir Julius frowned. 'Supporters of the King no doubt.'

'Denizens of the Parliament House,' said Christopher. 'Men who know the very nerves of state and who keep a close eye on each new faction that comes into being.'

'So?'

'Is it true that you have formed your own club?'

'That's my business,' said the other, curtly.

'I've been forced to make it mine.'

'Don't meddle in things you don't understand.'

'I understand danger when I catch a whiff of it.'

'What are you taking about?'

'You, Sir Julius,' said Christopher, sitting forward. 'Everyone I've spoken to has told me the same thing. You've been gathering men around you who share your aims and values. Susan has confirmed it. According to her, you hold meetings in this house that—'

'Enough!' shouted Sir Julius, getting to his feet. 'What happens under this roof is entirely my own affair.'

'I disagree.'

'Then you are being impertinent.'

'No, Sir Julius,' said Christopher, rising from his chair.

'And you begin to irritate me.'

'What happens in this house may be your own affair but yesterday, as we both well know, it spilled out into Knightrider Street.'

'Nobody regrets that more than I do.'

'It's a cause for fear rather than regret.'

'Fear?'

'Yes,' said Christopher with passion. 'Bernard Everett was an able man who might in time have caught the eye in the Parliament House. You, however, have already established your worth, so much so that you have attracted disciples.'

'I do not follow your argument.'

'Remember the weather.'

'The weather?'

'It was raining when we left that house yesterday. You and Mr Everett wore similar coats and hats. From a window in the Saracen's Head, it would have been impossible to tell you apart.'

'Someone apparently did so.'

'No,' declared Christopher. 'He made a mistake. From everything I've learned since then, I'm absolutely convinced of it. *You* were the intended victim. That man was hired to kill Sir Julius Cheever.'

He was momentarily stunned. It had never crossed Sir Julius Cheever's mind that his own life had been at risk in Knightrider Street. Since his friend had been killed so expertly with a single shot, he had assumed that Bernard Everett was the designated target. Now, he was forced to consider the possibility that he himself might have been murdered in cold blood on the previous day. He did not ponder for long. Having briefly looked at the evidence, he dismissed the idea completely, like a horse flicking its tail to rid itself of a troublesome insect.

'No,' he decided. 'I simply refuse to believe that.'

'Mr Everett did not pose a threat,' argued Christopher. 'You do, Sir Julius. You make your presence felt in the House of Commons.'

'That's why I was elected.'

'Your views are not universally popular.'

'I did not enter parliament in search of popularity.'

'You're a natural leader. Others are drawn to you.'

'Fortunately, there are still some men of integrity left in England. Bernard was one of them. He would have been a welcome addition to our little group.'

'That group would soon disappear if you were assassinated.'

'It will take more than some villain in the window of a tavern to get rid of me,' said Sir Julius, thrusting out a pugnacious jaw. 'Besides, I'm not persuaded that the crime has anything to do with me. There may be other reasons why Bernard was shot. We know little about his private life. It's not inconceivable that someone bore him a grudge.'

'No,' admitted Christopher, 'but it seems highly unlikely that they would wait until Mr Everett came to London before striking at him. If he has enemies in his home county, they would surely attack him there. I'm still strongly of the opinion that *you* were supposed to be the victim and that raises a worrying prospect.'

'Does it?'

'Having failed once, the killer will try again.'

'Upon my soul!' cried Sir Julius with exasperation. 'I don't know what nonsense your brother has put into your head but I'd advise you to forget every last stupid syllable of it.'

'Henry is very well-informed.'

'From what I've heard about your brother, he's a conceited fop who spends most of his time consorting with low company. Do you trust his assessment of the House of Commons over mine?'

'Of course not, Sir Julius.'

'Then cease this pointless line of argument. I detest most politicians to the height of my power and I daresay that they, in turn, detest me. But that does not mean they'd seek my life. Back-stabbing is the order of the day in parliament but only in the metaphorical sense. I have absolutely no fears for my safety.'

'You should,' said Christopher.

'Stop badgering me, man.'

'Precautions must be taken.'

'The only precaution that I'll take is to ignore everything that your idiot brother has told you.'

'I'm not relying solely on Henry's advice,' said Christopher, hurt by the antagonism towards his brother. 'I spoke to two Members of Parliament as well – Ninian Teale and Roland Askray. They agreed that you were perceived in some quarters as a dangerous firebrand.'

'I have the courage of my convictions, that's all,' announced Sir Julius, truculently, 'so I'm bound to cause a flutter in governmental dovecotes. And I have to tell you that I resent the way that you've gone behind my back in this matter.'

'It was for your own good, Sir Julius.'

'My own good! In what way can discussing me with your imbecile brother, and with two Members of Parliament who clearly deride me, be construed as my own good? This is a gross intrusion on my privacy.'

'I acted with the best of intentions,' said Christopher.

'And the worst of results.'

'Sir Julius—'

'I'll hear no more of this,' yelled the old man, interrupting him with a vivid gesture. 'Instead of pestering me, you should be out there, trying to catch the man who killed Bernard Everett.'

'I only came to issue a warning.'

'Then let me give you one in return. If you dare to bother me again in this way, you'll no longer be allowed into this house.'

'That's unjust.'

'Good day to you!'

Fuming with anger, Sir Julius turned on his heel and left the room. Christopher could hear his footsteps, ascending the staircase. Shortly afterwards, Susan came into the parlour.

'Whatever did you say to Father?' she wondered.

He swallowed hard. 'Sir Julius and I had a slight disagreement,' he replied. 'Nothing more.'

'He swept past me without a word.'

'I must take the blame for that, Susan.'

'Why? What happened in here?'

'I inadvertently upset him.'

'But he was in such good humour when he arrived home,' she recalled. 'What can have happened to deprive him of that?'

'A few ill-judged words on my part.'

'On what subject?'

'That's immaterial.'

'Not to me, Christopher. This is the second time you've called here today and only something of importance could make you do that. Is it connected with the murder?'

'Yes,' he conceded.

'Then why did it put my father out of countenance?'

Christopher was in a quandary. Wanting to tell her the truth, he knew how distressed she would be if she heard that someone was stalking Sir Julius Cheever. Susan's immediate reaction would be to tackle her father about it and that would expose her to the kind of brutal rebuff that Christopher had just suffered. For her own sake, she had to be protected from that. He decided, therefore, to leave her in the dark.

'I asked you a question,' she pressed. 'Why?'

'Because your father was unhappy about the way the investigation is going,' he said, trying to put her mind at rest.

'These things take time and Sir Julius is demanding instant results.'

'And that's all it was?'

Christopher took a deep breath. 'That's all it was, Susan.'

It was the last call of the day and, though it involved a long walk to Cripplegate Ward, Jonathan Bale did not mind the exercise. On the trail of a murder suspect, he never complained about sore feet and aching legs. As he strolled up Wood Street, he was interested to see the changes that had been made. Like other wards in the city, Cripplegate had been devastated by the Great Fire of 1666. Robbed of its churches, its livery halls and its houses, it had also lost much of its earlier character. The rebuilding had started immediately and Bale was intrigued to see how many streets, lanes and alleyways had risen from the ashes.

The man he sought lived in Aldermanbury Street, a thoroughfare in which several fine residences had already been completed. He had come to the home of Erasmus Howlett, a leading brewer in the city, and it was evident from the size and position of the house that Howlett's business was an extremely profitable one. Bale was admitted at once and shown into the parlour. Howlett soon joined him.

'You've come from Baynard's Castle Ward, I hear,' he said.

'Yes, sir,' replied Bale.

'What brought you to the north of the city?'

'A murder inquiry, Mr Howlett.'

The other man gulped. 'Murder? Can this be so?'

Bale told him about the crime in Knightrider Street, and, being a friend of Francis Polegate, the brewer was visibly disturbed. Nearing fifty, Erasmus Howlett was a portly man of medium height with a chubby face and a voluminous paunch only partly concealed by a clever tailor. His podgy hands kept twitching involuntarily.

'These are sad tidings, Constable,' he said, 'but I don't understand why you felt the need to bring them to me.'

'I came on another errand, Mr Howlett.'

'Ah, I see. In that case, perhaps you should sit down.'

'Thank you,' said Bale, taking a chair. 'Yours was the last name on my list. That's why I'm here.'

'List?' repeated Howlett, sitting down.

'Of people who might be able to help me.'

'I'm more than ready to do that.'

'Thank you. I called on Mr Polegate first thing this morning, before he set off to Cambridge. What perplexed me from the start,' Bale went on, 'was how the killer knew that his victim would be in the house on that particular day. Mr Everett had never stayed in London before. The first time that he does, he is shot dead.'

'Quite horrifying!'

'I asked Mr Polegate to give me the name of anybody – anybody at all – to whom he may have mentioned that his brother-in-law would be coming to celebrate the opening of the business. At first, he could think of nobody until he remembered dining with some friends a week ago.'

'That's right,' said Howlett. 'I was one of them.'

'I've spoken to the other two gentlemen, sir. They all agree that Mr Everett's visit was mentioned in the course of the meal.'

'It was, constable. I recall it myself.' He laughed heartily. 'You surely do not think that any of *us* was responsible for the crime, do you?' He extended his trembling palms 'With these wretched hands of mine, I could not even hold a weapon, let alone pull the trigger.'

'I didn't come here to accuse you, Mr Howlett.'

'That's a relief.'

'And I'm sorry about your ailment.'

'Three physicians have tried to cure it and each one has failed.'

'It must be an inconvenience.'

'One learns to live with one's disabilities,' said Howlett, clasping his hands together. 'Most of the time, I hardly notice the problem. On the question of your errand,' he continued, 'why has it brought you to my door – if you've not come to arrest me, that is?'

'I wondered if you'd passed on the information to anyone else.'

'What – about the visit of Mr Everett?'

'Yes, sir.'

'I don't think so, Constable. To be honest, there's nobody in my circle who would be at all interested to hear about it. Until today, I'd forgotten that the subject had ever been raised. When I dine with friends,' he said with a chuckle, 'I like to drink my fill and that means I remember very little of what was said.' His brow furrowed and he pursed his lips in concentration. 'No,' he decided at length, 'I told nobody – not even my wife.'

'Then I'm sorry to have taken up your time.'

'Not at all, Mr Bale. I'm glad that you came. I must call on Francis and offer my condolences. He's off to Cambridge, you say?'

'Yes, sir. Mr Everett's wife and family have yet to be told.'

'My heart goes out to them.'

'I do not envy Mr Polegate's task.'

Howlett sighed. 'It's never good to be the bearer of sad news.'

'No, sir.' Bale got to his feet. 'I must be off.'

'Give me your address before you go, constable.'

'My address?'

'Yes,' said Howlett, getting up from his chair. 'I'm fairly certain that I spoke to nobody about Mr Everett, but memory sometimes plays tricks on me. If, perchance, I *do* recall telling someone about his visit to Francis Polegate's house, then I'll send the name to you at once.'

The unexpected arrival of Lancelot and Brilliana Serle threw the house into a state of mild turmoil. Susan Cheever was taken by surprise.

'We had no idea that you would be coming today,' she said.

'Your letter more or less begged us to set out at once,' argued Brilliana. 'You may not have requested our help in so many words but I could read between the lines.'

'I merely sought to keep you abreast of developments, Brilliana.'

'A murder is more than a mere development.'

'I'll not gainsay that.'

'We are here now so you may count on our support.'

'Yes,' added Serle, doffing his hat. 'Delighted to see you again, Susan. This whole business must have been very trying for you.'

'Indeed, it has, Lancelot.'

Susan had the feeling that their presence would make it even more trying but she did not say so. Instead, she summoned up a smile and made an effort to be hospitable, inquiring about their journey and asking what their immediate needs were. Her brother-in-law, as ever, was polite, attentive and innocuous. Susan was very fond of him. She also pitied Lancelot Serle for taking on the dazzling burden that was Brilliana. Duty obliged her to love her sister but Susan had never been able to bring herself wholeheartedly to like her. Years of being under the thumb of her elder sibling had left their mark upon her.

Conducting the visitors into the parlour, she did her best to adjust to the fact that the house would be considerably noisier and more crowded from now on. Peace and quiet were alien to Brilliana. She liked to fill each day with inconsequential chatter. She was still complaining about the condition of the road to London when Sir Julius entered.

'Father!' she trilled, going to him.

'Good evening, Sir Julius,' said Serle.

'What the devil are you two doing here?' demanded Sir Julius.

'That's a poor welcome, to be sure!' protested Brilliana. 'Can you not even rise to a kiss for your daughter?' Her father reluctantly planted his lips on her cheek. 'That's better,' she said, standing back. 'Now, let me look at you properly. Has Susan been taking care of you?'

'I can take care of myself, Brilliana.'

'And you do it tolerably well, Sir Julius,' said Serle, hoping that a compliment might endear his father-in-law to him. 'I've never seen you in such fine feather.'

'Then you need spectacles,' chided his wife. 'Father is not well.'

'I was perfectly well until *you* appeared,' said Sir Julius.

Brilliana gave a brittle laugh. 'You always did have a weakness for a jest, Father,' she said. 'But the fact is that you look pale and drawn to me. Your diet is patently at fault. I need to take it in hand.'

'You'll do nothing of the kind.'

'No,' agreed Susan, smarting at the implied criticism of her. 'Now, why don't we all make ourselves comfortable?'

Brilliana chose the sofa and patted it to indicate that her husband should sit beside her. Sir Julius sat on the other side of the room. Susan occupied a chair that was midway between her father and her sister. An unlikely silence descended. It was broken, improbably, by Lancelot Serle.

'We are waiting to hear what happened yesterday, Sir Julius.'

'Are you?' grunted his father-in-law.

'All that we know is that a friend of yours was murdered,' said Serle. 'May one ask where you were at the time?'

'Not a foot from where Bernard was standing.'

'Heavens! Then you could so easily have been killed yourself.'

'I don't need you to remind me of that, Lancelot,' said Sir Julius with asperity. 'He was not the first man to perish beside me. Those of us who have fought many times in battle know the anguish of losing dear comrades – and that's what Bernard Everett was.'

'Yet he did not die in battle,' noted Serle.

'You're being pedantic.'

'Let father tell the story, Lancelot,' ordered Brilliana. 'He'll be able to be more explicit than Susan's letter.'

'How explicit do you wish me to be?' asked Sir Julius, sourly. 'One second, he was alive; the next, he was dead. Do you want to know how much blood was shed, Brilliana, or what a man's skull looks like when it's been split open by a musket bullet?'

'Father!' she protested.

'I thought not. I'll stick to the bare facts.'

He gave them a terse account of what had happened and told them what steps had been taken to catch the malefactor. Serle picked up on one of the names that was mentioned.

'Christopher Redmayne, did you say?'

'He was a witness to the crime.'

'Then you have fortune on your side, Sir Julius.'

'Do I?'

'Yes,' Serle went on. 'Mr Redmayne is a most resourceful young fellow. If he is involved, then it is only a matter of time before the villain is brought to justice.'

'I beg leave to doubt that,' said Sir Julius.

'Why?'

'He and I have contrary opinions as to what exactly happened in Knightrider Street yesterday. I fear that he will be misled into looking in all the wrong directions.'

'You're being very unkind to Christopher,' said Susan, hotly. 'I have more faith in his abilities. He has never failed before.'

'I endorse that,' said Serle. 'Have you so soon forgotten that it was Mr Redmayne – with the help of that constable, of course – who solved the murder of your own son, Gabriel?'

'Lancelot!' snapped his wife.

'It's true, isn't it?'

'There's such a thing as tact.'

Sir Julius blenched. He needed time to compose himself before speaking. A wound had just been reopened and the pain made him gasp. He had suffered so much remorse over the untimely death of his son that he tried to put it out of his mind. He glowered at Serle.

'Some things are best left in the past,' he said, pointedly, 'but I am saddled with a son-in-law who has a compulsion to haul them into the light of day. Please, Lancelot – spare me any further reminders.'

'He will,' promised Brilliana, calling her husband to heel with a malevolent glance. She conjured up a bright smile and distributed it among the others. 'Let's talk about something else, shall we?'

'What did you have in mind?' said Susan.

'What else but this attachment that Father has made?'

'This is not the time to bring that up, Brilliana.'

'I think that it is. Your letters have whetted my appetite.'

'Letters?' echoed Sir Julius, eyebrows bristling. 'Have you been spreading tittle-tattle about me, Susan?'

'No,' she replied, quickly. 'I simply mentioned that...' She paused to choose her words with care. 'Well, that someone has come into your life, and that you seem to spend a lot of time with your new friend.'

'Do you have any objection to that?'

'None at all, Father.'

'What Susan objects to,' said Brilliana with the boldness of an older sister, 'is that you pretend to be visiting your parliamentary friends when, in fact, you are sneaking off to be with Mrs Kitson. I don't think it's unreasonable of her, Father. Do you?'

Sir Julius scowled. The tension in the room was almost tangible. Susan braced herself for an explosion that would be largely aimed at her, and she wished that she had never even told Brilliana about their father's growing interest in a certain lady. It had been a serious mistake on her part. When she was kept safely down in Richmond, her sister was comparatively unthreatening. Brought to London, however, Brilliana Serle had an uncanny knack of introducing maximum embarrassment into any family discussion.

Susan closed her eyes in readiness but the expected onslaught did not come. Instead, repenting of his evasive behaviour, Sir Julius chose to be more honest with his daughters. He cleared his throat.

'You were right to upbraid me, Susan,' he confessed with a forgiving smile. 'My friendship with Dorothy – with Mrs Kitson – has been cloaked in too much secrecy. My only defence is that I feared our acquaintance would only be a short one, and that I would be left looking foolish if I had set too much store by it.'

'Tell us about her,' coaxed Brilliana.

'It's difficult to know where to start. Suffice it to say that she's one of the most remarkable women I've ever met. Mrs Kitson has so many accomplishments that she takes my breath away.'

'How old is she, Father?'

'Brilliana!' reproached Susan.

'It's a fair question,' said her sister. 'It would be insupportable if he were infatuated with someone who is younger than we ourselves.'

'Mrs Kitson does not fit into that category,' Sir Julius assured her, 'yet neither is she declined in years. I would describe her as being in the very prime of life.'

'Widowed, I presume?'

'Yes, Brilliana. Twice.'

'Comfortably off?'

Susan was shocked. 'You've no right to ask such a thing.'

'Nevertheless,' said her father, 'I'm happy to provide you with an answer. No, Mrs Kitson is not comfortably off.' He grinned as he saw the look that was exchanged between the sisters. 'She is *extremely* well provided for, so the pair of you can stop thinking that she is after my money. Mrs Kitson has more than enough of it herself.'

'That sounds promising,' observed Serle. 'May one inquire how you first met the lady, Sir Julius?'

'Through a mutual acquaintance who was at Newmarket one day. It was pure accident,' he said, 'but she has transformed my life. Mrs Kitson has been kind enough to say the same of me. That's why I'm glad that you and Lancelot have descended on us, Brilliana.'

'You were not so pleased a minute ago,' commented Susan.

'I was still trying to hide and dissemble then. Now that it's out in the open, I can speak freely at last.' He looked at his younger daughter. 'I know that you disapprove, Susan, but only because you have never met Mrs Kitson. That can soon be remedied. Only today,' he told them, 'when we dined together, she said how much she was looking forward to meeting my family. I'll arrange it at the earliest opportunity.'

Sarah Bale made no secret of her fondness for him. When Christopher Redmayne called at the house on Addle Hill that evening, she gave him a cordial welcome and ushered him into the little parlour as if he were an honoured guest. She then took her two young sons into the kitchen so that Christopher could speak to her husband alone.

'What sort of a day have you had, Jonathan?' said the architect.

'An exhausting one,' replied Bale.

'Did you find out anything of value?'

'No, Mr Redmayne. I've walked far but learned little.'

'Where exactly did you go?'

Bale told him about the three people whose names had been given to him by Francis Polegate, and how none of them recalled passing on the information to anyone else that Bernard Everett would be at the house in Knightrider Street on the previous day. Christopher felt a twinge of guilt.

'I owe you an apology, Jonathan,' he said.

'Why?'

'I may, unwittingly, have sent you on a wild goose chase.'

'But it's crucial for us to find out who was aware of the fact that Mr Everett would be at that address. That's why I tracked down those three friends of Mr Polegate.'

'You asked them the wrong question.'

'Did I, Mr Redmayne?'

'I think so,' said Christopher. 'Having made some inquiries on my own behalf, I'm not at all sure that the man at that window shot the person he was really after. My feeling is that he was there to kill Sir Julius Cheever.'

Bale blinked in surprised. 'Sir Julius?'

'He's the man who has caused such a stir in parliament, not Bernard Everett. If, as I believe, this murder has a political dimension, then Mr Everett was killed by mistake.'

He gave his reason for thinking so and told him of the conversation with his brother. Bale was sceptical. He found it difficult to place much reliance on the word of Henry Redmayne. Having met him a number of times, and being aware of the decadent existence that he led, he had the gravest reservations about Christopher's elder brother. In the constable's opinion, Henry symbolised all that was wrong with the Restoration, an event that Bale would never be able to accept as either necessary or in any way advantageous to his fellow-countrymen.

'Who were these other men you spoke to?' he asked.

'Roland Askray and Ninian Teale. Both have been Members of Parliament for several years.'

'And are they are close friends of your brother?'

Christopher smiled. 'If you mean that they are amongst Henry's many drinking companions,' he said, 'then I must concede that they are. But that does not disqualify them as shrewd judges of the political scene. Mr Askray has been talked of as a future Secretary to the Treasury and Mr Seal is part of the Duke of Buckingham's entourage.'

Bale was surprised. 'The Duke?'

'Yes, Jonathan, so he is close to the seat of power. Nobody has more influence over the King's councils than Buckingham.' He grinned as the other man gave a sniff of disapproval. 'Yes, I know that he would never win plaudits from you, Jonathan, but perhaps you should remember that he married the daughter of a Parliamentary general.'

'It's the Duke of Buckingham who needs to remember that,' said Bale, censoriously. 'Lord Fairfax's daughter deserves more respect from her husband. By all accounts, he leads the kind of life that makes a mockery of the marriage vows.'

Christopher did not contradict him. It was common knowledge that Buckingham was a notorious voluptuary, acquainted with every vice in a city where it flourished in abundance. But it was the way that he flouted the law that outraged Bale. In the previous year, Buckingham had killed the Earl of Shrewsbury in an illegal six-man duel, a scandal that was heightened by the fact that, before and after the event, the Countess of Shrewsbury was Buckingham's mistress. It worried Christopher that so much power had been vested into the hands of such a man. It appalled Bale. In his codex, Buckingham was Henry Redmayne writ large.

'I'm not asking you to admire Roland Askray or Ninian Teale,' said Christopher. 'Neither man is a saint. But you must accept that their experience of political matters commands attention.'

'Yes, Mr Redmayne.'

'They both told me how Sir Julius has a positive gift for making enemies, some of whom would like to see him forcibly removed from the Parliament House.'

'Then Mr Everett is to be pitied even more.'

'He is, Jonathan. He took the bullet that was supposed to kill another man. That means we have a second reason to catch the villain.'

'A second one?' said Bale.

'He needs to pay dearly for one murder, and be prevented from committing another. As long as the man is at liberty, Sir Julius's life is in danger.'

'Have you warned him?'

'I tried to,' admitted Christopher, 'but he refused utterly to believe that someone would wish to kill him. Indeed, he was so indignant that I should ever suggest such a thing that he threatened to ban me from his house. You can imagine how difficult that would be for me.'

'Yes,' said Bale, knowing of his attachment to Susan Cheever. 'It could make things very awkward. But, if you were unable to convince him that he was in jeopardy, why did you not ask his daughter to take on the office? From what I recall of the young lady, Miss Cheever knew how to deal with her father better than anyone.'

'That's certainly true.'

'Then entrust the task to her.'

'I dare not do so,' explained Christopher. 'It would only cause her grief and expose her to the sort of hurtful rebuke that I suffered. Susan would be terrified whenever her father stirred from the house.'

'He needs someone to keep watch on him.'

'He's too perverse to allow it.'

'Then what are we to do, Mr Redmayne?'

'Pursue the killer relentlessly and hope that we can overhaul him before he makes a second attempt on Sir Julius's life.'

'So my efforts today were in vain?'

'I take the blame for that, Jonathan. I should have stopped you.'

'What I should have asked Mr Polegate was whether or not he told those three friends of his that Sir Julius would be among the guests at his house yesterday.'

'That, too, would have been a futile exercise.'

'Why?'

'Because I suspect that it was not Francis Polegate who let the cat out of the bag,' said Christopher, seriously. 'Sir Julius himself would have told many people where he would be that day, though only a foolhardy man would dare to ask him who they were. I'd not be equal to the task. He'd bite my head off again. Then, of course, we have to consider his daughter. Susan may well have mentioned to friends that she would be going to Knightrider Street with Sir Julius.'

'You might have done the same, Mr Redmayne.'

'I did – no question about it.'

'Do you have a record of the people to whom you spoke?'

'No,' said Christopher. 'I let slip the information in a coffee house when I was talking to a client of mine. Several people could have overheard the name of Sir Julius Cheever and taken an interest. Do you see what that would mean?'

'What?' asked Bale.

'Indirectly, I'd be responsible for the death of Bernard Everett.'

'I think that very unlikely, Mr Redmayne.'

'Unlikely, perhaps – but not out of the question.'

'You'd be wrong to let it prey on your mind. The chances are that this is nothing to do with a remark you made in a coffee house. All you need to think about,' said Bale, solemnly, 'is how we can track down the villain who fired that shot.'

'We'll find him,' vowed Christopher, gritting his teeth. 'I owe it to Mr Everett's family. And I owe it to Susan to make sure that her father doesn't suffer the same fate. We've testing days ahead, Jonathan. I know that we've had some success in the past but this case – I feel it in my bones – will really put us on our mettle.'

The Saracen's Head served food as well as drink and Bridget McCoy made sure that its meals were of good quality. Instead of delegating the task to anyone else, therefore, she did all of her own shopping so that she could run a knowing eye over any meat, fish, poultry, vegetables and bread before buying it. Her companion on such expeditions was her son, Patrick, named after his father but entirely devoid of his charm and lively sense of humour. Barely eighteen, Patrick McCoy was a hulking youth of limited intelligence, pleasant, amenable but only fit for the most menial tasks. All too aware of his deficiencies, his mother loved him nonetheless.

It was on trips to market that Patrick really came into his own, able to carry heavy loads with apparent ease and acting as an escort for his mother. Before they set out early that morning, Bridget had to remind him time and again to bring the two large baskets. They came out of the tavern and began their journey, soon joining many others who were heading in the same direction. Before the Great Fire, there had been many markets in London, spreading indiscriminately along streets and lanes, and causing intense congestion. Such haphazard development had now been replaced by a more ordered arrangement.

Of the four new markets that had been created, the one in Leadenhall Street was the grandest, comprising a bewildering array of stalls in a quartet of extensive open courtyards. It was the major market for meat. A hundred stalls had beef for sale and even more were devoted to mutton, veal and poultry. Rabbits were also available, strung up in rows like so many hanged felons. Patrick McCoy liked the constant noise and bustle of Leadenhall with its sense of immediacy and its compound of pungent aromas. Taking it all in, he lumbered obediently behind his mother as she searched for bargains.

The four courtyards were, as usual, thronged with customers, and vendors competed for their attention with ear-splitting cries. Street hawkers also tried to sell their wares and Patrick bumped by mistake into a pretty young girl with a basket of dead pigeons on her head. Raising his hat in apology, he gave her a vacant grin but she was already threading her way through the jostling crowd. Bridget stopped at a stall, appraised its selection of beef, checked the price, then haggled so tenaciously that the vendor agreed to a discount simply to get rid of her. She put the beef into one of the baskets and they pressed on through the tumult.

Slow in speech and movement, Patrick was nevertheless extremely wary of thieves and pickpockets. When someone tried to steal the beef from his basket, he knocked the man summarily to the ground. The sly youth who attempted to slip a hand into Bridget's purse got a kick in the buttock from Patrick that sent him yelping away in pain. It was a normal market day for her so Bridget did not even notice these random moments of violence. She took it for granted that her son would protect her.

By the time they had finished, both baskets were bulging with meat and Bridget was carrying a brace of dead rabbits. It was time to move on so that they could purchase fruit and vegetables elsewhere. Side by side, they picked their way through the forest of bodies. They had not gone far before Bridget saw a face that she thought she recognized. It was only a fleeting glimpse but the broken nose was too distinctive to miss. A cry burst from her lips.

'That's him!'

'Who?' asked Patrick.

'Mr Field. The man who rented that room.'

'What room, Mother?'

'After him,' she ordered, pushing her way forward.

Patrick grinned helpfully. 'Is he a friend?'

'No, he's a murderer.'

'Ah.'

'Catch him up,' urged Bridget. 'We must see where he goes.'

They tried to move faster but it was virtually impossible in such a crowd. When they finally reached the place where she had seen the man, he was no longer there. Bridget stood on tiptoe to look around her but to no avail. Mr Field had been swallowed up in the swirling mass of bodies. In sheer frustration, she swung the dead rabbits viciously against the side of a wooden cart.

'A pox on it!' she exclaimed. 'We've lost the lying bastard!'

Christopher Redmayne's day began with a surprise. His brother called to see him shortly after breakfast, thereby setting a remarkable precedent. Having caroused half the night away, Henry Redmayne rarely woke before mid-morning and, as a rule, it was almost noon before his barber ventured to shave him. Yet there he was, as large as life, dressed in his finery, dismounting from his horse in Fetter Lane when the clock was barely past the eighth hour of a bright new day. Seeing him through the window, Jacob, the ever-reliable old servant, went out of the house to take charge of Henry's horse. He indicated the door.

'Please go in, Mr Redmayne,' he said.

'Thank you.'

'Your brother has been up for hours.'

'He always is,' said Henry, bitterly. 'Such an disgusting habit.'

Swaying slightly, he went into the house and found Christopher in his study, poring over his latest design with a pencil in his hand. His brother looked up in astonishment. Face haggard, shoulders sagging, eyes barely managing to remain open, Henry slumped into the nearest chair and let out a groan of disbelief.

'Why on earth am I up at this ungodly hour?'

'I was about to ask the same thing,' said Christopher.

'Then address your question to the Surveyor at the Navy Office. He will tell you why I've been hauled so cruelly from the comfort of my bed. I'm in deep disgrace, Christopher,' he said with an exaggerated roll of his eyes, 'because of some trifling error that I made in the accounts for the victualling contracts. To make amends, I've been ordered to work in the mornings for the next two weeks. It's a barbaric demand. My constitution will not hold out.'

'I disagree. It could be the making of you.'

'That's an absurd suggestion!'

'It's the very one that your physician has made,' Christopher reminded him. 'He's always urging you to keep more regular hours for the sake of your health.'

'Such a regimen would be the ruination of my health. It was never like this when Sir William Batten was Surveyor,' said Henry, sounding a nostalgic note. 'He understood that a gentleman could not possibly be expected to arrive for work until afternoon. Sir William – God rest his soul – had many faults and the old sea dog could hardly get through a sentence without sprinkling it with foul language, but he was a merry soul when he chose to be. We spent some joyful times, drinking with him at the Dolphin in Seething Lane.'

'I'm certain of that, Henry, but I'm equally certain that you did not come here to reminisce about Sir William Batten.'

'Too true. I'm here to tell you about last night.'

'I'm impressed that you are wide awake enough to remember it.'

'Leave your gibes aside. I came to help you.'

'In what way?'

'I supped last night with Ninian Teale,' said Henry. 'Afterwards, we joined some friends for a game or two of cards and dear Ninian was kind enough to lose a creditable amount to me.'

Christopher sat up hopefully. 'So you are now in a position to repay the debts you owe me?'

'Alas, no. Hard on my good fortune, I had a run of bad luck and my winnings disappeared before I had time to count them properly.'

'It was ever thus.'

Henry was peevish. 'Stop interrupting me, Christopher. I found out something that may be of use to you. Did you not beseech me to keep my ears open on your behalf?'

'Yes, I did.'

'Then listen to what they picked up,' said his brother, using the back of his hand to stifle a dramatic yawn. 'Ninian is an intimate of mine. I know that you conversed with him at length, but there are things he'd confide in me that you could never elicit.'

'Such as?'

'The fact that Sir Julius Cheever's camp has already been under attack. Does the name of Arthur Manville sound familiar?'

'No, Henry. Who is he?'

'Another troublesome Member of Parliament with revolutionary notions. Last year, he and Sir Julius were hand in glove. Then the assault occurred.'

'Assault?'

'One dark night, Manville had his nose slit open.'

'By whom?'

'He has no idea,' said Henry, 'but it did force him to moderate his political opinions. He's no longer the raging dissident that he once was. And Manville was not the only loss that Sir Julius sustained.'

'No?'

'Lewis Bircroft also fell away from the group.'

'Bircroft,' said Christopher, thoughtfully. 'Now where have I heard that name before?'

'You probably read it in a newspaper. There was a report of the incident. It happened in Covent Garden a few months ago, when Mr Bircroft was unwise enough to take a stroll down an alleyway on his own. Bullies set upon him with cudgels. They not only cracked several bones,' said Henry, 'they broke his spirit as well. Like Mr Manville, he has not been agitating quite so enthusiastically for the removal of the monarchy.'

'Were the two attacks the work of political opponents?'

'What else could they be?'

'All sorts of things,' said Christopher. 'Mr Manville could have been the victim of a private quarrel, and Mr Bircoft would not be the only man to fall foul of ruffians who lurk in Covent Garden.'

'I prefer to trust Ninian Teale's opinion.'

'Which is?'

'That dire warnings are being sent to Sir Julius.'

'He's far too stubborn to heed them.'

'Then someone needs to counsel him before it is too late,' said Henry with a meaningful look at his brother. 'There's a pattern here that he cannot ignore. Arthur Manville has his nose slit, Lewis Bircroft has his bones broken, then Bernard Everett, the latest of Sir Julius's parliamentary creatures, is shot dead in the street.'

'Each time the punishment is more severe.'

'Point that out to the counterfeit knight.'

'Sir Julius is no counterfeit,' said Christopher, stoutly. 'He earned the title by his outstanding service to the Commonwealth.'

Henry Redmayne was harsh. 'The only outstanding service he could render now,' he observed, tartly, 'is to get himself killed for voicing his incendiary views in the House of Commons. If he persists, that will surely happen and I, for one, will be delighted to see him go.'

'Are you quite sure that it was him, Mrs McCoy?' asked Jonathan Bale.

'I'd take my oath on the Bible,' she replied.

'How far away from you was he?'

'Ten or fifteen yards.'

'It would be easy to make a mistake at that distance.'

'Not if your eyes are as sharp as mine,' said Bridget McCoy. 'His face was only there for a second but I knew it at once, didn't I, Patrick? I saw that broken nose of his.'

'She did, Mr Bale,' confirmed Patrick. 'Mother saw him.'

The constable had met them in Knightrider Street on their way back from market. Bridget was still holding the pair of rabbits that had been thrashed against the side of the cart, and her son was carrying two large baskets brimming with provender. Only someone with Patrick's strength could have borne such a heavy load so far. Now that they had paused to talk to Bale, it never occurred to the lad that he could put the baskets on the ground to give his arms a rest.

'What was he wearing, Mrs McCoy?' said Bale.

'I only saw his face.'

'What about a hat?'

'He was wearing a cap.'

'Was it the same one he had on at the Saracen's Head?'

'No,' said Bridget, 'that was very different. The cap was much smaller so I had a good look at the whole of his face.'

'For an instant.'

'That's all it takes, Mr Bale. If you run a tavern, you have to keep your wits about you. Patrick – my husband, that is – taught me that. You must be able to weigh people up at a glance. Most of the time, I can do that. But I failed badly with Mr Field,' she confessed, 'and that hurt my pride. It rankled with me. Patrick – my son, that is – will tell you how quick I am to pick out a troublemaker at the Saracen's Head, yet I was deceived by a ruthless killer.'

Bale took her through the story again, trying to establish the exact point where the man had been sighted in Leadenhall Market. If he was a regular customer there, one of the meat traders might know his name. The constable had a rough description but it would not enable him to identify the wanted man with any degree of confidence. When he went to the market, Bale would have to take Bridget McCoy with him.

'Thank you for telling me,' he said to her. 'This could turn out to be very valuable.'

'Only if you catch the devil, Mr Bale.'

'We'll catch him eventually. Handbills have been printed with the description that you gave me of Field. A large reward has been offered for information leading to an arrest. That usually brings in results.'

'I'd like to break that ugly nose of his all over again!'

Patrick had been staring at Bale with a mixture of envy and veneration. A smile spread slowly across his unprepossessing features.

'I want to be a constable one day,' he announced.

'There's always a place for new men, Patrick,' said Bale.

'Well, my son is not going to be one of them,' affirmed Bridget. 'He'll be too busy helping his mother to run the tavern.'

'I'd be a good constable,' boasted the youth.

'Put that nonsense out of your head.'

'But I want to be like Mr Bale.'

'You don't have the brains for it, Patrick.'

'I can learn, Mother,' insisted the youth. 'Can't I, Mr Bale?'

'Yes, lad,' said Jonathan, kindly.

'Don't encourage him,' warned Bridget. 'Patrick is spoken for.

Besides, what use is a constable who can neither read nor write nor even remember what day it is half the time?' She used her free hand to give her son an affectionate pat. 'You're *my* constable, Patrick. Your job is to look after the Saracen's Head.'

Patrick was determined. 'I want to work with Mr Bale.'

'One day, perhaps,' said the constable, knowing that it would never happen. 'One day, Patrick.'

One surprise succeeded another. No sooner had Christopher Redmayne bade farewell to his brother than he had a second unexpected visitor at his house. Spurning both safety and convention, Susan Cheever had ridden unaccompanied to Fetter Lane, an address to which she normally travelled by coach. While his master took her into the parlour, Jacob once again acted as an ostler, leading her horse to the stables at the rear of the premises.

Christopher was thrilled to see her again so soon. Seated beside her on the couch, he noted how the ride had put some colour in her cheeks and how the breeze had disturbed the ringlets of hair that peeped out from under the front of her bonnet. He also saw the slight anxiety in her eyes.

'Is something amiss?' he asked.

'I have tidings that might interest you, Christopher. Word came late yesterday that Mr Everett's body was ready for removal. Father intends to accompany it to Cambridge later this morning.'

'Is he travelling alone?'

'No,' replied Susan. 'Mrs Polegate and her children will share the coach with him. Mr Polegate is already there, of course. The whole family will stay for the funeral tomorrow.'

'Thank you for telling me,' he said, worried that Sir Julius would be unprotected on the road. 'I'd like to pay my last respects to Mr Everett as well. What time are they leaving?'

'Not until eleven o'clock.'

'Then I'll bear them company.'

'I had a feeling that you might wish to do that.'

'As long as Sir Julius does not object. He and I did exactly not part on friendly terms yesterday.'

'I think you'll find him a changed man today.'

'I'm glad to hear it, Susan,' he said. 'Your father can very irascible when his views are challenged. What's brought about the change?'

'That's what I came to tell you,' she confided, lowering her head for a moment as she gathered her thoughts. When she looked up, she forced a smile. 'I have an apology to make, Christopher.'

'Why?'

'Because I lied to you.'

'I don't believe that.'

'I did and I hated myself for doing so. I suppose the truth is that I hoped that the problem would disappear of its own accord. You deserved better from me. I'm very sorry.'

'You mentioned a problem.'

'Yes,' said Susan, uncomfortably. 'It's one that I stupidly tried to conceal from you. Father has met someone who has made a deep impression on him. Her name is Mrs Kitson – Mrs Dorothy Kitson. He's been spending a lot of time with her.'

'Ah,' he said as realisation dawned, 'so that accounts for his benign mood in Knightrider Street. I saw him go off into a reverie more than once. Sir Julius is in love.'

'I'm not sure that it has reached that stage yet.'

'Whatever stage it's reached, it's obviously a source of pleasure to him. In what way is that a problem, Susan?'

'Father is too set in his ways to embark on a romance.'

'That's a decision only he can make.'

'Mrs Kitson is a distraction,' she argued. 'Father came to London to attend parliament, not to be beguiled into an attachment.'

'Have you met this lady?'

'Not yet.'

'Then how do you know it was she who beguiled *him*?' he asked. 'Could it not be that it was he who has actually enchanted her?'

'Hardly – you've met him.'

'Stranger things have happened, Susan. Look at my brother, for instance. Henry is very far from being what most people conceive of as handsome yet he's somehow bewitched a whole series of gorgeous ladies in his time.'

'Your brother is still relatively young – father is nearly sixty.'

'Age has no meaning in affairs of the heart.'

'But I'm not certain that this is what it is.'

'You can only make a proper judgement when you meet Mrs Kitson in person. Is your father ready for you to do that?'

'Yes,' she said. 'He wishes to introduce both of us to her.'

'Both of you?'

'Brilliana arrived from Richmond without warning. Subtlety, alas, was never her strong suit. She confronted Father at once and demanded to know what was going on in his private life. In the end, he capitulated. We are to meet Mrs Kitson before long.'

'Then all of your doubts may soon be eradicated.'

'I still feel uneasy about it, Christopher.'

'Why?'

'Father was perfectly happy as he was.'

'He leads a very full life, I grant you that.'

'It's far too full,' she argued. 'Father never stops. When we are at home, he busies himself with the running of the estate. And the minute we arrive in London, he has endless meetings with other Members of Parliament. He has no *time* for a dalliance.'

'Sir Julius obviously thinks otherwise. Besides, how do you know that's it's merely a dalliance? It may be more serious than that.'

Susan was about to reply but she thought better of it. Simply talking about the situation had introduced a sharpness into her voice that was rather unbecoming. Christopher noticed it at once. What interested him was that she sounded less like a daughter, talking about her father, than an apprehensive mother, trying to shield a wayward son from an artful female. Years before, Sir Julius Cheever had been rocked by the death of his wife and he had leaned heavily on his younger daughter as a result. While Christopher admired her devotion to her father, it did prevent him from asking Susan to share her life with him instead. As long as she looked after one man with such dedication, she would keep another at arm's length.

'I wonder if you are being altogether honest with yourself,' he said.

'What do you mean?'

'You've taken against this lady, Susan, haven't you?'

'I'm bound to have fears.'

'But they concern you rather than Sir Julius. Whenever you talk about him, you sound proprietary. He is *yours*. You've no wish to yield him up to another woman.'

'I have a *duty*,' she said, igniting with passion. 'When she was on her death bed, my mother made me promise that I would take care of him. I gave her my word, Christopher. I can't go back on that now.'

'You can if someone else lifts the burden from your shoulders.'

'Father is no burden.'

'He's no child either,' he pointed out. 'You can't make up his mind for him, especially on something as personal as this. Sir Julius will follow his instincts and you must let him do that.'

'Not if he's making a terrible mistake.'

'You've no proof that he's doing that, Susan.'

'No proof, maybe,' she admitted, 'but I have my suspicions. Don't ask me to explain what they are, Christopher, because I'm not able to put them into words. Father could be in danger, that's all I know.'

It was the ideal cue for him to tell her about a more immediate peril faced by her father but he drew back from doing so. At a time when she was already distressed, it would hurt her even more. It would also reveal that he had deceived her and Susan would feel aggrieved at that. There was an awkward silence. He wished that he could reach out and enfold her in his arms but there was an invisible barrier between them. Two names suddenly popped into his head.

'Did you ever meet a man called Arthur Manville?' he asked.

'Why, yes,' she replied. 'He used to come to the house.'

'Used to?'

'We've not seen him for a long time. He and Father probably fell out. Mr Manville had robust opinions. He tended to express them at the top of his voice. I heard father shouting him down on occasion.'

'What about Lewis Bircroft?'

'Why do you ask about him?'

'Curiosity. My brother happened to mention his name.'

'Mr Bircroft also took part in regular meetings at our house in Westminster,' she said, 'but, for some reason, he stopped coming as well. I was sorry about that. He was a pleasant man, very intelligent, and something of a philosopher. Mr Bircroft wrote many political pamphlets. Father had a great admiration for him.'

'Did he say why the man stopped visiting your house?'

'No, Christopher, but, then, he never talks about politics with me. He says that I could not even begin to understand what goes on inside the walls of the Parliament House.'

Susan was being deliberately misled. In order not to alarm her, Sir Julius had said nothing about the violence inflicted on his friends. He kept her ignorant of the hazards of political life for someone with views similar to his own. Christopher elected to do the same. Given her deep concern over her father's romantic friendship, he reasoned that Susan had enough to worry about.

'Well,' she said, rising from the couch, 'I suppose that I had better return home. They will be wondering where I am and, if you are going to Cambridge for a couple of days, you'll need time to pack some things.'

Christopher stood up. 'Jacob will do that for me,' he said, 'so I've plenty of time in hand. Tarry a little and I'll ride back to Westminster with you. Fine horsewoman that you are, I don't like the idea of your going abroad on your own.'

'Then I'll wait until you're ready.'

'Shall I ask Jacob to get you some refreshment?'

'No, thank you. I've not long had breakfast.'

'I had mine some hours ago,' said Christopher. 'Since I need to give so much time to this investigation, I'm attending to my own work early in the morning. Though I'm willing to play the constable, I can't forget that I'm also an architect. So,' he went on, 'your sister is staying with you, is she? Is her husband with her?'

'Yes, she and Lancelot came together.'

'I hope that I have the chance to spend time with them.'

Susan looked embarrassed. 'It might be better if you didn't,' she suggested. 'At all events, I think that you should avoid Brilliana.'

'Why – does she disapprove of me?'

'Quite the opposite.'

'Oh?'

'Brilliana likes to exert control over people,' said Susan.

'That was the first thing I noticed about her. She enjoys power. Your sister is a very beautiful woman but I do not envy Mr Serle.'

'Lancelot is content to be dominated by her.'

'Most men would resent that.'

'Not only men, Christopher. I've suffered more than anyone at her hands. When she cannot persuade, Brilliana will hector. When that fails, she'll resort to abuse. It can be very painful.'

'Why are you telling me this?'

'Because my sister turned her attention to me last night,' said Susan with obvious discomfort. 'Or, to be more precise, she's decided to use her influence on us.'

'Us?' said Christopher, mystified. 'We are the best of friends. Surely, your sister appreciates that? She has no call to interfere. How can she possibly use her influence on us?'

Susan said nothing but her silence was an explanation in itself.

Jonathan Bale acted swiftly. He gave Bridget McCoy and her son time to leave their provisions at the Saracen's Head, then the three of them drove back to Leadenhall Street in a borrowed cart. Bale took the reins and Bridget sat beside her. Patrick was perched at the back of the cart, his legs dangling over the edge, his whole body burning with excitement at the thought that he was helping a parish constable. If he could prove his worth on this occasion, he told himself, then his dream of becoming an officer might one day be fulfilled. When they reached the market, however, he was disappointed to learn that he had to guard the horse and cart. He could hardly demonstrate his prowess from there.

The market was still very busy and the pandemonium as deafening as ever. Barking dogs added to the cacophony. Bale had to raise his voice to make himself heard.

'Take me to the exact spot where you saw him, Mrs McCoy.'

'I will,' she said.

'And if, by chance, you do recognise him again, just point him out to me. I'll take over from there.'

'But I want to wring his neck for him.'

'Let the law take its course,' advised Bale. 'If you charge at the man, you'll only frighten him off and we'd have missed our opportunity. I need to creep up on the fellow. Do you understand that?'

'Yes, Mr Bale,' she said, reluctantly.

He buffeted his way through the crowd with Bridget at his heels. When they reached the place where she had spotted the man she took to be Field, she tapped Bale's shoulder and he stopped. She indicated where Field had been at the time. A woman of her height would not have been able to see much over the bobbing heads of the throng and the constable began to have doubts. Bridget McCoy was insistent.

'I know what I saw, Mr Bale,' she said, confidently. 'It was him.'

'In which direction was he going?'

She pointed a finger. 'Towards that lane.'

'Then let's talk to the stall holders between here and there,' said Bale, 'in case one of them knows the man.'

There were dozens of carts, stalls and booths in the vicinity but that did not deter Bale. He was methodical. After working their way down one side of the courtyard, they came back up the other. They asked if anyone was acquainted with a Mr Field and gave a description of the man. Their efforts were fruitless. When they enlarged the area of their search, they met with equal lack of success. Nobody recognised the name or identified the nasal abnormality. In a city where drunken brawls were a daily event, a broken nose was a common sight.

What hampered them was that vendors were too busy serving customers to talk to Bale and Bridget for more than a few seconds. They were there to sell their produce, not to engage in conversation with an angry Irishwoman and an inquisitive constable. In certain cases, Bale feared, even if they had known the wanted man, some vendors would not have admitted it. They would have protected a friend. Bale and Bridget pressed on until they finally had a more promising response.

'Field?' said the old woman. 'Would that be Gamaliel Field?'

'It could be,' replied Bale.

'Then, yes, I do know him.'

'Was he here this morning?'

'Of course. Gamaliel is always here.'

'And is he about my age and build?'

'With a broken nose?' added Bridget, starting to believe that they had eventually picked up a scent. 'A proper brute of a man.'

'Some would say so,' decided the old woman.

She had a poultry stall and had just sold the last of her stock – a goose in a wooden cage – when they approached her. Bale put her in her sixties and poor eyesight made her squint, but her voice was clear enough even if it did crack. She gave them a toothless grin.

'What business have you with Gamaliel?' she said.

'We just need to speak to him,' explained Bale, squeezing Bridget's arm to stop her from blurting out their real intention. 'We believe that Mr Field may be able to help us.'

'He's not here now, sir.'

'Then where is he?'

'Drinking at the Black Horse, if I know him.'

'And where's that?' asked Bridget.

'I know where it is,' said Bale. He nodded at the old lady. 'Thank you very much. You've been very helpful.'

She grinned again. 'Tell Gamaliel that I'll see him tomorrow.'

'No, you won't!' said Bridget under her breath.

The two of them walked along Leadenhall Street until they came to an alleyway. Once through that, they turned into a narrow street that curved its way north. The Black Horse was only one of a number of taverns in the street, and it occupied a position between a warehouse and a carpenter's shop. Bale told his companion to stand directly opposite so that she could have a good view of anyone who came out. He then slipped down the passageway at the side of the building so that he could enter it at the rear.

Bridget McCoy waited impatiently, wishing that she had a weapon about her so that she could wreak her revenge. In using the Saracen's Head as a place from which to commit murder, Field had left the place tainted. It would always bear a stigma. The reputation that she had struggled so hard to maintain in the wake of her husband's death had been vitiated by a man with a broken nose. Bridget wanted the satisfaction of seeing him hang from the gallows so that she could hurl abuse at him. Her only regret was that she could not put the noose around his neck herself.

The longer she waited, the more incensed she became, letting her rage build until it was difficult to contain. Where was Jonathan Bale? Why was he spending so much time in the Black Horse? Had he met with resistance? Or had Gamaliel Field overpowered him? Concern mingled with fury to leave her throbbing with emotion. Having tracked the man down, they must surely not let him escape.

Bridget was on tenter-hooks. Her blood was racing. She had just reached the point where she could endure it no longer when the front door of the Black Horse opened and Bale led out a burly man for her inspection. She identified him at once and she scurried across the street to attack him.

'That's the man!' she yelled. 'Arrest him, Mr Bale.'

Before he could move, Gamaliel Field was held in a bear hug then swung round quickly to face the tavern so that Bridget could not pummel him with her fists. She continued to screech and it took a while to calm her down. When she agreed not to assault the prisoner, Bale pulled him round so that she could have a closer look at him. Bridget was dismayed. Overwhelmed with eagerness for him to be the killer, she had been too hasty. The man was the same age and height as Bale but he was much fatter. His face was covered in a dark beard and his broken nose was nothing at all like the one owned by the killer who had rented a room from her at the Saracen's Head. It was an agonising setback.

'Let him go, Mr Bale,' she said, quietly. 'That's not the man.'

Before they left the house, Christopher Redmayne wrote to Jonathan Bale, explaining that he was going to Cambridge for the funeral and suggesting that the constable make certain inquiries during his absence. The letter was given to Jacob so that he could arrange delivery. Christopher then went off down Fetter Lane with Susan Cheever at his side. It was several weeks since they had been out riding together and, although they were simply going to Westminster, they both took great pleasure from the journey, moving at a trot in order to stretch out the time spent alone in each other's company.

When they reached the Strand, the traffic thickened noticeably and they had to wend their way past coaches, carts, countless other riders and dozens of ambling pedestrians. The wide thoroughfare seemed to be alive with people, streaming to and from the city.

'It will be a long ride to Cambridge,' she noted.

'Mr Everett lived in a village just this side of the town.'

'Even so, you'll be in the saddle for hours.'

'Any discomfort that I suffer is irrelevant,' said Christopher. 'I feel impelled to go, whatever the distance. I take my example from the King.'

'The King?'

'Yes, His Majesty can ride all morning and afternoon without showing any strain. It must be forty miles or more to Newmarket, yet he'll go there and back in a day just to see the races.'

'I'd rather you didn't mention Newmarket,' said Susan.

'Why not?'

'That was where Father met Mrs Kitson.'

'You may live to be grateful for that, Susan.'

'Grateful?'

'Any woman who can make Sir Julius mellow a little must have quite exceptional qualities. I'd cultivate this friendship between them. It might be in everyone's interest.'

'I wish that I could be so sanguine about it.'

'Will this lady never overcome your objections?'

'It's unfair of me to resent her when we've never actually met,' she conceded. 'To be honest, it's not Mrs Kitson who concerns me. It's my father. I think it's rather unseemly of him to behave this way at his age – especially after the vow he gave.'

'What vow?'

'It was when Mother died. He swore that he'd never marry again because he knew she was irreplaceable.' Susan lifted her chin with indignation. 'Yet now he's allowed himself to become entranced with someone he met at a racecourse.'

'Would it have made a difference if they'd met in a church?' Her eyes flashed and he wished that he had not made the comment. It was clearly a sensitive topic for her and best avoided. 'That was a crass remark,' he said, immediately, 'and I take it back.'

Continuing on their way, they turned, by mutual consent, to the more neutral subject of the weather. The English obsession with the vagaries of the climate led them to endless speculation and they arrived at the Cheever house still wondering if it would be wet or fine for the funeral. The coach stood ready outside the front door but it was the horse and cart that caught Christopher's eye. In the back of the cart was an object that was covered in a dark tarpaulin. It was the coffin that contained the body of Bernard Everett and it gave both of them a start.

Sir Julius Cheever came waddling out of the house to greet them.

'Wherever have you been, Susan?' he asked, switching his gaze to Christopher before she could reply. 'And why have you come back again, young man? I need no more lectures from you.'

'It was Mr Everett who brought me here,' said Christopher, indicating the cart. 'I wish to attend the funeral and, since you are travelling to Cambridge today, I thought that I'd accompany you.'

'My coach is full enough.'

'Then I'll ride beside it, Sir Julius.'

'There's no need for you to come.'

'Christopher feels that he must,' said Susan, taking over from him. 'After all, he designed the house for Mr Polegate. That's what brought his brother-in-law to London in the first place. Christopher is implicated, Father.'

'That's true. He was there at the time.'

'I promise to keep out of your way,' said the architect.

'Well,' decided Sir Julius, stroking his jaw, 'I suppose that I can hardly stop you. And an extra person will help to deter any villains who might be tempted to rob us.' He took note of the sword and dagger that hung from the other man's belt. 'And you are armed, I see.'

Christopher patted his saddlebag. 'I carry a pistol as well.'

'Then you are welcome to travel with us.' His eyes twinkled. 'Now I know why my daughter rode off with such eagerness this morning. Susan went to warn you what was happening.'

'Christopher had a right to know,' said Susan.

'I accept that.'

'I'm also looking forward to seeing a little of Cambridge,' said Christopher. 'I hear that it's a place that every architect should study. But my principle reason for going, of course, is to attend the funeral. I liked Mr Everett. He was entertaining company. Even on such a brief acquaintance, I could see that he was a very able man.'

'A truly estimable fellow.' Looking towards the cart, Sir Julius heaved a sigh. He became businesslike. 'We are by no means ready to leave yet. Come inside and meet everyone else.'

Christopher dismounted then helped Susan down from the saddle. He was rewarded with a warm smile of gratitude. A servant took care of the horses and they went into the house, stepping from bright sunshine into a funereal atmosphere. Hester Polegate was seated in the parlour with her twin sons either side of her. All three were dressed in black. Though she was the sister rather than the widow of the deceased, Hester wore a peaked black headdress that helped to obscure her face. She looked up at the newcomers.

There was a muted flurry of greetings and expressions of sympathy from Christopher and Susan. Hester Polegate was touched to hear that the architect was making the journey with them. Her two sons, only fourteen years of age, were still too shocked by the violent death of their uncle to speak. Also in the room were Brilliana and Lancelot Serle. They were pleased to see Christopher again but, because of the pervading mood of sorrow, they were unable to engage in a proper conversation with him. Christopher was relieved. Warned by Susan, he was glad to escape the threatened ambush from her sister.

Twenty minutes later, the travellers left the house and climbed into Sir Julius's coach. Mounting his horse, Christopher noted that both a coachman and a footman were making the journey, and that two men were accompanying the coffin in the cart. All would be armed, making the little cortege an uninviting target for any footpads or highwaymen they might meet on their way. Brilliana and her husband came out to wave them off but Christopher's gaze was directed at Susan. After exchanging a private smile with her, he set off behind the coach and the cart. The vehicles rumbled along, their iron-rimmed wheels resounding on the hard road. When they hit open country, Christopher knew, ridges, depressions and potholes would make Bernard Everett's last journey a very undignified one.

Heading north up King Street, they were all lost in thought. Inside the coach, Hester Polegate and her children were consumed with grief while Sir Julius Cheever searched for words to console them. In the light of what he had been told, Christopher wondered what sort of woman had managed to attract a choleric old knight who had seemed so entrenched in his bachelor existence. He hoped that he would have the opportunity of meeting the lady in the fullness of time. Meanwhile, using his artistic skills, Christopher drew a series of conjectural portraits of her in his mind. None sat easily beside the image of Sir Julius Cheever.

So diverted was he by the exercise of bringing Dorothy Kitson to life that he did not realize that they were being followed. The lone rider stayed well back, knowing the route that they would have to take and biding his time. It was simply a question of choosing his moment.

Chapter Six

After driving Bridget McCoy and her son back to their tavern, Jonathan Bale returned the horse and cart to the blacksmith from whom he had borrowed it. He then strode to his house on Addle Hill.

'I'm glad that you're home,' said his wife as he came through the door. 'There's a letter for you from Mr Redmayne.'

'When did it arrive?'

'Half an hour ago, at least. I expected you earlier.'

'I had to go to Leadenhall Market.'

'Whatever for?'

'I'll tell you later,' said Bale, looking around. 'Where's the letter?'

'On the kitchen table.'

He went into the kitchen and snatched up the missive, breaking open the seal to read it. Sarah saw the consternation in his face and hoped that it was not bad news. As she had discovered years ago, the problem with being a parish constable was that good tidings were few and far between. Reports of murder, theft and assault were far more likely to be brought to the door. Bale was also frequently called upon to intervene in disputes between neighbours or – as if he did not have enough crime to occupy him – to rescue pet animals from the precarious situations into which they had got themselves. Whatever else the letter contained, Sarah mused, it was not another plea to haul an injured dog from a stinking quagmire.

'Well?' she asked as he put the letter aside.

'Mr Redmayne's gone to Cambridge for the funeral,' he explained. 'He wants me to talk to someone while he's away.'

'Who is it?'

'A man called Lewis Bircroft. He's a Member of Parliament.'

She was impressed. 'A politician? Does that mean you'll have to go to the Parliament House?'

'In the first instance. I'll also need to find out where this man lives when he's staying in London.'

'Why must you speak to him, Jonathan?'

'He's a friend of Sir Julius Cheever,' said her husband, concealing from her the information that Bircroft had been savagely beaten in an alleyway in Covent Garden. 'He may be able to tell us something that throws a light on this present case.'

'I see.' She recalled his earlier remark. 'But what's this about going to Leadenhall Market?'

'Oh, that was Mrs McCoy's doing.'

'Bridget McCoy from the Saracen's Head?'

Bale nodded. Lowering himself on to one of the wooden chairs that he had made himself, he told her about their search for the man who had been seen at the market earlier. While she listened, Sarah started to prepare dinner, reaching for some bread to cut into thick slices. Like her husband, she was sorry that the trail had gone cold. She was interested to hear that Patrick McCoy had been involved.

'That lad is so unlike his father,' she noted.

'I disagree, Sarah. He's the image of him.'

'He may *look* like him but that's as far as he goes. Patrick, his father, was such a quick-witted man and so amiable. The son can barely hold a conversation. Whenever I see him,' she went on, 'I thank God that our boys are not like that. They go to school. They learn things. All that Patrick McCoy has learned is how to clear the tankards off the tables at the Saracen's Head.'

'It's not his fault.'

'I know, Jonathan. I feel sorry for the poor lad.'

'Anyway, he does more than simply clear away the tankards. His mother keeps most of her customers under control but, if one of them does start to cause mischief, it's Patrick who throws him out, young as he is. The lad's as strong as an ox.'

'Yes,' she confirmed. 'I saw him lift a beer barrel off a cart the other day. Most men would have rolled it along the ground but he carried it as if it was as light as a feather.' She shook her head worriedly. 'What's Bridget McCoy going to do with him?'

'Keep him at the tavern where she can watch over him,' said Bale. 'Mind you, that's not what the lad wants himself.'

'No?'

'He has an ambition, Sarah.'

'To do what?'

'My job – he wants to be a parish constable.'

She spluttered. 'Patrick McCoy?'

'Everyone's entitled to dream.'

'He could *never* do what you do, Jonathan.'

'The lad's eager and that's a good start. I've met too many officers who've been pushed into it against their will. If you resent what you have to do, how can you do it properly?'

'There are not many parish constables like you,' she said with an admiring smile. 'You love the work *and* do it well. And you're fit enough for the post. Constables in some parishes are almost decrepit.'

'I know at least three who are disabled, Sarah, yet they're kept hard at it because nobody else will come forward to take their place.' Clicking his tongue, he repeated a familiar complaint. 'No wonder there's so much crime in London when there are so few able-bodied men employed to prevent it. What's the point of laws if we lack the means to enforce them? We need more constables on the streets.'

'Could that lad possibly be one of them?'

'It's unlikely, I agree.'

'He's not clever enough.'

'Tom Warburton is hardly known for his brains.'

'Maybe not but Tom has other qualities.'

'So does Patrick – he's strong, honest and God-fearing.'

Sarah looked him in the eye. 'Would *you* like to work with him?'

'If it was a case of talking to people, or looking for clues, or reading documents of some sort, then the lad would be hopelessly out of his depth. But if I had to patrol the riverbank on a dark night,' said Bale, meeting her gaze, 'then I'd be more than happy to have him walking beside me.'

They had gone the best part of ten miles before they stopped at a wayside inn. While the horses were rested and watered, the travellers went inside for refreshment. Hester Polegate and her sons were too locked in their private anguish to be capable of any conversation so they dined alone in a corner. Christopher Redmayne shared a table with Sir Julius Cheever. It gave him an opportunity for time alone with the other man. Mindful of their last encounter, he kept off the subject that had so enraged his companion earlier.

'Having your daughter arrive from Richmond must have been a very pleasant surprise for you,' he began.

'I do not like surprises.'

'But this one must have gladdened your heart, Sir Julius.'

'Must it?'

'Mrs Serle is a member of your family.'

'Yes,' agreed Sir Julius, 'Brilliana does indeed have that claim on my affections. The trouble is that, where Mrs Serle goes, Mr Serle is always compelled to follow.'

'Do you not enjoy your son-in-law's company?'

'What is there to enjoy? Lancelot has neither wit nor affability.'

'I've always found him extremely affable.'

'That's because you've never had to endure his presence for any length of time. There's hardly any subject that I dare raise with him. If we discuss the way he manages his estates, I end up quarreling with him about his farming methods. And if he unloads his political opinions on me, I want to strangle the fellow with my bare hands.' He gave a mime by way of illustration. 'Last time I visited Richmond, he had the gall to tell me that the King was a credit to the Stuart dynasty.'

'I admire his bravery in doing so, Sir Julius.'

The old man glared at him. 'You share his sentiments?'

'Not entirely,' said Christopher. 'But if I did, I'd not have the courage to voice them so boldly in front of you. That must surely make you respect your son-in-law.'

'I'd respect him far more if he kept Brilliana from snapping at my heels whenever we meet. Children,' he continued. 'That's what she needs more than anything else – children. And where are they? There's no sign of them. After years of marriage, I've still not been presented with my first grandchild. It's unnatural, Christopher.'

'Perhaps your daughter does not wish for a family.'

'It's every woman's wish,' asserted Sir Julius, flatly. 'The fault lies not with Brilliana but with that milksop of a husband. He's clearly unequal to the office of fatherhood.'

'That's unkind,' said Christopher, defensively. 'Mr Serle does not deserve your scorn. Apart from anything else, he's made himself into a fine swordsman. I've had a few bouts with him and he's improved beyond all recognition.'

Sir Julius was grudging. 'I suppose that's in his favour.'

'He has many other good qualities and you must surely be grateful to any man who makes your elder daughter so happy.'

'Brilliana's happiness depends on having her every whim satisfied. There's no more capricious human being in the whole kingdom. I think that she should be challenged rather than indulged but Lancelot has chosen the easier path through life.'

'And seems content to do so.'

'Yes, I'll admit that.'

Talking about his family had helped to relax Sir Julius. He had not forgotten his recent confrontation with Christopher but he was ready to set it aside. It was as if a truce had been declared between them. As time passed, his manner softened even more and Christopher was tempted to explore the limits of their truce.

'Parliament sits in a few days, I believe,' he said.

'Yes,' said Sir Julius, sadly, 'and I'd hoped to introduce Bernard Everett to the chamber. It was not to be, I fear. But I'm sure that he'll forgive me if I rush back to London as soon as the funeral is over.'

'Mr Everett may have gone but you have other loyal friends there.'

'I thank the Lord for it.'

'One of them, I gather, is Lewis Bircroft.'

'Bircroft?' The old man's eye kindled. 'What do you know of him?'

'Only that he was a staunch supporter of you, Sir Julius.'

'You've been listening to that lunatic brother of yours again.'

'Henry is no lunatic.'

'He's a blabbering gossip.'

'He did tell me about the accident that befell Mr Bircroft,' admitted Christopher, 'that much is true. I wonder that you did not perceive a connection between that and what happened to Mr Everett.'

'Be warned, young man.'

'That's the very advice that you should take, Sir Julius.'

'Silence!'

'It's not only Mr Bircoft's fate that needs to be remembered. Arthur Manville must also be borne in—'

'Enough – damn you!' Sir Julius cut him short, growling in an undertone so that he did not disturb the three members of the Polegate family at the other table. 'Are you determined to test my temper?'

'Not at all, Sir Julius.'

'Well, you are going the right way about it.'

'I am bound to be concerned for your safety.'

'If you bother me again,' said Sir Julius, 'then you'll need to be concerned for your own safety. Keep away from me. I thought you were coming with us to pay to your respects to Bernard Everett but I see now that it was just a ruse to hound me.' He got up and towered over Christopher. 'Stand off, sir. Oblige me by holding your tongue in future. I've nothing more to say to you.'

The truce was over.

Patrick McCoy was industrious. The Saracen's Head stayed open for long hours and he worked tirelessly throughout that time, fetching and carrying, sweeping and clearing away, dealing firmly with the occasional obstreperous customer and doing all the other tasks that his mother assigned to him. Cheerful, willing and good-natured, he laboured without the slightest complaint. What he lacked in intelligence, he made up for in sheer application.

It was during a lull that afternoon that he spoke to his mother.

'Mr Bale thought I could be a constable one day,' he said.

'He was only being kind to you, Patrick.'

'It's no more than I do here, Mother.'

'It is,' she said. 'A parish constable has a lot of responsibilities. He has to keep his eye on so many different things. He has to make reports and appear in court. You could never do that.'

'I could if Mr Bale showed me how to do it.'

'Your place is here,' she said, cupping his chin in her hand. 'I need you beside me, Patrick. What would I do without my son?'

'Find someone else.'

'There's nobody like you.'

Bridget spoke with an amalgam of fondness and practicality. She loved her son deeply and depended on him completely. Had he been more competent, she would not have thwarted his ambition but she was aware of all the things that were beyond him. Ever since he had been born, she had been protecting him from mockery and doing her best to build his confidence. At the Saracen's Head, he had an important role. Anywhere else, his limitations would be cruelly exposed.

'What if I was to catch him?' he asked.

'Catch who?'

'The man with the broken nose.'

'You've no idea what he looks like, Patrick.'

'You do, Mother.' The vacant smile surfaced. 'Do you remember what you used to do when I was little?'

'I played with you whenever I could. So did your father.'

'You were much better at it than he was.'

'Better at what?'

'Drawing pictures for me,' he said. 'You drew pictures of animals and people and ships on the river. I liked them.'

'That was years ago, Patrick.'

'You can still do it.'

'I haven't the time,' she said. 'Besides, why should I bother?'

'Because it would help me.'

'I think you've outgrown childish pictures.'

'But it would show me what he looked like, Mother.'

'Who?'

'The man who fired that musket from upstairs,' he told her. 'If you drew a picture of his face, I'd know who he was if I saw him at the market. I'd be able to catch him for you. That's what you want, isn't it?'

She was taken aback. 'Yes, Patrick. It is.'

Bridget embraced him lovingly. It was not because she believed for a moment that he could ever apprehend the wanted man. It was because he had just given her an idea that might possibly assist the hunt for the killer. As a young mother, Bridget McCoy had indeed had a moderate skill as an artist. It had been employed in those days to amuse a demanding son. All that she used it for now was to design placards that went in the window to advertise the cost of drinks and accommodation. In the corner of each one, she always drew a smaller version of the Saracen's Head that adorned the signboard hanging outside the tavern. Customers had remarked on the accuracy of her portrayal. If she could recreate one head, she could surely copy a second from memory.

'Yes, Patrick,' she said. 'I will draw a picture of the man.'

'Will you give it to me? Can I take it to market tomorrow?'

'We'll show it to Mr Bale first.'

And she gave him another impulsive hug.

'At your age, I was already married,' Brilliana Serle proclaimed. 'It's high time that *your* mind turned in that direction.'

'That's for me to decide,' said Susan Cheever.

'It's my duty as an elder sister to advise you.'

'And it's my right to ignore that advice, Brilliana.'

'Married life can bring true fulfilment to a woman.'

'Not only to a woman,' Lancelot Serle interjected. 'It's the same for a man as well. I had no conception of what happiness really was until I met and married Brilliana. My whole world has been enlarged.'

'I'm delighted for both of you,' said Susan, looking from one to the other, 'but my situation is different. Brilliana was free to wed. I am not. As long as Father needs me, then he will always have first call on my love and time.'

'And what about your love for Christopher Redmayne?' asked Brilliana, aiming the question at her like a stone. 'Not to mention his patent adoration of you.'

Susan blushed. 'That's a private matter between the two of us.'

'Has he made a declaration?'

'He makes it every time they are together,' said Serle with a gentle smile. 'You can see it in his eyes and hear it in his voice. Christopher Redmayne is spellbound.'

'Excuse me,' said Susan, anxious to terminate the conversation. She reached across him to snip some roses with her shears. They were in the formal garden at the rear of the Westminster house, and Susan was collecting flowers for display in the parlour. Compared to the extensive gardens at their home in the Midlands, it was relatively small but it allowed her to grow a whole range of flowers and fruit. During their time away, men were employed to tend the garden. When she and her father were in residence, however, Susan liked to supervise them. For her, the garden had two major attractions. It was a pretty, secret, tranquil refuge from the ceaseless commotion of London, and, more important in her opinion, Christopher Redmayne had designed it.

It was ironic. She thought about him every day and longed to be with him. Yet now that her sister wanted to talk about the architect, Susan was rather unnerved. Strolling across the lawn, she hoped that she had curtailed the discussion but Brilliana was not so easily shaken off. She pursued her sister without mercy.

'Have you met his family?' she said.

'Yes, Brilliana.'

'They must have found you eminently acceptable.'

'They were not asked to accept me in the sense that you imply,' said Susan, adding some lavender to her basket. 'His father is the dean of Gloucester cathedral and his elder brother, Henry, works at the Navy Office.'

'The father is above reproach then. What of the brother?'

'He and Christopher are very different.'

'But the fellow is respectable, I trust?'

Susan faced her. 'Brilliana, I resent this interrogation.'

'We can't have anyone who lowers our family's standards. Before I even consented to have Lancelot as a suitor, I took very careful note of his people. That was imperative.'

'Fortunately,' said Serle, joining them, 'we survived your scrutiny. I'm certain that Christopher's family will do the same.'

'That remains to be seen, Lancelot.'

'No, it does not,' said Susan, turning to face her. 'There's no need for scrutiny of any kind. You are taking far too many things for granted, Brilliana. My place is here beside father. Christopher and I have made no plans whatsoever.'

'You'll lose him if you dither.'

'Yes,' agreed Serle. '*Tempus fugit.*'

'He'll slip right through your fingers, Susan.'

'I'll not be rushed into anything before I am ready,' asserted Susan, 'so I'll thank you to stop pressing me on the matter. Christopher and I are close friends. That situation contents both of us for the moment. I find it indelicate of you even to raise the matter.'

'My only concern is for your well-being,' said Brilliana.

'You may safely leave that in my own hands.'

'Things may soon change,' Serle pointed out. 'If Sir Julius should, by chance, marry, then your occupation's gone. A step-mother will replace you, Susan. You'll be in the way.'

'I don't foresee that happening,' said Susan.

'You must at least allow for the possibility.'

'Lancelot's point is a telling one,' said Brilliana, touching his arm in acknowledgement. 'Father is clearly enthralled with Mrs Kitson and a woman of her age would not encourage his advances unless the feeling between them were mutual. In due course, I suspect, what is now a mere possibility might well evanesce into a probability.'

Serle grinned. 'Sir Julius married again! Who'd have thought it?'

'We've not even met the lady yet,' Susan reminded them. 'When we do, she will understand what is at stake. In addition to taking on a third husband, she will also be acquiring two stepdaughters. Some people might find that rather daunting.'

'There's nothing remotely daunting about me,' claimed Brilliana, striking a pose. 'I'm the most agreeable person I know. Lancelot?'

'You are extremely agreeable, my dear,' he said, taking his prompt. 'And highly desirable as a stepdaughter – as, indeed, is your sister.'

'There were are, then – it's settled. Oh, how satisfying!' Brilliana rubbed her hands together. 'Father will wed Mrs Kitson and Susan will be free to accept a proposal from her inamorato.'

'Christopher is only a friend,' said Susan with exasperation.

Serle beamed. 'That's all I was when your sister and I first met,' he said, 'and look at us now. Cynics may cry that marriage is a form of enslavement but I found it an act of liberation. Brilliana has enabled me to do a whole host of things that I thought were completely outside my compass. She has empowered me.'

'That's why you must take the next step forward,' said Brilliana, imperiously. 'You must cut a figure in parliament, Lancelot. You are more than ready for it now.'

'You've made me *believe* I am ready, my dear. When you first mentioned the idea, I was anxious and hesitant but not any more. Your confidence in me has provided the fire I needed.'

Susan had never met anyone less fiery than her brother-in-law but she did not say so. Instead, she had an upsurge of sympathy for him. Lancelot Serle was an educated man with a range of talents but he was hardly suited for the bear pit of political life. Brilliana was trying to force him outside his natural milieu and he would suffer as a result. Living with her father gave Susan an insight into the physical and mental strains of parliamentary activity. Stronger men than her brother-in-law had been broken on its relentless wheel. There was another factor to be taken into account.

'You'd find yourself in opposition to Father,' remarked Susan.

'On some issues,' he said.

'On every issue, Lancelot.'

'What of that?' challenged Brilliana. 'My husband will stand up for his principles just as Father does. If that means they will clash in the House of Commons, so be it.'

'Diversity of opinion is inevitable,' said Serle, philosophically. 'It would be a dull Parliament House if we all agreed with each other. Out of discord comes forth compromise – and I am a master of that.'

'Then I wish you the best of luck,' said Susan, hiding her fears for him. 'What I would suggest, however, is that you do not reveal your ambitions to Father just yet.'

'He would not listen if I did. Sir Julius rarely listens to me.'

'His mind is on other things at the moment,' said Brilliana with a smile of approval, 'and that means he will listen to nobody. All that he can think of is his future wife, Mrs Dorothy Kitson.'

Dorothy Kitson stirred her cup of tea before tasting it. After taking a few sips, she set cup and saucer down and looked across the mahogany table at her brother.

'What objections do you have, Orlando?' she asked.

'They are not so much objections as lingering reservations.'

'You lawyers will play with words!'

'Then let me be more blunt, Dorothy.'

'I'd prefer that to all this equivocation.'

'First,' said her brother, counting his reasons off on his fingers, 'Sir Julius Cheever has the most abhorrent political views.'

'It's something we never discuss.'

'Second, his estates are in the wilds of Northamptonshire.'

'I'm given to believe that it's a county of some appeal.'

'Third – and you wish me to be honest – the fellow is too rough and ready for someone of your fine sensibilities. He's a farmer, Dorothy – and a soldier to boot. There's an uncouth air to him and he blusters. You have absolutely nothing in common with him.'

'Then why do we delight in each other's company?'

'Witchcraft!'

Dorothy laughed. Though she loved her brother, and leaned heavily on his advice, there were moments when he seemed hopelessly out of touch with normal human behaviour. She put it down to the fact that he had never married, or fathered a child, or ventured a single step outside the legal realm. Orlando Golland was a fleshy man in his sixties with heavy jowls that shook as he spoke, and a ginger wig that sat askew his overly large head. A brilliant lawyer in his day, he was now a justice of the peace in the city. His benign features concealed the fact that his habit of issuing unduly harsh sentences to those who appeared before him was legendary.

'Four,' he concluded, 'I do not like the fellow.'

'You did not like my first husband either,' she recalled.

'I came to appreciate his few recognisable virtues.' She laughed again. 'You sought my opinion and I've given it with clarity. I'm sorry that you ever met Sir Julius.'

'Then you should not have introduced me to him.'

'It was Maurice Farwell who did that.'

'Yes,' she riposted, 'but it was you who took me to Newmarket.'

'My horse was running there.'

'You must accept some of the blame, Orlando.'

'Not one iota.'

Brother and sister were in the parlour of Dorothy Kitson's house in Covent Garden, a stately mansion that was only one of four properties that she owned. The table at which they sat was cushioned by an expensive Turkish carpet and caught the light from the sash window. Two large, ornate, matching mirrors stood either side of a display cabinet that contained oriental porcelain. Large and well-proportioned, the room was an accurate reflection of her taste and her evident prosperity.

'Sir Julius does not belong *here*,' contended Golland. 'He would be totally out of place, Dorothy.'

'He has properties of his own.'

'Yes – the main one is in Northamptonshire!'

'It is not the end of the world.'

'It seems so to me. No,' he said, fussily. 'I could not possibly let you live there. It would be unbearable.'

'For whom?'

'For you, for me and for everyone who cares about you.'

'I appreciate your concern,' she said with a smile, 'but your assumptions are premature. All that I've told you is that Sir Julius and I have become friends and you immediately throw up a barricade across the aisle. Can one not have friendship without proceeding to marriage?'

'Of course.'

'Then your strictures become irrelevant.'

'The man is not *good* enough for you, Dorothy.'

'You hardly know him.'

'I know him by repute.'

'You are reputed to be the most ruthless magistrate in London,' she said, 'but it would be unfair to judge you solely on your record in court. I know that you have a more compassionate side to your character. The same is true of Sir Julius.'

'You'll never convince me of that.'

'Then I'll not waste time trying.'

'Beware, Dorothy!'

'Of what – my brother's false counsel?'

She sipped her tea and Golland lifted his own cup to his lips. Since he had never shown any serious interest in the opposite sex – still less in his own – he could not understand the passions that moved others. Horses were his only love. They had a graceful simplicity about them. Attraction between two people had always baffled Orlando Golland. Each time his sister had married, she had chosen men whose charm he had been quite unable to comprehend. He accepted them because at least they came from the same privileged background as his sister. Nothing would persuade him to welcome Sir Julius Cheever into the family.

'The wonder is that Maurice Farwell even spoke to the man,' he said as he remembered their visit to Newmarket. 'I'd have cut him dead.'

'Maurice is a gentleman. He treats his opponents with respect.'

'That disgusting old reprobate deserves no respect.'

'Sir Julius is younger than you, Orlando,' she pointed out, 'and he is neither disgusting nor a reprobate. He's a surprisingly cultured man, well-read and well-informed.'

'He helped to overthrow the monarchy, Dorothy.'

'That's all in the past.'

'Men like that never change.'

'And neither do you,' she said, fondly. 'I knew that it was a mistake to consult you. I needed guidance, not a recitation of Sir Julius's faults. In truth, I do not know what my feelings are for him. In talking to you, I hoped that I might find out. But that was far too much to ask. You put on your judicial robes and condemned him on sight.'

He was penitent. 'I am rightly chastised.'

'I forgive you.'

'Have you arranged to see him again?'

'Not yet.'

'But this friendship is set to develop?'

Dorothy was cautious. 'We shall see,' she decided. 'We shall see. After my second husband died, I vowed never to marry again but I did so at a time when I was overcome with grief. That is no longer the case.'

'You cannot mourn forever.'

'I know. As for Sir Julius, I will have to wait until he returns.'

'He has left the city?'

'Yes, Orlando,' she said. 'I had a note from him this morning. He is travelling to Cambridge to attend a funeral.'

They faced a problem. Eager to press on at a reasonable speed, they had to show respect for the dead. Even though he was hidden under a tarpaulin, Bernard Everett could not be hurried. The measured pace of a funeral was not required but neither was a headlong dash to their destination. At the behest of Sir Julius Cheever, coach and cart moved at a comfortable speed that would get them there eventually without causing any offence to the mourners who rode with him.

They were still in Hertfordshire when they made their second stop of the day. The inn gave them a chance to seek light refreshment and to answer any calls of nature. Horses that had become lathered in the hot sun could have a welcome rest in the shade. The coachman and the footman were glad of the chance to slip off their coats. The two men on the cart also relished the cover of the trees. Christopher Redmayne was the last to reach the inn, dismounting and tethering his horse close to the others. Determined not to upset Sir Julius again, he stayed outside and strolled off through a stand of oaks and elms.

It had been an uneventful journey. Moving at such a moderate speed had given him an opportunity to study the landscape with a degree of leisure. Hertfordshire was one of the smallest counties in England. Rivers and streams abounded, crisscrossing the terrain in almost every direction and forcing them to make use of various bridges and fords. It was a granary for London, providing corn for its bread and hay fodder for its horses. Many fields were given over to beef cattle, some of the herds having been driven down from the north to be fattened on the lush grass before sale in the capital.

Christopher had also noticed how many watercress beds they passed in the villages. An antidote to the scurvy that afflicted so many Londoners, watercress was always in great demand. Of more interest to the architect was the large number of country houses he had seen, rural retreats from the stench and squalor of the city, places of escape from the regular outbreaks of plague. Helping to rebuild London after the ravages of the Great Fire, his concerns were exclusively urban. He was fascinated to see how houses could be designed to blend into the landscape, and how fine architecture could, in turn, be enhanced by its surroundings. The journey was also a learning process for Christopher.

Emerging from the trees, he saw yet another stream, meandering lazily through the grass before disappearing in a spinney. Ahead of him, in the distance, was a building that arrested his gaze at once, a magnificent prodigy house, constructed in the previous century by someone with high ambition and unlimited capital. Burnished by the sun, it stood on a rise that commanded a panoramic view. Its array of gables, turrets and pinnacles gave it the appearance of a fairytale palace. A banner fluttered from the flagpole on top of the tower.

'That's what you should be designing,' said a voice behind him.

Christopher looked over his shoulder and saw, to his surprise, that Sir Julius was coming through the trees. The long ride in a stuffy coach seemed to have drained much of the hostility out of him.

'A place like that,' continued the old man, surveying the house with approval, 'could make you rich and famous.'

'But it would take so long to build that I would soon tire of it. I prefer to design houses in a city,' said Christopher, 'places that are likely to be completed in a year rather than in twenty or thirty. London is the greatest city in the world and I feel honoured to be able to make a small contribution towards reshaping it.'

'Would you not like to have created *that* house?'

'No, Sir Julius.'

'Why not? It looks superb.'

'But it was designed long ago when such a style was in fashion. Had I been its architect,' said Christopher, 'I would now be well over a hundred years old.' Sir Julius chortled. 'I'll settle for smaller projects with more immediate results.'

'Like the house you designed for me in Westminster?'

'My memory is that *you* designed it, Sir Julius. I merely executed your wishes. Not that I disagreed with any of your specifications,' he added, hastily, 'but I'll not take full credit for a property that sprang largely from your fertile brain.'

'I knew what I wanted.'

'That makes you almost unique among my clients.'

Christopher was relieved to be back on speaking terms with him but Sir Julius had not come for conversation. He was there to stretch his legs and to enjoy a pipe of tobacco while he could. Leaving the architect, he sauntered down to the stream then followed its serpentine course for thirty yards or so. He paused to light his pipe and inhaled deeply. There was an air of contentment about him. Peering down into the water, he seemed to Christopher to be far more at ease in a rural setting. London was anathema to him. Sir Julius was, in essence, a country gentleman, a rogue politician who could set a corrupt parliament by the ears but who was happiest when at home on his estates.

Studying the father, Christopher became acutely aware of the daughter. Susan Cheever also loved the country. That was where she could be a free spirit. She came to London under duress and only found it tolerable because of Christopher's friendship. What he did not know was whether that friendship was strong enough to entice her to stay. His future lay in the city, her hopes resided in the country. Christopher feared that those competing calls might gradually ease them apart.

He was still meditating on the unresolved problem when he

saw something out of the corner of his eye. Turning his head in the direction of the spinney, Christopher observed a brief flash as the sun glinted off an object half-hidden in the undergrowth. He sensed danger at once and responded. Drawing his sword, he charged towards Sir Julius and yelled at the top of his voice.

'Get down!' he shouted. 'Get down on the ground!'

The warning was a fraction too late. As Sir Julius spun round to look at him, a musket was fired from the spinney and the old man was hit. Before Christopher could reach him, he let out a cry of pain and stumbled backwards, losing his balance and falling into the stream with a loud splash. Spat from his mouth, the clay pipe was carried along by the rippling water, a thin wisp of smoke still rising from it until the bowl tipped over and the tobacco was swallowed up in one liquid gulp.

Chapter Seven

Christopher Redmayne was momentarily stopped in his tracks, not knowing whether to go to the aid of the victim or to pursue the man who had shot him. He soon made his decision. Sir Julius was flailing about in the water, clearly in difficulty but very much alive. Sheathing his sword, Christopher ran down to the stream and plunged straight in, wading swiftly across to him.

'I'm coming, Sir Julius,' he called.

'Get me out of here!' spluttered the other.

'Are you hurt?'

'I can't swim.'

When Christopher reached him, he took him hold of his shoulders but Sir Julius let out a grunt of pain and put a protective hand to his left arm. Seeing where the wound was, Christopher instead grasped him around the waist and pulled him towards the bank. Others came running to help. Having heard the shot, the coachman and the footman darted through the trees and made for the stream. Christopher was glad of their assistance. Between them, they hauled Sir Julius on to the bank and laid him gently on the grass.

The musket ball had grazed his upper arm, tearing his sleeve and the shirt beneath it, and producing a spurt of blood. Stung by the shot, Sir Julius was more alarmed by the fact that he had gone under the water for a few seconds. He was sodden from head to foot and he twitched on the ground like a giant fish caught in a net. Christopher insisted on easing off the coat so that he could examine the wound. When he saw that it was a deep gash, and that no bone had been shattered, he removed his own coat. He tore a long strip from his shirt, using it to bind the wound and stem the flow of blood.

'What happened?' asked Sir Julius, still dazed by it all.

'Someone fired at you,' said Christopher.

'Who was the devil?'

'That's what I hope to find out.'

Satisfied that Sir Julius was now safe, Christopher hared across the grass towards the spinney and vanished into the trees. His sword was back in his hand and he did not mind that he was dripping wet to the waist. He blamed himself for being caught off guard. Determined to make amends, he searched the spinney thoroughly, using his sword to push back shrubs and bushes. But the attacker had fled. As he came out of the trees on the other side, Christopher found a set of hoof prints gouged in the earth, suggesting a speedy departure. The man could be half a mile away by now.

Filled with remorse, he trudged back towards the others, fearing how Susan Cheever would react when she learned what had happened to her father. Christopher had not forewarned her of the danger that Sir Julius faced and that was certain to horrify her. There would be fierce recriminations. It was only by luck that Sir Julius had not been killed. In responding to Christopher's yell, he had turned almost simultaneously as the shot was fired. That sudden movement had saved his life but it was no use pointing that out to his younger daughter. She would want to know why Christopher had not confided in her beforehand so that she could have insisted her father take more care on the journey.

Sir Julius was sitting up as Christopher approached.

'Any sign of the villain?'

'None,' replied Christopher. 'He got clean away.'

'A pox on him! Look at me,' said Sir Julius, indignantly. 'I was almost drowned, my arm is on fire, my coat has been ruined, and my pipe has floated off downstream.'

'It could have been worse, Sir Julius. Someone tried to kill you. It's only by the grace of God that you are not making the rest of the journey beside Mr Everett.'

'Do you think I don't know that? Get me up.'

'Are you sure that you can stand?'

'Of course, man. It's only a flesh wound. I've had far worse.'

Taking care not to touch the injured arm, Christopher lifted him to his feet with the help of the coachman. Water was still dripping copiously from Sir Julius. He let out a snort of disgust.

'Thank heaven I have some fresh apparel with me!'

'It might be better if you changed in private,' advised Christopher.

'I was not intending to strip naked in front of an audience.'

'What I meant is that Mrs Polegate and her children would be shocked if they learned what had happened. To spare them any further distress, it might be politic to say nothing.'

'I agree.' Sir Julius glanced at the other men. 'Not a word of this, do you understand?' Both gave a nod of assent. 'We'll give out that I fell in the river by accident and that Mr Redmayne rescued me. Now – fetch some blankets from the inn. Nobody should see us in this state.'

The coachman and the footman went off. Sheathing his sword, Christopher glanced towards the spinney. Unbeknown to them, they had been followed. When they stopped at the inn, someone had worked his way around them then lurked in the trees ahead on the off-chance that his target would come into view. Christopher had one tiny consolation. Sir Julius would no longer be able to deny that he was in jeopardy. It was, however, certainly not the time to emphasize that point.

'How do you feel now, Sir Julius?' he inquired.

'Very wet.'

'What about your arm?'

'It hurts like blazes,' said Sir Julius, 'but that's the least of my worries. My main concern is for Hester Polegate and the boys.'

'Why?'

'I'm a marked man, Christopher. The rogue who failed to kill me will surely try again. As long as they travel with me, Hester and her sons are imperilled. I'm knowingly putting them at risk.'

'There's no need to feel guilty, Sir Julius.'

'How can I help it?'

'By remembering the man in the trees.'

'What do you mean?'

'His shot knocked you off your feet and into the stream,' said Christopher. 'From where he was standing, it must have looked as if he'd killed you. That's why he made such a rapid escape. You can forget about him altogether now. He's riding back to London to tell his paymaster that Sir Julius Cheever is dead.'

Because the man was a Member of Parliament, involved in the government of the nation, Jonathan Bale had assumed that he would have a distinguished address in London. This was not the case at all. When the House of Commons was sitting, and his presence was required in the capital, Lewis Bircroft, who hailed from Norfolk, lodged with friends in their modest house in Coleman Street. Bale had an immediate affinity with the district. In earlier days, the place had been a well-known stronghold of Puritanism.

He was admitted to the house by its owner and asked to wait in the little parlour while Bircroft was summoned. It was some time before the man actually appeared because he had some difficulty descending the staircase. Expecting someone with an air of authority about him, Bale was surprised to meet a short, stooping, emaciated old man with tufts of grey hair sprouting above a prominent forehead like patches of grass on a cliff top. There was a hunted look in Bircroft's eyes and his face was lined with concern. Using a walking stick, he also held his neck at an unusual angle as if it had been twisted out of shape.

Bale introduced himself and explained that he had been to the Parliament House to discover where Bircroft was staying in London. He apologised for calling but said that it was necessary to do so. The other man was extremely wary.

'What do you want with me, Constable?' he asked.

'A few minutes of your time, sir.'

'Then I must sit down.'

'Of course, Mr Bircroft.'

'Bear with me.'

What was a simple movement for Bale was a more complicated exercise for the other man. Shuffling to a chair, he lowered himself with agonising slowness on to it, his limbs poking out at odd angles as he settled down. He was clearly in constant pain. Sitting opposite him. Bale felt sorry for the man. However, he had been sent to get information and did not wish to leave without it.

'Do you know a man named Bernard Everett?' said Bale.

'Yes, he lives near Cambridge.'

'Not any more, I'm afraid. He died some days ago.'

'Dear me!' exclaimed Bircroft. 'What a terrible shame! Bernard was about to join us in the Parliament House. I only arrived here yesterday so I was quite unaware of this news. Had he been ill for long?'

'It was not a natural death, Mr Bircroft. He was murdered.'

The old man gurgled and looked as if he were on the point of having a seizure. Bale had to wait a long while before Bircroft felt able to continue. The visitor explained what had happened in Knightrider Street and how he had become part of the hue and cry that had been set up.

'I'll not abide it, Mr Bircroft,' he said, grimly. 'I'll not have people shot dead in Baynard's Castle ward. However much time and effort it takes, we'll find this villain and see him hang.'

'I admire your commitment, Mr Bale, but I fail to see how I can be of any assistance to you. I did not know Bernard Everett well.'

'But you were a close friend of Sir Julius Cheever.'

'I was,' confessed Bircroft, 'at one time.'

'Are you no longer associated with him?'

'Only in the loosest way.'

'I believe that you and he shared so many common objectives,' said Bale. 'May I ask why the two of you fell out?'

Bircroft looked away. 'That's a private matter.'

'You were wont to visit his house.'

'Yes, I was.'

'Did you lose faith in your ideals?'

'No!' retorted Bircroft. 'I would never do that and I find your question offensive. I repudiate nothing.' He was trembling with passion. 'Do you know where you are, Mr Bale?'

'Yes, sir – in Coleman Street.'

'And are you aware of its reputation?'

'Of course, Mr Bircroft. I rejoice in its Puritan values.'

'In 1642, when the King's father was on the throne, he sought to silence opposition in parliament by arresting five of its leaders. Those men – Pym, Hampton, Hesilrige, Holles and Strode – had to flee for their lives. They hid here in Coleman Street. A week later, they were able to return in triumph to Westminster.'

'I'm familiar with the story, sir.'

'Then do not accuse me of lacking ideals. I stay in this part of the city because this is where I belong, politically and in every other sense. I may not have the same strength to champion my beliefs in the House of Commons, but I can work by other means to achieve my ends. I write pamphlets, I speak to clubs in private, I disseminate ideas.'

'Yet you withdrew from the group that is led by Sir Julius.'

'I admit it freely.'

'And another man who fell away was Mr Manville.'

'Arthur had his own reasons.'

'Was it because he had his nose slit?' said Bale, repeating the question he had read in Christopher's letter. 'And were you, in turn, frightened away by the men who attacked you with cudgels?'

Bircroft shuddered as harrowing memories flooded back. Two hideous minutes in an alleyway had left his body permanently distorted and he would never be able to walk properly again. Yet he tried to cling on to a shred of dignity.

'Violence will never change my fundamental ideals.'

'But it can stop you expressing them.'

'I was foolish,' claimed Bircroft. 'When I walked through Covent Garden that day, I did not keep my wits about me. Those bullies fell on me because I was an easy prey. Once they'd knocked me senseless, they stole my purse and made off. Anyone else who'd been alone in that alleyway would have suffered the same fate.'

'So you did not see the beating as a kind of warning?'

'No, Mr Bale.'

'What about the attack on Mr Manville?'

'Ask him about that,' said Bircroft, knuckles tightening on his walking stick. 'Arthur was too reckless. He courted a particular lady even though she was married. Her husband learned of it. I think that *he* paid for the disfigurement.'

'Is that what Mr Manville thinks?'

'Yes.'

'And was the husband in question a politician, by any chance?'

'What difference does that make?'

'Was he, Mr Bircroft?' pressed Bale.

The old man shifted uneasily in his chair. 'Yes,' he said.

'But not of your persuasion?'

'Good Lord – no!'

'So it could have been an attack on a political opponent?'

'Why are you bothering me with these questions?'

'Because we see a link here,' said Bale.

'Between what?'

'All three of you, sir.'

'I do not follow.'

'You, Mr Manville and Mr Everett,' said the constable. 'It's too much of a coincidence. One by one, Sir Julius Cheever's supporters have been whittled away. Mr Manville does not speak in parliament any more, you are in no condition to do so, and Mr Everett was never even allowed to take his seat. The same person is behind all these outrages. You must have some idea who he might be.'

Lewis Bircroft tried to summon up a look of defiance but it simply would not come. Instead, his body drooped, his face crumpled and tears began to roll slowly down his cheeks.

Brilliana Serle was an enterprising woman. Failing to get what she felt was adequate cooperation from her sister, she decided to take matters into her own hands. Accordingly, she and her husband set off in their coach to find out what they could about the Redmayne family. Susan had been so reticent about Christopher's brother that her suspicions had been aroused. Truth needed to be sought. While Brilliana was in high spirits, her husband was having doubts about the expedition.

'Would it not be better to wait until Christopher returns?' he said.

'No, Lancelot.'

'But it would be quite improper of us to arrive on his brother's doorstep without the courtesy of a warning.'

'We do not have to enter the building,' she explained. 'I merely wish to see it from outside. A house can tell one so much about its owner and I would like to learn all that I can about Henry Redmayne.'

'What if Susan were to find out what we've done?'

'Then we'll deny it hotly.'

'But that would be a deception.'

'It would be a white lie and therefore of no consequence,' she said, flicking away his objection with a peremptory gesture. 'We are acting in my sister's best interests, Lancelot. Keep that in mind.'

'Yes, Brilliana.'

'If I knew where Mrs Kitson lived, I'd suggest that we perused *her* residence in passing as well.'

'That would be quite wrong,' he argued. 'We are not spies.'

'We are intelligencers for our family, and that entitles us to take whatever steps we decide.'

'Whatever steps *you* decide, I fancy.'

'Someone has to make the decisions.'

Their coach was part of the traffic that rattled along the Strand but it soon swung left into Bedford Street, a wide thoroughfare with handsome buildings on either side. The coachman drove up to the end of the street then stopped so that its occupants could alight. Taking her husband's arm, Brilliana strolled back down the street with him until she found the house that she was after. They paused in order to appraise it. Henry Redmayne's home was a tall, elegant, stone-built structure with a pleasing symmetry and a good location. Well outside the reach of the Great Fire, it had sustained none of the damage that afflicted most of the city. Over the years, it had weathered well.

Serle felt embarrassed to be staring at someone else's house but his wife wanted to see her fill. She ran her eyes over every inch of the building before she gave her verdict.

'It's the home of a gentleman,' she announced.

'May we return to the coach now, Brilliana?'

'Though it's in need of repair in one or two places.'

'We are not surveyors, my dear,' he said, trying to lead her away. 'Now that you have satisfied your curiosity, let us withdraw.'

The clatter of hooves made them turn towards the Strand and they saw a horseman approaching at a canter. He reined in his mount only yards away from them.

'Why are you peering at my house?' he inquired, eyeing them

with faint suspicion. 'Do you have business here?'

'Am I speaking to Henry Redmayne?' said Brilliana.

'You are.'

'I see little resemblance to your brother.'

'Your are acquainted with Christopher?'

'My name is Brilliana Serle,' she said, 'and this is my husband, Lancelot. We are staying in London at the home of my father, Sir Julius Cheever. I believe that you've met my sister.'

'Briefly.' Henry dismounted and doffed his hat with a flourish. 'I'm pleased to meet you, Mrs Serle – and you, sir.' His gaze remained on Brilliana. 'I can see a clear likeness to Susan.'

'In character,' Serle volunteered, 'they are poles apart.'

'And rightly so. It would not do if sisters were exactly the same, and I think it imperative for a man to be as different from his brother as he can possibly contrive. Variety is needed in a family – don't you agree, Mrs Serle?'

'I do, Mr Redmayne,' she said, studying him shrewdly.

'You work at the Navy Office, I hear,' said Serle.

'I've just returned from there,' said Henry, sparing him no more than a glance. 'When one lives on an island, as we do, the maintenance of a strong navy is vital. I'm proud to assist in that important mission.'

'Then I commend you, sir.'

Henry did not even hear him. He was too busy contemplating Brilliana, noting how irresistibly fetching she looked in a dress of blue and gold, colours that enhanced her beauty. For his part, Henry wore less flamboyant apparel than was usual but he was still a model of ostentation beside the more soberly attired Lancelot Serle. His dark periwig threw the paleness of his face into relief. Brilliana accorded him the same close scrutiny as the house. Older than his brother, his features were sharper, more mature and, in her opinion, far more interesting. It was a face that, self-evidently, had seen a great deal of life and it somehow gave her an unexpected thrill.

'What brought you to London?' said Henry.

'News of that foul murder in Knightrider Street,' she replied. 'My father was inadvertently caught up in it.'

'So was my brother.'

'We know.'

'As a matter of fact, I was able to furnish him with information that may in time lead to an arrest. I have many friends in the political arena,' he went on, airily, 'and my attendance at court has widened my circle even more. Christopher often trades on my knowledge of the great and good of England.'

Brilliana was intrigued. 'You belong to the court?'

'His Majesty has been kind enough to include me among his many acquaintances. We have always been on excellent terms.'

'You hear that, Lancelot?'

'What, my dear?' said Serle.

'Mr Redmayne moves in high places. It's the sort of thing that you should be doing.' She turned back to Henry. 'My husband has ambitions to enter parliament. To move in court circles as well would be an even greater achievement.'

'But well outside my reach, Brilliana.'

'I disagree.'

'What would your father say? You know his opinion of monarchy.'

'I'm only concerned with *my* opinion,' she said, proudly, 'and I'm an admirer of His Majesty. What do you think, Mr Redmayne? Would it be possible for someone like my husband to enter the portals of the Palace?'

'If he were introduced by the right person,' replied Henry, unable to keep his eyes off her. 'But why are we discussing such lofty subjects out here in the street? Since you have taken an interest in my house, perhaps you would like to see its interior as well. It would be an honour to welcome you as my guest.' He and Brilliana exchanged a prolonged smile. Henry then remembered that someone else was there. His head swung round to Serle. 'And you, too, sir. Pray, follow me.'

Accustomed to rising early, Christopher Redmayne was up not long after dawn to wash, shave and eat his breakfast. The funeral was to be held in the parish church of a village some four miles south-east of Cambridge. Since there was no room at the Everett household for either of them, Christopher and Sir Julius were staying at an inn nearby. The injury sustained by the latter had been concealed from everyone else, though Sir Julius had taken the precaution of finding a local doctor who had examined and dressed the wound for him. Since the old man's enemies would presume that he was dead, Christopher felt that his companion was out of immediate danger. That encouraged him to slip quietly away from the inn while Sir Julius was still snoring contentedly in his bed as he dreamed of Dorothy Kitson.

Cambridge looked majestic in the early morning light, a seat of learning that was also a display of architectural excellence over the centuries. Christopher found it breathtaking. He knew Oxford well but this was his first visit to its rival in the fens. Peterhouse, the oldest college, had been founded in 1280 and by the time of the Reformation, fourteen more colleges had been added. But it was not only the university that defined the town. Churches, chapels, halls, houses, civic buildings and extensive parks made their contribution, and the River Cam was an ever-present landmark. Christopher felt that he was stepping back in time to a more scholarly era when men were untroubled by the religious and political upheavals that had shaken the Stuart dynasty to its foundations.

Permitting himself only a few hours, he did not waste a second of it. He went everywhere, saw everything and drank it in like fine wine. As a practising architect, he never travelled without his sketchbook and it came out of his saddlebag as soon as he arrived. Any feature that caught his eye was duly recorded, more for its own intrinsic worth than because he could ever make use of it in his own work. He savoured the talents of stonemasons, wood carvers, blacksmiths, tapestry-makers, glaziers and carpenters. He marvelled at the minds of the master builders who had conceived the various edifices.

Most of all, he loved the higgledy-piggledy nature of the town, its narrow, twisting, cobbled streets, its jumbled confusion, its pervading sense of improvisation. And there at the heart of it, reminding him that this was somewhere to live, eat and drink as well as to study, was a thriving marketplace, filled with noise, smells and all the paraphernalia of commerce. By the time that he had completed his tour of Cambridge, his sketchbook was brimming with memories and his heart was pounding at the thought of belonging to a profession with such a noble heritage. Christopher had only come to the funeral in order to protect Sir Julius Cheever. Three hours in the university town was a more than ample reward for the vicissitudes of the journey.

Jonathan Bale had just left his house when he saw someone coming down Addle Hill, waving a piece of paper in his hand like a flag. It was Patrick McCoy and his face was glowing with excitement.

'It was my idea, Mr Bale,' he bragged. 'It was my idea.'

'What was, Patrick?'

'This.'

He thrust the paper into Bale's hands. The constable looked down at a rough portrait in charcoal of a man's face. Bridget McCoy was only an innkeeper but she had a good eye and a deft hand. The picture was striking. She had put enough detail and character into it to make it more than a crude sketch. The broken nose dominated but she had also recalled the man's large ears and the mole on his right cheek. Within her strict limitations, she had brought him to life again.

'That's him,' said Patrick.

'So I see.'

'I know who to look for now.'

'Does your mother think it's a fair likeness?'

'Yes, Mr Bale. She spent hours over it. Mother must have done five or six drawings before she was happy. This is the man,' he said, jabbing a finger at the portrait. 'This is the killer.'

'Then his face ought to be on some handbills.'

'There's no need for that.'

'I could go straight to the printer's now.'

'No,' protested the youth. 'That would be unfair.'

'Unfair?'

'He's ours, Mr Bale. We don't want anyone else to catch him.'

'Someone might identify him from this,' said Bale. 'They

could tell us where we could find Mr Field.'

'But we know where to find him.'

'Do we, Patrick?'

'Yes, at Leadenhall Market.'

'That may just have been a chance visit on his part.'

'It wasn't,' said Patrick. 'I know it for sure. He'll be there again one day. All we have to do is to wait and watch.'

'I can't spend every morning in Leadenhall Street.'

'I'll do it for you, Mr Bale.'

'No, lad.'

'It will be a test for me.'

'Test?'

'I can show you how good a constable I can be. Let me be your lookout, Mr Bale. Let me work with you.'

'Tom Warburton does that.'

'I'm stronger than Mr Warburton. I'm younger and faster.'

'That's true,' said Bale, 'but you don't have Tom's experience. We know how dangerous Mr Field is. He may well go abroad armed. Tom and I know how to overpower such a man.'

'So do I.'

'No, Patrick. This man is no reeling drunk at the Saracen's Head. You can't just grab him. He's a killer. He needs to be stalked.'

'Then let me stalk him.'

'Leave him to us. We know what to do.'

'But I want to *help*,' insisted Patrick.

'You already have helped, lad.' Bale held up the drawing. 'If this really was your idea, then you deserve praise. It shows that you can think like a constable even if you're not old enough to be one yet.'

'I will be old enough one day.'

'Go back to your mother and thank her from me.' He patted the youth on the shoulder. 'And tell her that she has a very clever son.'

The funeral took place late that afternoon. Customarily, funerals tended to be held in the evenings when light was falling and it was a common complaint that undertakers only encouraged the practice so that they could increase their profits by providing the candles. It was Bernard Everett's widow who decided to have her husband buried at the earliest opportunity so that it could remain essentially a private affair. Since he represented the county in parliament, Everett was known far and wide and, had all his friends and acquaintances come to mourn him, the funeral would have been so well-attended that the widow could not have coped. A service of remembrance for a much larger gathering could be held at a later date. What Rosalind Everett required now was a swift, simple ceremony.

Christopher Redmayne stayed on the fringe of the event. He was invited into the house for drinks before the funeral and introduced to the various family members. The chief mourners wore black attire and the hearse, in which the coffin was draped in black, had black horses with black plumes to pull it. The service was both moving and disquieting. Though the priest heaped fulsome praise on Bernard Everett, his words brought little solace. Instead of thinking about his life, the congregation was preoccupied with the manner of his death. The widow bore up well throughout and it was Hester Polegate who collapsed in tears. She was taken aside and soothed by her husband, the London vintner.

Everyone returned to the house for refreshments after the service but Christopher and Sir Julius soon took their leave so that they could travel at least part of the way back to London by nightfall. Since the Polegate family elected to remain at the Everett house for a few days, the coach only had one occupant on the return journey. Christopher was delighted when Sir Julius invited the architect to join him. With his horse tethered to the rear of the vehicle, Christopher sat opposite the other man as they drove towards London. From the time when they had first arrived, he had taken care not even to mention the attack upon Sir Julius. The subject now had to be discussed and it was the man himself who broached it.

'I must tender my apologies, Christopher,' he said.

'There's no need for that, Sir Julius.'

'There's every need. I was rude, inconsiderate and stupid.'

'I felt that I had to warn you,' said Christopher.

'You were so wise to do so. And how did I respond? Was I grateful that you had such concern for my safety? Was I glad that you had taken the trouble to inquire about political colleagues of mine who had suffered for their ideals? No,' admitted Sir Julius. 'I was too busy pretending that it could never happen to me.'

'And now?'

'I know better, Christopher.'

'Mr Everett died in your place. The shot was intended for you.'

'I accept that.'

'What happened by that stream proves it.'

'Indubitably,' said Sir Julius. 'Every time I feel a twinge in my left arm, I'm reminded of the incident. Zounds! Though he failed to kill me, I could easily have drowned in that water, had you not pulled me out. Ugh!' he went on, grimacing. 'I can still taste the stuff. I must have drunk a gallon of it as I went under.'

'As long as you take full precautions in future,' urged Christopher.

'Oh, I will, I will.'

'Go out as little as possible.'

'I must to the Parliament House when the session opens.'

'From what Susan tells me, Sir Julius, your own home is a veritable Parliament House. It's a pity you cannot conduct business there, well away from danger.'

'I'm not afraid, Christopher. I need to be *seen*. I have to show my enemies that I'm not put to flight by a stray musket ball.'

'They'll have a shock when they realise you are still alive.'

'I'll give them even more shocks when they're unmasked!'

'Go armed at all times,' advised Christopher.

'I do.'

'I see no weapon about you.'

'Stand up.'

'What?'

'Get to your feet so that you may raise the seat.'

Christopher obeyed the order and lifted the cushioned seat. Lying beneath it was a blunderbuss and a supply of powder and ammunition.

'I keep it loaded,' said Sir Julius. 'It's a great persuader if any

highwayman should deign to stop us. Lower it down.'
Christopher did so and resumed his seat. 'What I'll not do again
is to be caught out in the open, alone and unguarded.'

'That's music to my ears.'

The old man leaned forward. 'I value your discretion.'

'Discretion?'

'Susan was told nothing of your fears. Otherwise, she'd have
done her best to stop me going to Cambridge. Thank you,
Christopher.'

'I did not wish to alarm her.'

'You spared her much anguish.'

'I'll be blamed for doing that, Sir Julius. When she hears about
the attack on you, Susan will be very angry with me.'

Sir Julius grinned. 'My daughter will be more than angry. She
has Cheever blood in her veins. You concealed something from
her that she had a right to know. Susan will want you hanged,
drawn and quartered.'

'I'm not looking forward to telling her.'

'Then why do so?'

'Something as important as this cannot be hidden.'

'Yes, it can,' said Sir Julius, indicating his left arm. 'My sleeve
will cover the wound and Susan will be none the wiser.'

'But what if she should learn the truth by other means?'

'What other means? The coachman and the footman have
been sworn to secrecy. The only other person who knows about
the attack was the man who fired that musket, and he's unlikely
to tell her. No,' Sir Julius went on, 'we must conspire together for
her peace of mind. Why cause her unnecessary upset? There's no
way that Susan will ever find out that her father's life is in danger.'

Lancelot Serle was too honest a man to nurse a guilty secret for
long. After a day of brooding, and in spite of warnings from his
wife, he blurted it out over supper that evening.

'We met Christopher's brother yesterday,' he volunteered.

'Did you?' Susan was astonished. 'Why did you not say so
when you returned from your drive?'

'Because it was only a casual encounter,' said Brilliana,

shooting her husband a venomous look, 'and hardly worth mentioning.'

'Where did this encounter take place?'

'Outside his house.'

'And inside, Brilliana,' said Serle, determined to make a clean breast of it. 'We went to Bedford Street to look at his house from outside when Mr Redmayne came riding home.'

'It was a happy accident,' said Brilliana.

'I call it bare-faced audacity,' cried Susan, looking across the table at her sister. 'Whatever possessed you to go near Henry's house?'

'We were only acting on your account.'

'I did so with great reluctance,' said Serle.

'Keep out of this, Lancelot,' advised his wife in a tone of voice that suggested he would be severely reprimanded later on. 'You've already said too much.'

'I'm glad that Lancelot spoke,' Susan continued, her anger rising. 'It's bad enough that you should do such a thing. Hiding your treachery from me only makes it worse.'

'No treachery was involved, Susan.'

'You went there behind my back.'

'Only because you'd never have sanctioned a visit.'

'I'd have resisted the notion with every breath in my body.'

'When you spoke about Henry Redmayne,' said Brilliana, 'I felt that you were hiding something and I wanted to know what it was. A first step was to look at the house where he lived.'

Serle nodded. 'We were doing that when the gentleman rode up.' He caught another glare from his wife. 'You tell it, Brilliana.'

'As it was,' continued his wife, 'Mr Redmayne – Henry – was kind enough to invite us in so that we could see the inside of the house. In fact, we stayed there for some time.'

'Talking about me, I suppose?' said Susan, clearly upset.

'Your name did come into the conversation.'

'Brilliana, this is quite unforgivable! How dare you intrude into my private life? Even by your standards, this is shameful behaviour.'

'My standards have always been impeccably high.'

'Well, they sank to the depths yesterday.'

'I was acting on your behalf, Susan. Don't you understand that? If we are to be more closely allied to the Redmayne family, it behoves me to find out more about it.'

'And where is your next port of call?' asked her sister with biting sarcasm. 'Do you intend to bang on the doors of Gloucester cathedral and demand to see the dean?'

'No. Henry is much more entertaining company.'

'Though I deplore his taste in art,' Serle put in.

'I found it rather diverting.'

'Brilliana, how can you say such a thing?' He turned to Susan. 'The first thing you see as you enter the hall is a depiction of a Roman orgy, and there's hardly a room where naked females do not adorn the walls. They are painted with great cunning, I grant you, but are they suitable for public exhibition?'

'You are too narrow-minded, Lancelot.'

'Would you hang such obscenities in our home?'

'That's neither here nor there,' said Susan, irritably. 'The simple fact is that you should never have gone anywhere near Bedford Street. As for being invited into the house so that you could discuss my private affairs, that was unpardonable.'

'But we learned something of importance about Father.'

'It was the reason why I had to speak out,' said Serle. 'Since you actually share the house with Sir Julius, it would be wholly unfair to keep it from you a moment longer. The wonder is that you did not hear it from Christopher.'

'Hear what?' asked Susan.

'Henry Redmayne has been advising his brother with regard to the murder investigation.'

'Yes,' said Brilliana, admiringly. 'Henry is remarkable. He knows everyone in London who is worth knowing, from His Majesty downwards. After the tragedy in Knightrider Street, he had a visit from his brother. Christopher asked him about any enemies that Bernard Everett might have in parliament.'

'Mr Everett had not even taken his seat.'

'Exactly – that was why Christopher was so puzzled by the murder. His worst suspicions were confirmed by Henry and by

Members of Parliament introduced to him by his brother.'

Susan was perplexed. 'Christopher told me of no suspicions.'

'Well, he certainly entertained them,' said Brilliana, 'and with justification. Henry confirmed what his younger brother feared. Bernard Everett was mistaken for someone else and died in his place. There's not a shadow of doubt about it. That man was hired to kill Father.'

Patrick McCoy was single-minded. Having decided that he would one day be an officer of the law, he thought about nothing else. Jonathan Bale may have taken the final crude portrait but there were half-a-dozen others that Bridget McCoy had drawn and her son had kept all of them. After careful study of each one, he felt that he had a good idea of what Field had looked like. Even though the Saracen's Head would need no more provisions for days, Patrick decided to go to Leadenhall Market that morning. In his pocket were the sketches of the killer and he referred to them constantly.

It was a long walk and he was still well short of the market when he was distracted by a commotion. Jeering and laughing, a small crowd was walking along the street. When he saw what they were carrying, Patrick soon understood why they were so excited. At the heart of the crowd, a man was being dragged along to the pillory by two constables. What the onlookers were waiting for was the chance to pelt the prisoner with the various missiles they had collected on the way. Rotten fruit was preferred by most of them but some had stones or pieces of wood, and there was even a dead cat being held in readiness.

The prisoner was a scrawny man in his twenties, protesting his innocence and begging for mercy. The constables ignored his pleas. When they reached the pillory, one of them unlocked it and lifted up the top half so that the man's head and hands could be thrust into the rough shapes carved out of the wood. Because he was so short, the prisoner had to stand on tiptoe to reach the pillory and he was obviously in great discomfort. No sympathy was shown. The top half was slammed down and locked, securing him immovably in a position that would gradually become more and more agonising.

One of the constables read out the charge but it went unheard beneath the baying of the mob. No sooner had the officers stood back than the real punishment began. Missiles of all kinds were flung at him from close range. A ripe tomato splattered across the prisoner's nose and a piece of brick took the skin off the knuckles of one hand. When he yelled for mercy, he was hit full in the face by the putrid cat. Unable to defend himself, he was exposed to the ridicule and cruelty of the crowd. Sticks, stones, fruit, vegetables, and even a live frog were hurled at him.

Patrick watched it all with absent-minded interest. When he was younger, he had helped to bait such malefactors and take his turn at throwing anything that came to hand at a hapless target. The treatment meted out was brutal. Those trapped in the pillory could be cut, bruised, blinded, deprived of teeth or, in some cases, killed by the ferocity of the attack. They were fair game to any passing citizen and the ordeal might last all day. Patrick decided that this particular man was getting off quite lightly. He sidled across to one of the constables, a sturdy man in his forties with a thick brown beard.

'What's his offence, sir?' asked Patrick.

'Sedition,' replied the other.

'What's that?'

'Speaking against the King and his government.'

'Is that what he did?'

'Yes,' said the constable. 'In the presence of witnesses, this villain swore that His Majesty was a creeping Roman Catholic, that he went to Mass six times a day and that he and his bloodsucking ministers were in the pay of the Pope. That was sedition.'

'Then he deserves what he gets.'

'Every last minute of it.'

Patrick thrust out his chest. 'I'm going to be a constable one day.'

'Are you?' said the other with amusement.

'I'll enjoy putting rogues like him in the pillory.'

Snatching up a handful of offal from the street, he flung it hard at the man's head and secured a direct hit. The prisoner did not even feel it. He had already been knocked unconscious by a well-aimed horseshoe.

It was still morning when they finally returned to London. Having stayed overnight at an inn, they completed the rest of their journey and pulled up outside Sir Julius Cheever's house in

Westminster. As on the previous day, Christopher Redmayne travelled in the relative comfort of the coach, listening to his companion's strong political views while feeling unable to challenge them. He was grateful to be released from the litany.

As soon as the coach appeared, Susan and Brilliana came out of the house to greet their father and to ask if he had had a safe journey. Christopher had intended to ride back home but a glance from Susan kept him there. He could tell at once that she knew. The plan to keep her ignorant of what had been going on was instantly abandoned. Christopher felt chastened.

Brilliana made much of her father before sweeping him into the house. Susan was left alone with Christopher. He was subjected to a long and hostile stare before being invited into the house. She led him into the drawing room and shut the door firmly behind them. Hands on her hips, she rounded accusingly on her friend.

'I think that I owe you an explanation,' he said, apologetically.

'It's too late for that.'

'Susan, I did not want you to be hurt.'

'What is more hurtful than being deceived by the one person in my life that I thought I could trust? Really, Christopher,' she said. 'This has made me look at you in a whole new light.'

'I'm still the same person.'

'You mean that you were always given to lies and dissembling?'

'No, of course not.'

'I begin to think so.'

'Then let me put your mind at rest on that score.'

'Put it at rest?' she returned, harshly. 'You've set it ablaze.'

'There was no point in telling you about my anxieties with regard to your father,' he explained. 'I needed to find more proof.'

'Your own brother did that.'

'Henry?'

'He told you from the start that Mr Everett was an unlikely victim of any political plot. Father is the man with sworn enemies. Henry even arranged for you to speak to two Members of Parliament.'

'How do you know all this?'

'Brilliana had a long conversation with your brother.'

'But they've never even met.'

'They have now,' explained Susan. 'Having decided to push the two of us closer together, my sister took it upon herself to discover more about your family background. She and her husband went off to see what sort of a house your brother owned.'

Christopher was aghast. 'Are you telling me that they arrived in Bedford Street and knocked on Henry's door?'

'Even Brilliana would not be that impudent. They just happened to be there when your brother returned from the Navy Office. They fell into conversation. When he realised who they were, Henry invited them in. And that,' said Susan, bitterly, 'is how I came to hear something I should have been told days ago.'

'I concede that.'

'So why did you mislead me?'

'It was an error of judgement, Susan.'

'It was more than that,' she rejoined. 'It was proof that you neither understand nor care about me in the way that I'd naively assumed.'

'I *do* care about you,' he declared, going to her with outstretched arms. 'How can you possibly doubt that?'

'Then why did you betray me like this?'

'Susan—'

'Am I so weak and tender that I'm not able to hear bad news? Do you think that I'll burst into tears if you tell me that Father is in danger? Your memory is wondrous short, Christopher,' she went on, shaking with emotion. 'When my brother, Gabriel, was murdered, I did not take to my bed in a fit of despair. I did my best to help you in tracking down the man who was responsible.'

'You showed amazing courage.'

'I was the only member of the family who kept in touch with him.'

'That, too, was an example of your steadfastness.'

'It has not fled,' she told him. 'Had I been warned in advance that my brother's life was at risk, I'd have gone to any lengths to protect him. The same is true of my father. I love him. I'd do anything to save him. But only if I knew in advance that he was in jeopardy.'

'This is all true,' he confessed. 'I deserve your reproaches.'

'Supposing that he'd been killed in the last few days?' she said. 'How do you think I'd have felt when I learned that you were already aware of the fact that someone sought his life?'

It was a sobering question and he could find no immediate answer. Instead, he wrestled with his conscience. Should he tell her about the attempted murder of Sir Julius, or suppress the information? Should he risk upsetting her or should he compound his earlier mistake by hiding something from her yet again? Looking into her eyes, he saw the swirling confusion in them. Susan wanted to trust him yet she felt hurt and disregarded. He could deny her no more.

'I only went to the funeral to keep an eye on your father,' he said.

'Without a single word of it to me.'

'I failed, Susan. We were followed.'

He told her about the incident and how he had agreed with her father to say nothing about it. As a result of the conversation with her, Christopher had changed his mind. Shocked by the revelation, she did at least give him credit for confiding in her at last and she wanted to know every detail of what had occurred on their journey. Some of the vehemence had gone from her voice. He was relieved.

'I'll take the matter up with Father,' she said.

'No, no. Let me speak to him first.'

'The pair of you have done enough whispering together. I'll not be led astray again. Thanks to your brother, I know the truth. Brilliana had the whole story from him.'

'That surprises me.'

'Why?'

'Because I'd not have thought that she and Henry would have been in any way compatible. To speak more plainly, I'd have expected Brilliana to be less than complimentary about my brother and the sort of life that he leads. If she went into the house,' said Christopher, 'she must have seen some of those lurid paintings that he favours.'

'Brilliana saw them and liked them.'

'*Liked* them?'

'It was Lancelot who found them scandalous. He could not stop talking about a picture of a Roman orgy. As for Henry, my sister was very impressed. Brilliana had never met anyone remotely like him.'

'No,' said Christopher, sighing, 'I suppose that Henry does have a uniqueness about him. It's always been a cause for profound regret to me. On the other hand,' he added, keen to state one thing in his brother's favour, 'he can be extraordinarily helpful. He seems to know almost everyone in London.'

'Including Dorothy Kitson.'

Christopher blanched. 'Henry is acquainted with *her* as well?'

'He knows *of* the lady,' said Susan, 'and had actually met her last husband. According to Brilliana, he spoke very highly of Mrs Kitson. It made me feel rather contrite.'

'Contrite?'

'I'd had some unkind thoughts about her.'

'Only because you'd never had the advantage of meeting her, Susan. It was natural that should want to shield your father from any inappropriate advances.' He gave a short laugh. 'Though I pity any woman bold enough to make such an approach to Sir Julius.'

'He loves Mrs Kitson,' she said. 'I ought to accept that.'

'Only one question remains, then – does Mrs Kitson love *him*?'

The Parliament House was part of the Palace of Westminster. It was situated in what had been, before it was secularised, St Stephen's Chapel, a tall, two-storied building with high turrets at the four corners and long stained-glass windows that reflected its earlier sacred function. Irreverent language was now more likely to be heard in the former chapel, and some of the rituals observed would have been regarded as profanities on consecrated ground. Maurice Farwell had been a Member of Parliament for many years and had risen to occupy an important place on the Privy Council. The House of Commons was his second home. As he alighted from his coach, he saw many familiar figures walking towards the chamber. The man who first accosted him, however, was not a politician.

'You have a lot to answer for, Maurice,' said Orlando Golland.

'I'm not responsible for all the legislation that comes out of parliament,' replied Farwell, pleasantly. 'Do not call me to account for it, Orlando.'

'This has nothing to do with the statute book.'

'Then why do you look so sullen?'

'Because I am deeply worried about my sister.'

'There's no novelty in that,' said Farwell. 'You've spent an entire lifetime, worrying about Dorothy. When she was single, you feared that she might never wed. And when she did take a husband – on two separate occasions – you felt that they were palpably unworthy of her.'

'They were saints compared to her latest suitor.'

'And who might that be?'

'Sir Julius Cheever, of course,' said Golland. 'When we met him at the races, you not only acknowledged the rascal, you introduced him to Dorothy and set catastrophe in motion.'

'What can you mean?'

'He wishes to marry her.'

Farwell's jaw dropped. 'Marry her? I'm astounded.'

'It was you who played Cupid to this bizarre romance.'

Well into his forties, Maurice Farwell was tall, rangy and passably handsome. There was an air of conspicuous prosperity about him and a natural dignity that came into its own during parliamentary debates. The last person he had expected to waylay him was Orlando Golland.

'Have you been waiting to ambush me?' he asked.

'No,' said Golland. 'I had legal business at the Palace today. When I saw your coach arrive, I felt that I had to speak. This development has been more than worrying, Maurice. It's a daily torment.'

'Put it out of your mind.'

'How can you say that?'

'Because I cannot believe that someone as refined and well-bred as your sister would let a boor like Sir Julius anywhere near her. He may want to marry Dorothy – London is full of men who would happily fling themselves at her feet – but there's not the slightest danger that she would accept his proposal.'

'But there is, Maurice.'

'Surely not.'

'Dorothy has agreed to meet his children.'

Farwell's eyebrows shot up. 'Good gracious!'

'And she has had a number of clandestine meetings with him.'

'With that grotesque old buffoon? It verges on indecency. What can possibly have attracted her?'

'Whatever it is,' moaned Golland, 'I fail to see it. He's a roaring bear of a man. The only thing I can say in favour of him is that he's a good judge of horses. Sir Julius picked the winner in almost every race at Newmarket that day – including my own filly.'

'And is that when this unlikely friendship started?'

'Apparently.'

'Then I suppose that I must take the blame,' said Farwell with a shrug. 'Had I known that this would happen, I'd have kept Dorothy well away from him.' He became pensive. 'It's rather curious, though.'

'What is?'

'My wife may be more prescient than she knows.'

'Prescient?'

'Yes,' said Farwell. 'Adele has never shown any gift for prophecy before. When we got back from the races that day, however, she told me that she had a strong impression that your sister was ready for marriage again. Adele sensed it.'

'She could not have sensed that Sir Julius would be the husband.'

'Never in a hundred years!'

'What am I to do, Maurice?' said Golland, anxiously. 'I can hardly speak to her as a man of the world. Dorothy has been married twice whereas I regard holy matrimony as the grossest intrusion of privacy.'

'Yes, you like to have control of your life.'

'A wife would insist on rearranging it for me.'

'But she would bring many compensating virtues,' said Farwell with a fond smile. 'That's what Adele has done for me. She's a perfect helpmeet, a true partner.' He pondered. 'As to the best course of action with regard to your sister,' he resumed after a while, 'I know exactly what you should do.'

'What?'

'Nothing.'

'Nothing?'

'Let it runs its course, Orlando.'

'But what if she gets hopelessly entangled with Sir Julius?'

'I have more faith in Dorothy than you.'

'She seems to be genuinely enamoured of him.'

'It will pass,' said Farwell, smoothly. 'She'll soon see through that blundering fool. Ha! Your sister ought to be here this afternoon so that she could watch the bloated oaf pontificate. That would teach her what an irritating fellow he is. Later on, I'll be jousting with Sir Julius Cheever once more. He'll lead strong opposition to a bill that we mean to introduce.'

'How do you know?'

'He's a born rebel. Whatever we propose, he'll raise endless and unnecessary objections. I'll have to do battle with the old curmudgeon yet again. He's a menace, Orlando.'

'And he may end up as my brother-in-law.'

'Marry him?' he said with a laugh. 'If Dorothy knew him as well as I do, she'd run a mile from Sir Julius Cheever.'

'Stay here, Sir Julius,' she pleaded. 'Remain where you are safe.'

'I'll be out of harm's way at the House of Commons.'

'How do you know that? That man tried to kill you. He may do so again. I care for you too much to let you put your life at risk again.'

'Thank you,' he said, enjoying her attention and glad that he had decided to confide in her. 'But I'll not present such an easy target again. Now that I know what to expect, I'll have eyes in the back of my head.'

Sir Julius Cheever had called at the house in Covent Garden to let Dorothy Kitson know that he had returned, and to test her affection for him by telling her about the ambush he had survived. The news had jolted her and, for the first time, she had reached out to touch him in a spontaneous gesture of concern.

'Did you receive my letter?' he said.

'Yes,' she replied, 'and I was pleased to hear that both of your daughters are in London. I'm ready to meet them whenever they wish.' She gave him an inquisitive smile. 'What have you told them about me?'

'Only that you are the most wonderful woman in the world.'

'That was very silly of you, Sir Julius.'

'I was only speaking the truth.'

'But you were not being very tactful,' she pointed out. 'For any daughters, the most wonderful woman in the world is their mother. I could never compete with your wife. Nor would I wish to do so.' He nodded soulfully. 'Be more judicious in future. If you praise me to the skies, your daughters are bound to find me wanting.'

'You are entirely without fault, Dorothy.'

'I've learned to hide my shortcomings, that's all.'

'Mine are all too visible,' he confessed. 'But I fear that I must away,' he added, moving to the door. 'I've work to do in that yapping menagerie we call a parliament.'

'Take care, Sir Julius.'

'I'll be Caution itself.'

'And speak to my brother about this outrage you suffered.'

'What can Mr Golland do?'

'Orlando can arrange some bodyguards for you.'

'I have one waiting for me beside my coach. And like me,' he said, opening his coat to reveal the pistol that he carried, 'he is well-armed and primed for action.'

'I find this all so troubling.'

'You may rest easy, dear lady. Nothing can touch me now. I have a more potent weapon at my disposal.'

'Oh? And what's that?'

'A young friend who has helped me in the past. He has a genius for hunting down villains. Christopher will not fail me. It's only a matter of time before this killer is behind bars.'

Within minutes of arriving back at his house, Christopher Redmayne had a visitor. Eager to speak with his brother, Henry was even more peevish than usual. He adopted a tone of rebuke.

'Where on earth have you been, Christopher?' he complained. 'This is the third time today that I've called.'

'I thought you were shackled to your desk at the Navy Office.'

'Fortunately, the hateful Surveyer has gone to Chatham. I was able to sneak away – and I expected you to be *here*.'

'I was attending a funeral in Cambridgeshire.'

'That's a paltry excuse.'

'Nevertheless, it accounts for my absence. I went with Sir Julius Cheever to see his friend, Mr Everett, laid to rest.'

Henry sneered. 'It's a shame that there was no room in the grave for Sir Julius himself. No, no,' he corrected immediately, 'I withdraw that calumny. It's unjust. Any man who can bring such glory into the world deserves respect.'

'What are you talking about, Henry?'

'His daughter. She is a positive divinity.'

'I agree,' said Christopher with a warm smile. 'Susan is the most gorgeous woman alive.'

'Then you have obviously not seen her sister.'

'Brilliana?'

'An angel in human form,' said Henry, fervently. 'A queen of her sex. Beauty personified.'

'Brilliana cannot compare with Susan.'

'She can, Christopher. You may be drawn by the virginal charm of the younger sister but it pales beside the seasoned excellence of the elder. I've never met such an alluring creature.'

'You should not have met her now,' said Christopher.

'It was destiny!'

'It was unwarranted curiosity, Henry, and her sister has told her so in blunt terms. Brilliana had no call to pry into my private life. What right did she have to pester my brother?'

'Every right,' said Henry. 'I grant it freely.'

'You should have behaved with more discretion.'

'In the face of such a temptress? It was impossible. The hour we spent together was magical.' A nostalgic beam lit up his face. 'Dare I hope that Brilliana enjoyed her visit to Bedford Street?'

'It seems that she was rather impressed with you, Henry.'

'Wonder of wonders!'

'But I doubt if the same can be said of Lancelot.'

'Who?'

'Her husband,' said Christopher, pointedly. 'Not that you even noticed him, I daresay. Lancelot was horrified by your taste in art.'

'How strange! Brilliana approved of it.'

'That amazes me.'

'It shows that she and I have a close affinity.'

'Henry, she's *married*. She's beyond your reach. I refuse to let you entertain libidinous thoughts about her. Brilliana Serle is not available.'

'Many women think that until they feel the first hot pang of desire. As for marriage, no man could have more respect for the institution. It's an inexhaustible hunting ground for me,' he boasted. 'I've helped to rescue many a bored wife from a dull husband.'

'Well, you'll not add Brilliana Serle to your list of conquests,' said Christopher, sternly. 'I can tell you for a fact that she is neither bored nor trapped in a dull marriage. More to the point, she is Susan's sister and that means I have a strong personal interest here.'

'I would not dream of embarrassing you.'

'You've already done so – many times.'

'One sister is surely enough for any man. Leave the other to me.'

'No, Henry!'

'I'll move stealthily. Nobody will ever know.'

'*I'll* know,' said Christopher, 'and so will the lady herself. You misjudge her completely. Brilliana will not welcome your blandishments. She'll be very distressed.'

'She was not distressed by my paintings. They awakened her.'

'No more of this. I forbid you to continue.'

'Pish, man! Don't moralise. When you have designs on one daughter, it ill becomes you to climb into the pulpit about another. Besides, I have enough sermons from our benighted father. I came here for one simple reason,' said Henry, briskly. 'I need a brother's help. Contrive a situation so that I can meet Brilliana once again – without the distracting presence of her husband this time. Have I not helped you with regard to this murder investigation in which you are embroiled?'

'You have,' said Christopher. 'I am very grateful.'

'Then display that gratitude by doing what I ask.'

Henry turned on his heel and sailed gracefully out of the room.

Christopher was dumbfounded. Wanting to remonstrate with his brother, he saw how pointless his strictures were. He was also aware of how prudish he sounded when he tried to warn Henry about the pitfalls of a dissolute life. Christopher felt the same natural impulses as all men but he had learned to control them instead of being at their mercy. Henry was different. Having rejected the homilies of his father, the dean of Gloucester, he would hardly listen to the warnings of a younger brother.

It was disturbing for Christopher. Any pursuit of Brilliana was doomed. If she rejected Henry – as was most likely – she would turn against the whole Redmayne family. If, on the other hand, she chose to encourage his interest, then the consequences were unthinkable. Either way, Christopher's friendship with Susan would be adversely affected and he resolved that that must never happen. Were she to discover that Henry was harbouring lustful thoughts about her sister, Susan would be truly appalled. And if the information ever reached the ears of Sir Julius, nothing short of disaster would follow.

Christopher heard voices in the hall. Thinking that Henry might not, after all, have left, he went out to challenge him, only to discover that one visitor had been replaced by another. Jonathan Bale had just been let into the house. Christopher was pleased to see him. After the abrasive meeting with his brother, he needed stable companionship. He led the constable into the parlour and they sat down.

'When did you return, Mr Redmayne?' asked Bale.

'This morning. Sir Julius and I stayed overnight in Essex.'

'Did everything go without incident?'

'No, Jonathan.'

'Oh?'

'Someone tried to kill Sir Julius.'

He explained what had happened. Bale was reassured to hear that Sir Julius Cheever had escaped with only a minor injury. Like his friend, however, he feared that a third attempt might be made to shoot him.

'Will he take more care in future?' he asked.

'He has a bodyguard with him at all times,' said Christopher, 'and he'll remain vigilant. His daughters only consented to let him out of the house if he took precautions.'

'Good.'

'But what about you, Jonathan? Did you get my letter?'

'Yes. I called on Lewis Bircroft in Coleman Street.'

'An apposite address for him for a Puritan.'

'At first, he refused to accept that his beating had any political connection but I sensed that he was lying. I pressed him hard.'

'And?'

'I eventually squeezed some of the truth out of him,' said Bale, taking a piece of paper from his pocket. 'Mr Bircroft told me that it was to do with a political pamphlet. Here,' he went on, handing the paper to Christopher. 'I asked him to write down the title because there was no way that I could remember it.'

Christopher read it out. '*Observations on the Growth of Popery and Arbitrary Government in England.* I've heard of this before. There were references to it in the newspapers.'

'It caused a scandal, Mr Redmayne.'

'I know. I remember a huge outcry against the pamphlet. It was published anonymously, wasn't it?'

'Nobody would dare to put his name to it. A reward of £200 was offered for information that would lead to the arrest of the author.'

'And did Mr Bircroft tell you who that was?'

'No,' said Bale, sadly, 'but he did admit that many people thought it was his work. He's been an assiduous pamphleteer in the past and is very critical of the government.'

'So that's why he was attacked.'

'They tried to beat a confession out of him with cudgels. Though he swore that he was not the author, they refused to believe him. It took him months to get over his injuries and he now uses a walking stick.'

'The pamphlet must have been very seditious.'

'Yet it was not written by Lewis Bircroft.'

'Who *was* responsible for it, Jonathan?'

'He could not tell me. However, one thing he did know.'

'Go on.'

'Suspicion has now moved to Sir Julius Cheever. Some people are convinced that he wrote that pamphlet. They are so enraged,' said Bale, 'they they've taken the law into their own hands. They want him executed for what he did.'

'Sir Julius has said nothing to me about the pamphlet.'

'Then he may not be its author.'

'The title certainly bears his stamp,' said Christopher, 'but he is not a man to hide behind anonymity. Also, of course – if the pamphlet really had been his – he would not have told me in case I tried to collect that reward.'

'You'd never have done that, Mr Redmayne.'

'I know that. Sir Julius, perhaps, may have doubts about me.'

'Even though you've done your best to protect him?'

'Even then.' Christopher put the paper aside. 'You've done well, Jonathan. We finally have a motive. Sir Julius may be wrongly accused but that will not make his enemies stay their hand. A pamphlet that somebody else wrote may bring about his downfall.'

'That's unfair, sir.'

'Granted, but it's the situation with which we have to deal. Before he can strike again, we simply must catch the killer between us.'

'We may have some assistance.'

'From where?'

'The Saracen's Head. Mrs McCoy drew a picture of the man who rented a room there. She says it's a good likeness. Her son cannot wait to go in search of the man. For some reason,' he explained, 'Patrick wants to be a constable like me. He's determined to find Mr Field for us.'

They set out even earlier than usual. Bridget McCoy was not optimistic.

'He'll not be there,' she said, gloomily.

'He may be, Mother. You never know.'

'He was not at the market when you went there yesterday.'

'He might have been,' said Patrick, lumbering along beside her. 'I could easily have missed him in the crowd. That's why it needs two of us to catch Mr Field.'

'That's not his name, Patrick.'

'How do you know?'

'Because I've been thinking about it,' she said. 'If a man was about to commit a terrible murder, would he give his real name to me? No, it would be foolish of him. A name can be used to hunt someone down.'

Patrick was bewildered. 'If his name is not Mr Field,' he said with a frown, 'then what is it?'

'We may never know.'

'We will if we catch him today. I'll make him tell us the truth.'

'No, Patrick.'

'He lied to you, Mother. That was wrong.'

'Yes,' she agreed, 'and he deserves to be punished but it's not for us to touch him. That's Mr Bale's job. I made that mistake the first time. When I saw him in the market, I ran after Mr Field – or whatever his name was – and he must have seen me coming. I scared him off.'

'I can run faster than you.'

'He may have a weapon.'

Patrick held up his fists. 'I have two.'

'They're no use against a dagger or a pistol,' she said. 'Save them for rowdy customers at the tavern. This is a job for a constable.'

'That's what I'll be one day, Mother.'

'One day – perhaps.'

They walked on in silence. Bridget felt it would be too unkind to dampen his enthusiasm by reminding him of some of the other aspects of a parish constable's occupation. All that Patrick thought about was the pursuit and arrest of criminals. On the previous day, he had returned in a state of exhilaration because he had watched a prisoner being locked in the pillory by two constables. It was a task that he relished doing himself. It simply required brute force. When it came to giving evidence in court, or to interrogating a suspect, it was a very different matter. Patrick would flounder badly. He would be a figure of fun once again.

'I could have brought a cudgel,' said Patrick, bravely. 'I took one off that man I had to throw out last Saturday. He tried to hit me with it. With a cudgel in my hand, I could take on anybody.'

'You'd only get hurt.'

'Not if I get in the first blow.'

Bridget was firm. 'No, Patrick. All that we can do is to find him. We have to leave it to Mr Bale and Mr Warburton to arrest him.'

'We can't let him get away.'

'No, we'll follow him. We'll find out where he lives and then report it to the constables.' Her despondency returned. 'If we ever catch sight of him, that is, and I don't believe we will. He's gone forever. That lousy, scurvy, villainous son of a pox-ridden whore may not even be in London.'

They walked on. While his mother was unhopeful, Patrick was full of confidence. He felt certain that they would see the man this time. He straightened his shoulders and marched along with pride. It was almost as if he were on patrol as a parish constable. The market was already busy by the time they reached Leadenhall Street and all four courtyards were swarming with people. In such a heaving multitude, it would not be easy to pick out one person.

Beginning with the courtyard where the man had been seen before, they walked slowly through the crowd. Bridget wished that she were taller so that she could see over the heads of the people all around her. Unable to retain a mental picture of the suspect for long, Patrick kept taking out one of the pictures that his mother had drawn in order to refresh his memory. When he looked up again, his eyes searched for a broken nose and a mole. As they moved from one courtyard to another, he saw both frequently but they were never on the same person. Having taken the crumpled drawing from his pocket for the tenth time, Patrick resolved to rely on his mother. Bridget had seen and talked to the man. She would know him.

'He's not here,' she decided.

'The market is still young. More people are coming in all the time.'

'We can't stay here all morning.'

'I can,' he volunteered.

'No, Patrick. We've too much work to do.'

'What's more important than catching Mr Field?'

'Nothing,' she said. 'Nothing at all.'

'Then we stay.'

Bridget nodded. Bolstered by her son's resolve, she continued the search, going back to the first courtyard and starting all over again. It was painstaking work. The more faces that flashed in front of her, the more confused she became and the ear-shattering noise all around her was a further distraction. She seemed to be at the very heart of the turmoil. Pushed and jostled from all sides, Bridget started to lose faith in the whole enterprise yet again.

Then a man's face passed within a yard of her. It took her a moment to register the shape of his head, the large ears, the colour of his complexion, the hang of his lip, the ugliness of the broken nose and that mole on the cheek that she had noticed at their first encounter. When she put all the elements together, she was certain of his identity.

'That's him, Patrick!' she said.

'Where?'

'That man carrying the side of beef on his shoulder.'

'Are you sure?'

'As sure as I'll ever be – that's the rogue.'

'Then let me get him,' said Patrick, bunching his fists.

She held him back. 'No!'

'We can't miss a chance like this, Mother.'

'Follow him. See where he goes.'

'He could easily shake us off in this crowd.'

'Stay here!' she ordered.

But she had reckoned without the strength of his ambition. Patrick McCoy was a young man with little in life beyond the desire to better himself. And the only way he could conceive of doing that was to be a parish constable. Here was a chance to display his abilities. In a situation like this, Jonathan Bale would not hold back. Ten yards away was a man who had committed murder from the vantage point of the Saracens's Head. He had to be apprehended.

Pushing his mother aside, Patrick bullocked his way forward.

'Stop!' he yelled. 'Stop there right now!'

Like everyone else in the vicinity, the man with the side of beef over his shoulder turned to look in Patrick's direction. Then he noticed the woman who was trying to follow the youth and he realised who she was.

'Wait there!' shouted Patrick. 'I want a word with you, Mr Field!'

The man immediately took a defensive stance. As Patrick charged at him, he swung the side of beef so hard that it knocked his attacker to the ground. Flinging his cargo down on top of Patrick, he delivered several swift kicks to the youth's head to disable him. Then he fled at full speed into the crowd with a stream of abuse from Bridget McCoy filling his ears.

Chapter Nine

Crimes and disturbances did not obligingly cease in Baynard's Castle ward to allow Jonathan Bale to devote his whole time to the murder hunt. That morning, he and Tom Warburton were called to Great Carter Street to intervene in a violent quarrel. A customer had visited the barber-surgeon, who, among his many talents, was able to draw teeth. It was a painful exercise but less of a torment than the bad tooth that had infected the customer's whole mouth and made his cheek swell to twice its size. The extraction was swift and decisive. On only one small detail could the barber-surgeon be faulted. He had removed the wrong tooth.

When the constables arrived on the scene, the men were trading blows and roaring spectators were urging them on. Bale grabbed the barber, Warburton took hold of the customer, and they dragged the adversaries apart. Struggling for release, the two men continued the fight with robust language and dire threats. It was minutes before Bale was able to calm them down enough to hear the cause of their dispute. He was still trying to act as a mediator when he saw two people hurrying along the street towards him.

Bridget McCoy was flushed and agitated but it was her son who made the constable stare. A hideous bruise darkened one side of Patrick's face and there was an ugly swelling on his temple. One eye was almost closed. Even the disgruntled customer felt sorry for him. A lost tooth did not compare with a vicious beating. Leaving Warburton to sort out the argument, Bale detached himself to speak to the newcomers.

'What happened?' he said.

'We saw him,' replied Bridget. 'We saw that bastard again.'

'Where?'

'At the market.'

'Why did you not send word, Mrs McCoy?'

'It would have taken too long,' said Patrick. 'So I tried to arrest him myself. I tried to be like you, Mr Bale.'

Bridget indicated the wounds. 'You can see the result,' she said, rancorously. 'He almost kicked my son's head off. Wait till I catch up with the knave. I'll bite his balls off and spit them in the Thames.'

'Tell me exactly what happened, Mrs McCoy,' suggested Bale.

'I'll slice him into tiny bits and feed him to the dogs.'

'We have to apprehend him first, and we can't do that while you're railing against him. Now, then, let me hear the full story.'

Supported and sometimes contradicted by her son, Bridget gave a bitter description of events. The crowd had now abandoned the dental dispute and turned their attention to this new development. Given an audience, Bridget responded by introducing gruesome details, couched in the sort of language that most of them had never before heard coming from the lips of a woman. Bale seized on the salient details.

'He's a porter,' he concluded. 'Mr Field is a porter.'

Patrick rubbed his sore face. 'Mother says that's not his name.'

'I think that she's right, lad.'

'So we don't know who he really is.'

'But we know where he works.'

'Do we, Mr Bale?' said Bridget.

'Yes,' he told her. 'If he had a side of beef with him, he was delivering it to market. So we can guess where he took his name from.'

'Where?'

'Smithfield. He's a meat porter from Smithfield. Take out the Smith and what to you have left, Mrs McCoy?'

'Field.'

'I'll wager that's how he christened himself.'

'Let's catch him, Mr Bale,' urged Patrick. 'Let's go to Smithfield.'

'The only place you're going to is bed,' said his mother, tenderly. 'You must have a terrible headache. Wait until you see yourself in a mirror, Patrick. You shouldn't be abroad in a state like that.'

'I agree,' said Bale. 'Take him home. I have to tell someone else what you managed to find out. Then we'll need to speak to you again.'

'And to me,' insisted Patrick. 'I was there as well.'

'You need to rest, lad.'

'I only did what you'd have done, Mr Bale.'

'That was very brave of you.'

'He used our tavern for a murder. That was sinful.'

'It was a bloody disgrace!' asserted Bridget.

'Take him away, Mrs McCoy,' advised Bale. 'I think a doctor ought to look at those wounds of his. They were got honourably, Patrick,' he said, hoping to cheer him up. 'But it's time to step aside now, lad. Leave this fellow to us.'

'It's not a criticism, Brilliana,' said her husband. 'It's an observation.'

'Well, it's one that is quite uncalled for, Lancelot.'

'Do you deny that you paid excessive attention to Mr Henry Redmayne?'

'No, I do not.'

'Or that you praised his paintings?'

'I adored them,' said Brilliana.

'They were thoroughly indecent.'

'Nakedness can be beautiful in the hands of a skilful artist.'

'All I saw was filth and obscenity,' he argued, wrinkling his nose, 'and if that is an accurate reflection of the man's taste, I vote that we shun the society of Henry Redmayne forthwith.'

'Then you'll be cutting off your nose to spite your face.'

'In what way?'

'He can help you, Lancelot,' she said, kissing him softly on the cheek. 'That was the only reason I pandered to him. I did it for *you*.'

'Really?'

'Is a wife not allowed to advance her husband's interests?'

'Of course.'

'Then you should give me thanks instead of berating me.'

They were in the garden of the Westminster house, seated on a bench that occupied a little arbour. It was a fine summer's day. Insects buzzed happily around them and the mingled scent of flowers filled the air. Lancelot Serle was so unaccustomed to offering his wife even the slightest reproach that it had taken him a long time to work up the courage to do so. She was quick to defend herself.

'Henry Redmayne is a means to an end,' she explained. 'That's why I chose to flatter him. He attends Court and is on familiar terms with anyone of note in parliament. We must cultivate him, Lancelot. He is your passport to greater things.'

'But he ignored me completely.'

'He'll not do so again.'

'Those lecherous eyes of his never strayed from you.'

'I encouraged his interest,' said Brilliana, 'so that he would feel obligated to me. When I have a more secure hold on him, I'll ask Henry to introduce you to people who can assist your own political career. In due course, he will also present you at court. Would you not like to rub shoulders with the King?'

'Who needs a king when I live with a queen?' he said, gallantly.

'A pretty compliment but it evades my question.'

Serle was more forceful. 'Then my answer is this: yes, I would like to enter parliament. Yes, I do want to have my say in the government of the country. And yes, moving in court circles would be – if you'll forgive a crude pun – the crowning achievement. However,' he went on, seriously, 'I'd like to do it by my own efforts, Brilliana, and not be beholden to a man who nurses improper thoughts about my wife.'

'Henry does not have improper thoughts.'

'Judging by those paintings, he never has any other kind.'

'His father is the dean of Gloucester Cathedral.'

'I discerned no ecclesiastical leanings in his elder son.'

'Lancelot,' she said, stamping a foot, 'I cannot help you if you will not be helped. Knowing the right people is everything.'

'My suspicion is that Henry Redmayne knows all the wrong ones.'

Brilliana gasped. 'What has possessed you?'

'I'm sorry, my dear. I know that you mean well but I think that there are other ways to fulfil my ambitions. Dangling the person I love as tempting bait in front of another man is not one of them, especially when the man in question is Mr Henry Redmayne.'

She stared at him with a mixture of annoyance and admiration, piqued that he should deny her a role in his political advancement yet stirred by the boldness with which he had spoken. Brilliana did not know how to respond. The need to do so was removed by the arrival of Susan.

'Ah, there you are,' she said. 'Am I interrupting anything?'

'Yes,' replied Serle.

'No,' overruled his wife, putting a hand on his knee. 'Lancelot and I were engaged in idle gossip, nothing more. Do join us, Susan.' Her sister held her straw hat as she ducked under the arbour. 'You look as if you've brought news.'

'I have,' said Susan, taking a seat beside her. 'A message has come from Father. He's called on Mrs Kitson again.'

'I thought that he went straight to the Parliament House.'

'He could not resist going to Covent Garden first, even though it took him right out of his way. His message is simple. We are to expect Mrs Kitson this evening.'

'Splendid!' said Brilliana, clapping her hands.

'And it seems that her brother will be coming as well.'

'Her brother?'

'Mr Golland. He's a justice of the peace.'

'I've always wanted to sit on the bench,' said Serle, alerted by the news. 'I look forward to meeting him.'

'We must not let Father down,' warned Brilliana. 'We must be on our best behaviour. Her brother as well, you say? It sounds as if it will be quite a party. Listen, Susan,' she said, artlessly, 'perhaps you should invite Christopher to join us.'

'I think not,' said Susan, 'this is a family affair.'

'Well, he is practically one of the family.'

'Not yet, Brilliana.'

'But he's such a presentable young man and would add some interest for Mrs Kitson. And I have an even better idea,' she continued. 'Since we are enlarging our number, why not add one more and include Christopher's brother as well? I should like to meet Henry again.'

Henry Redmayne could not get her out of his mind. Though he appeared to be working at the Navy Office that morning, his thoughts were with Brilliana Serle and that bewitching smile she had given him as they parted. She had come into his life at an opportune moment. Spurned by one wife, he had met the ideal replacement. She was womanhood in all its glory and he coveted her madly. There was the small problem of her husband but Henry had had great experience in circumventing spouses. No obstacle would be allowed to stand in the way that led to paradise.

Bent over his desk, he was lost in contemplation of Brilliana Serle when a voice broke into his reverie. Henry looked up at Maurice Farwell.

'Mr Farwell,' he said, leaping obediently to his feet. 'Good day to you, sir. This is an unexpected pleasure. It's not often that you stray this far from parliament.'

'I've come for ammunition, Mr Redmayne.'

'We do not keep any cannonballs here.'

'I know,' said Farwell with a quiet smile. 'That's not the kind of ammunition I had in mind. We are to debate naval procurements this afternoon, and I need to have the relevant details at my fingertips. I'm told that you could provide them.'

'Why, yes,' said Henry, burrowing among the papers that littered his desk. 'I have everything you need here. You've been such a friend to us in the past that you can always count on our help.' His hand closed on some documents. 'This is what you require, I believe.'

Farwell took the documents. 'Thank you,' he said, perusing them.

'You may borrow them, if you wish.'

'There's no need, Mr Redmayne. I have an excellent memory and it always impresses the house if one can speak without notes. Yes,' he went on, nodding in appreciation as he read on. 'These facts and figures are quite unanswerable.' He turned to the second page and scanned it with a sharp eye. When he had read the last page, he was content. 'With these at my disposal, I'll be able to bring Sir Julius crashing down.'

'Sir Julius Cheever?'

'That's the fellow – though I fancy that he prefers to see himself as another Julius Caesar. He's a stubborn Roundhead yet he has strangely imperial ambitions.' Farwell gave the documents back to him. 'Someone should remind him what happened to Caesar.'

'Do you see much of Sir Julius in parliament?'

'Far too much. I do not mind lively debate – it's the essence of our democracy – but I do draw the line at personal invective. Respect for one's political opponents is important, I feel. When the business of the day is done, we should be able to shake hands and act as gentlemen.'

'I cannot imagine Sir Julius shaking hands with a government minister,' said Henry. 'He would sooner amputate his whole arm.'

'It makes for so much unnecessary hostility.'

Henry did not know him well but he had followed Farwell's career with interest. The man's rise had been swift and sure. Unlike most successful politicians, he seemed to have held himself aloof from the cabals and conspiracies that animated the Parliament House. Maurice Farwell was above such things. Henry had never once heard his name connected with skullduggery or corruption.

'In some ways,' admitted Farwell, 'I admire him. We need men of Sir Julius's calibre. He has a simple integrity that shines like a candle in the darkness. But he does not, alas, treat us with any regard,' he said. 'Full-throated abuse is all that we hear. And there is such a ring of defiance about him. He still seems to think that the Lord Protector will walk into the chamber at any moment.'

'Cromwell is dead – thank goodness! Those dark days are over.'

'You would not think so to listen to Sir Julius.'

'He has supporters, I hear.'

'A ragbag of hangers-on. Nobody of any standing follows him. Though he could have counted on Bernard Everett,' he conceded. 'Now, *he* would have been a much more formidable opponent. His death was untimely. By repute, he was a master of debate. I would have enjoyed locking horns with Mr Everett.'

'My brother is involved in the pursuit of his killer.'

'Indeed? More power to his elbow.'

'Christopher was the architect who designed Sir Julius's house.'

'Then he earned his fee,' said Farwell, approvingly. 'I've seen the place. It's a fine piece of architecture.' He lowered his voice. 'I trust that your brother does not share his client's political opinions?'

'He finds them repellent.'

'Too strong a word – Sir Julius is misguided, that is all.'

'Christopher tells me that he has mellowed slightly of late.'

'We saw no sign of it in parliament yesterday. He was as bellicose as ever. A debate is always another battlefield to him. However,' he added with a chuckle, 'I do believe that there's been something of a change in his private life and I, unwittingly, was the cause of it.'

'Are you referring to Mrs Kitson?'

'You've heard about the attachment?'

'One of his daughters told me about it. I was thunderstruck. It's hard to think of a more eccentric liaison.'

'My wife more or less prophesied it,' said Farwell, proudly. 'Adele warned me some time ago that Dorothy Kitson was ready to consider marriage once more and – lo and behold – along comes Sir Julius.'

'I pity the poor lady.'

'There's obviously a mutual attraction of some kind.'

'Sir Julius has the appeal of a gargoyle.'

'I disagree. Some might consider him to have a rugged charm. And I'm told that he has two very beautiful daughters.'

Henry pounced on his cue. 'No, Mr Farwell,' he said, beaming, 'I dispute that. One is beautiful but the other is quite exquisite.'

'Clearly, you know them both.'

'Not as well as I would wish.'

'Do they take after their father?'

'Happily – no.'

'It looks as if they may soon acquire a stepmother,' said Farwell, 'and I give my wholehearted blessing to the match. Dorothy Kitson is a delightful person. If anyone can tame Sir Julius, then it is she. He might yet be redeemed by the love of a good woman.'

* * *

Jonathan Bale was an indifferent horseman and the ride was a trial for him. Conscious of his friend's discomfort, Christopher Redmayne took them along at a steady trot. A canter would have troubled the constable. A hell-for-leather gallop would have hurled him from the saddle of the borrowed animal. After speaking with Bridget McCoy at the Saracen's Head, the two men were on their way to Smithfield. Both she and her son were ready to go with them but Christopher declined the offer. Patrick needed rest and the sight of his mother would only put their quarry to flight again. With the drawing of the killer in his pocket, and with the certainty that the man worked as a Smithfield porter, Christopher felt that they had enough information to run him to ground themselves.

'You are handling the mare well, Jonathan,' he said.

'I'd rather not handle her at all.'

'It's the quickest way to get to Smithfield.'

'I'd sooner crawl there on my hands and knees,' said Bale, holding on to the reins as if his life depended on it. 'It feels so unsafe up here.'

'You'll get used to it.'

Covering over ten acres, Smithfield had been the city's largest meat market for centuries. It was famed for its turbulence and as the site of many executions. Smithfield was the home of the annual Bartholomew Fair, an occasion for unbridled rowdiness and debauchery. So notorious was it as a place of fighting and duelling that it was known as Ruffians Hall. In an attempt to impose a degree of order, the area had been paved and provided with sewers and railings, but old habits died hard. It was still pulsing with danger.

Christopher and Bale became aware of it long before it came into view. Slaughtermen had been working in earnest and the stink of blood and offal was carried on the light breeze. It made them both retch. The noise, too, came out to meet them. Crazed cattle, sheep and pigs set up a constant din as they scuttled here and there in a vain attempt to avoid their grisly fate. When the riders got to Smithfield itself, the stench was indescribable. Everywhere they looked, axes were being swung and doomed animals were sending their last cries of protest up to heaven.

It was no place for the faint-hearted or for the unwary. As soon as they dismounted, the first thing that Christopher did was to employ a young boy to look after their horses, promising to pay him when they returned so that they could guarantee he would still be there. A ghastly scene confronted them. Blood-soaked men were loading meat into carts. A fresh supply of cattle was just arriving. A barking dog was chasing some sheep. A mischievous drover, much the worse for drink, let loose a large bull and it rampaged around the market, scattering all and sundry, before disappearing into one of the shops to cause even more havoc. It was a typical day at Smithfield.

They talked to anyone who hired porters. A description was given, the drawing was shown and Christopher hinted at a reward for any help. Their efforts brought little result at first. People either did not recognise the man or protected him out of a false loyalty. It took them an hour before they finally found someone willing to assist them. He was a squat individual with a porcine face and thick forearms. After staring at Bridget McCoy's art for some time, he gave a nod.

'Yes, I know him,' he said. 'Dan Crothers.'

'Are you certain of that?' asked Bale.

'I should be. He works for me.'

'Is he here now?'

'No,' said the man. 'He disappeared. Dan's like that.'

'Could he have been in Leadenhall Market earlier on?'

'That's where I sent him with the cart. He had meat to deliver. Dan brought the cart back then vanished.'

'Has he always worked here?' said Christopher.

'On and off.'

'Was he ever in the army?'

'Yes, sir. Eight years, he served.'

'So he'd be used to handling weapons?'

'Sword, dagger, pistol, musket – Dan knows them all.'

'I see,' said Christopher with a meaningful glance at Bale. 'Has he been here all this week?'

'No,' grumbled the man, wiping his nose with the back of his hand. 'Dan went off somewhere for a day or two. I only employ him, of course, so he didn't bother to tell me. When he got back, I swinged him soundly. If he kept going off, I warned him, I'd find another porter.'

Christopher tried to contain his excitement. Everything he had heard confirmed that they might have found the elusive Mr Field at last. He had been in Leadenhall Street that morning so could well have encountered Bridget McCoy and her son. He had also been away from his work at the very time when Sir Julius Cheever had been ambushed in Hertfordshire. As a former soldier, Crothers would be proficient with a musket. If he were only a humble porter, being paid to commit murder would have a strong temptation for him.

'Where does he live?' said Christopher.

'Old Street,' the man told him. 'Hard by St Luke's Church. Are you going to pay Dan a visit, sir?'

'Yes.'

'Then tell him not to come back here. I'll not take him on again.'

'You won't be able to,' said Bale, solemnly.

Christopher dropped some coins into the man's grubby hand. After collecting their horses, they rode off towards Old Street, glad to escape the multiple horrors of Smithfield. Bale's face was expressionless but he felt the same inner thrill as Christopher. The hunt might be over. The killer who had desecrated the constable's beloved ward would now pay for his crime. So keen was Bale to get there that he forgot all about his fear of riding a horse.

When they reached Old Street, they soon found the house. It was little more than a hovel. Whatever he had done with his blood money, Dan Crothers had not used it to find more a comfortable lodging. They tethered their horses and approached with care. Christopher sent Bale around to the rear of the house before he knocked on the door. There was no reply. He pounded with his fist and, this time, the door swung back on its hinges.

'Mr Crothers!' he called. 'Are you there?'

Still there was no response. Taking out his sword, Christopher pushed the door fully open and stepped furtively into the house. On the ground floor, it comprised two small rooms and an evil-smelling scullery. They were all empty. He went slowly up the bare wooden stairs, trying to make as little noise as possible but unable to stop the loud creak of a loose step. Two rooms stood ahead of him. One door was ajar and he could see that there was nobody inside the room. When he turned to look at the other door, however, he sensed danger.

'Mr Crothers!' he called again. 'Dan Crothers!'

There was an eerie silence. Convinced that there was someone in the room, Christopher inched forward. It was no time for misplaced heroism. The man had a musket and he knew how to fire it. Christopher had to temper his eagerness with commonsense. He yelled once more.

'Mr Crothers – I'm coming in!'

Kicking open the door, he then jumped back quickly out of sight so that any shot would go harmlessly past him. As it happened, there was no resistance at all. Dan Crothers was in no position to offer it. He was lying on his back in the middle of the room. Christopher took out the drawing to compare it with the face of the dead man. Bridget McCoy's work was uncannily accurate. All his features were there. Mr Field was without doubt the alias of Dan Crothers. There was one significant difference between the drawing and the man on the floor. It was a detail that the Irishwoman might be pleased to add.

His throat had been cut from ear to ear.

'There's no need at all for you to be there, Orlando,' said Dorothy Kitson.

'I could not possibly let you go alone.'

'I do not require a chaperone.'

'I think that you do,' said her brother, fussily 'and that's why I insist on accompanying you. My presence will act as a needful restraint.'

Dorothy laughed. 'A restraint against what?'

'Impulsive action. It will also introduce some balance. If you went there alone, you would be hopelessly outnumbered.'

'This is an informal meeting, Orlando, not a skirmish.'

'Nevertheless, I'll not see my sister put at a disadvantage.'

Orlando Golland had called on her to find out what time they were bidden that evening. Ordinarily, he would strenuously have avoided the company of Sir Julius Cheever but circumstances compelled him to go. What surprised him was how calm and unflustered his sister was about the forthcoming event. Golland was already having qualms.

'I spoke to Maurice Farwell about it,' he said.

'About what?'

'This ludicrous friendship you have with Sir Julius.'

'It's not ludicrous,' she replied, sharply.

'Then what is it?'

'Something that has given me untold pleasure. As for Maurice, I think it very unkind of you to discuss my personal affairs with him.'

'I took him to task for introducing the pair of you at Newmarket.'

'Then talked about us as if we were two horses in the paddock, I've no doubt.' Dorothy took a moment to suppress her anger. 'Orlando, I have a pleasant friendship with a certain gentleman. That is all. It's not a source of gossip for you and Maurice Farwell.'

'But his wife foresaw it all.'

'What do you mean?'

'Adele had a distinct feeling about you.'

'She made no mention of it to me.'

'According to her husband, she sensed that you were ready to welcome a man back into your life again. The tragedy is that you chose Sir Julius.'

'I chose him as a friend – not as anything else.'

'He may have higher aspirations.'

'Well, he has not discussed them with me.'

'Maurice was as surprised as any of us.'

'I'm not interested in Maurice's opinion, or that of his wife.'

'He could not believe that Sir Julius could turn suitor at his age,' said Golland, 'and he found it even more difficult to accept that you should encourage his overtures.'

'Sir Julius has not *made* any overtures.'

'What else is this invitation but a declaration of intent?'

'For heaven's sake, Orlando,' she said, her exasperation showing. 'It's perfectly natural that Sir Julius should want me to make the acquaintance of his daughters. It will put a stop to any idle speculation on their part about our friendship. At least,' she continued, 'I hoped that it would. Your presence will probably only inflame it.'

'How?'

'They will interpret it as a sign that you are examining their family to see if a closer relationship with them is desirable.'

'I'm certain that it is not.'

'Only because you do not *know* Sir Julius.'

'Maurice Farwell does.'

'Leave him out of this,' she responded, tartly.

'He considers him to be an ogre.'

'Maurice's views are irrelevant. So, for that matter, are yours. I'll not let anyone else live my life for me. I'm old enough and wise enough to make my own decisions. And that, Orlando,' she said, looking him in the eye, 'is exactly what I intend to do.'

When he saw that the man was dead, Christopher Redmayne went to the window and summoned his companion. Jonathan Bale soon joined him and the pair of them bent over the corpse to inspect it.

'He has not been dead long,' decided Bale.

'How do you know?'

'Because I've seen too many murder victims in my time.'

'Yes, I'm sure.'

'The blood is still fresh and there's no sign of *rigor mortis*. That only starts to set in after four hours or more.'

'He was obviously a strong man,' noted Christopher, looking at the broad shoulders and the muscular arms. 'He'd not have been easy to overpower.'

'That's why he was knocked out first,' said Bale, turning the head of the corpse so that a gash became visible. Blood had stained the back of the scalp. 'I think that Mr Crothers was hit from behind before having his throat slit. What I don't know is why anyone should want to kill him.'

'It was because he failed, Jonathan.'

'Failed?'

'He had two attempts at shooting Sir Julius and, each time, his victim survived. It must have been very galling for his paymaster,' said Christopher. 'I was there when the second shot was fired and it looked as if Sir Julius was dead. That report would have been brought back to London. Imagine the shock for the man who employed Crothers when he realised that Sir Julius was, in fact, still alive.'

'He'd be very angry, Mr Redmayne.'

'I think he lost patience with his hired killer.'

'There's another thing,' said Bale. 'As long as Mr Crothers carried on his old job as a porter, there was always the chance that he'd be found in the end. He knew too much. Someone silenced him.'

'He may yet be able to tell us something.'

'Search his pockets.'

'I will. You see what else you can find.'

Bale looked around the room. It was small, dirty and poorly furnished. Dan Crothers had pathetically few possessions. Beyond a pile of old clothing, there was little apart from some bread, wrapped up in a cloth, and a flagon of beer. Hidden away underneath the bed, however, was a collection of weapons. Bale got down on his knees to pull out a dagger, a cudgel, a flintlock pistol and a musket. There was powder and ammunition for both firearms.

'This is the musket that killed Mr Everett,' said Bale, holding it in his hands. 'The murder's been solved. Mr Crothers is the guilty man.'

'Yes,' said Christopher. 'Unfortunately, someone has done the executioner's job for us. If we'd caught him alive, he might have been able to tell us who suborned him to commit the crime. That's the real villain, Jonathan – the man behind all this.'

'Was there anything in his pockets?'

'A piece of cheese and a few coins, that's all.'

'Have you felt inside the coat, sir?'

'I could find no pockets there.'

'Let me try,' said Bale, putting the musket aside and crouching beside the corpse. 'Criminals sometimes have secret pouches sewn into their coats where they can hide things.' He groped around until his hand closed on something. 'I thought so.'

'What have you discovered?'

'Not much, sir, but it may help us.' He withdrew his hand and opened his palm. He was holding two pieces of paper. 'Messages of some kind, I think.'

Christopher took them from him. The first one was a short letter, written in a neat hand, informing Crothers that Sir Julius Cheever would be travelling to Cambridge that very day. It was unsigned. A different correspondent had sent the other letter. Using a spidery scrawl, he simply gave a date and the name of the Saracen's Head in Knightrider Street. Christopher passed both missives to Bale to read.

'That's the date on which Bernard Everett was killed,' he said, pointing to the second letter. 'This is clear proof that someone gave Dan Crothers instructions to shoot Sir Julius.'

'Someone else sent the other message,' observed Bale, reading it. 'That means we have to look for two people.'

'Or even more. I think we'll find a conspiracy at work.'

'How do we expose it?'

'With a combination of patience and hard work, Jonathan. We caught up with one villain. Now we have to find the person or persons who paid him.' Christopher took the letters from him. 'This murder must be reported at once.'

'I'll do that, Mr Redmayne.'

'Thank you.'

'Sir Julius will need to hear about this as well.'

'I'll tell him that we found the man who tried to kill him on his way to Cambridge. But I'll urge him not to drop his guard,' said Christopher. 'One hired killer might be dead but there's clearly another at work. My fear is that he might turn his attention to Sir Julius now.'

'What about Mrs McCoy, sir?'

'I leave you to inform her – and to thank her for that drawing she made. It helped us to find the man. I think she'll be delighted to learn that he's dead.'

'Delighted or disappointed?'

'You know her better than I do, Jonathan.'

'Mrs McCoy is a woman of strong passions,' said Bale. 'She'd have preferred to cut his throat herself then have the pleasure of dancing a jig on his grave.'

When he stormed into the house with a dark scowl on his face, it was clear that Sir Julius Cheever had not enjoyed his day in parliament. His daughters greeted him in the hall.

'Welcome home, Father,' said Susan, guessing the reason for his irritability. 'Did you come off worse in the debate?'

'We had a moral victory,' he replied, 'but it was not reflected in the voting. Those lily-livered cowards were too frightened to stand up against the government.'

'What were you talking about?' asked Brilliana.

'Naval procurements.'

'What a dreary subject!'

'Far from it, Brilliana. It's a topic of national importance. It's not all that many years ago that we had Dutch vessels, sailing up the Medway and destroying part of our fleet. We need to make sure that it never happens again. One way to do that is to root out incompetence from the Navy Office.'

'Oh,' she said. 'That's where Henry Redmayne works.'

'He was partly responsible for my defeat this afternoon.'

'But he's not a Member of Parliament.'

'No, he isn't,' said Sir Julius, sourly, 'but he supplied privileged information to Maurice Farwell. Had I been in possession of those details, my case would have been strengthened. As it was, Farwell used them so skilfully me against me that I was tied in knots.'

'You cannot expect to win every debate,' said Susan.

'I had right on my side in this one.'

'Why did you not get Henry to help *you*?' said Brilliana.

'That popinjay would never assist me. He's in the pocket of men like Maurice Farwell, cunning politicians who surround themselves with flatterers. Redmayne is a sycophant.'

'I don't agree at all, Father. Henry struck me as his own man.'

'This is not the time to argue,' said Susan, conscious that their visitors would be arriving within the hour. 'Everything is ready. We had your note to say that Dorothy's brother would be coming as well.'

'I was not my idea to invite that dry old stick,' said her father.

'I believe that he's a chief magistrate.'

'Orlando Golland has no call to barge in.'

'I take is as a promising sign,' said Brilliana. 'It's an indication of how involved Mrs Kitson really is. Mr Golland is coming so that he can take a closer look at his future brother-in-law.'

'Arrant nonsense! I've told you a dozen times. Mrs Kitson is a friend and nothing more than a friend.'

'At the moment.'

'Brilliana!'

'You can't hide your feelings from me, Father,' she said, depositing a kiss on his cheek. 'I'll go and see if Lancelot is ready. He must look at his best if he's to impress Mr Golland.' She tripped up the staircase. 'My husband would sit upon the bench with real authority.'

'Authority!' said Sir Julius, turning to Susan. 'He lost all touch with that concept the moment he married your sister. Lancelot has to ask her for permission to breathe. However,' he continued, leading her into the parlour so that they could speak in private, 'let's forget them for a moment. I had some cheering news earlier.'

'From whom?'

'Christopher. While one member of the Redmayne family is trying to thwart me, another has actually tried to help. He intercepted me as I was about to leave the House of Commons.'

'What did he tell you?'

'They found the man who tried to kill me.'

'That's wonderful,' said Susan, taking his arms to squeeze

them. 'Who was he? How did they catch him? Where is the man now?'

'With the coroner. He was dead when they got to him.'

Her excitement disappeared. 'Dead?'

'Someone had slit his throat, Susan.'

'Heavens!'

'So the news is not entirely good,' he admitted. 'We still do not know who hired this man to come after me. In other words, they are free to set someone else on me. Say nothing of this to Brilliana and Lancelot,' he urged. 'I find their concern for my safety so irritating. Most of all, Susan, do not breathe a word of this to Mrs Kitson or her brother. It will only spoil the evening and I'm determined that it will be a success.'

Jonathan Bale had a good understanding of Bridget McCoy's character. His prediction was borne out. When he told her about their visit to Smithfield, and the discovery they had subsequently made, she felt cheated that Dan Crothers had escaped her retribution.

'Slit his throat?' she cried. 'I'd have taken his whole head off.'

'Show some respect for the dead, Mrs McCoy.'

'I save my respect for the living and that's more than he did. You saw what he did to Patrick. He knocked him down then kicked him in the head. A man like that deserves no mercy.'

'He got none,' said Bale.

'I want to see him.'

'No, Mrs McCoy.'

'I can help to identify the broken-nosed bastard.'

'Your drawing of him did that. Besides, now that we have his real name, we can call on several people from Smithfield to identify him. Dan Crothers was well-known there.'

'I'd still like to see him, Mr Bale. I'm entitled to gloat.'

'Do it in private. The coroner will not let you near the body.'

'But I was a victim of deceit.'

'That's the very reason you should be kept away from him,' said Bale, gently. 'It would only arouse you to evil thoughts. The man is dead, Mrs McCoy. Take comfort from the fact that you and Patrick helped us to find him. If you had not gone to Leadenhall Street today, we might still be searching for Dan Crothers.'

'That's right.'

'Your son behaved like a true constable.'

'No, Mr Bale,' she said. 'He rushed in too fast. You'd never have done that. Patrick has learned his lesson. He'll not be so rash again – I'll make sure of that.'

'How is he?'

'Still fast asleep in bed.'

They were in the taproom of the Saracen's Head. It was only half-full so Bridget was not kept busy serving beer. Angry that she had not been involved in the capture, she was grateful to Bale for bringing the news in person, and for showing a genuine interest in her son.

'Why do we never see you drinking in here, Mr Bale?' she said, giving him a nudge. 'Don't you like beer?'

'I like it very much, Mrs McCoy.'

'But you prefer another tavern to this one – is that it?'

'No,' he explained. 'I'd rather drink it at home in the company of my wife. And I never touch it when I'm on duty. What use would a drunken constable be?'

'None at all. But you'll have a tankard now, won't you?'

'No, Mrs McCoy.'

'It would be my way of thanking you.'

'That's very kind of you but I'll have to refuse. I've still got lots of work to do today. I must keep my head clear.'

'One drink won't hurt you,' she said, slapping the barrel on the counter. 'Howlett's beer is the best in London.'

Bale was suddenly alert. 'Howlett's beer?'

'We've always used his brewery.'

'Would that be Erasmus Howlett?'

'Yes, Mr Bale. He supplies good quality at fair prices, and you can't say that of some brewers. Do you know Mr Howlett?'

'I met him some days ago.'

'Then you know what a decent man he is.'

'Yes, I do.'

'He visits all the taverns that buy his beer,' she said.

'Does he?'

'Yes. In fact, he was here a week or so ago. A man in his position doesn't need to bother with the likes of us. He could send someone in his place. But Erasmus Howlett cares enough to come here himself. He's a real gentleman in every way. Well, you've met him.'

'I have,' said Bale.

But he was not thinking about the man's prowess as a brewer or of his courteous treatment of his customers. What occupied his mind was a memory of a scrawled letter that had been found in the pocket of a murder victim. When the constable had questioned him earlier, Erasmus Howlett had been friendly and gracious.

But his hands had never stopped shaking.

Chapter Ten

Christopher Redmayne was pleased to have made some progress but he was keenly aware of the fact that the most difficult part of the investigation might yet be to come. On his way back from the House of Commons, he had to ride along the Strand so he decided to call in on his brother, less out of any real desire to see Henry than in order to apprise him of the latest development. He hoped that by now his brother's infatuation with Brilliana Serle had either burned itself out or been replaced by another of Henry's temporary obsessions. In the past, prompted by a distant sense of shame, he had always tried to conceal Henry from the Cheever family. To have him pursue a female member of it with all the zest of a rampant satyr would be a calamity. First and foremost, it would jeopardise Christopher's precious friendship with Susan. At all costs, that had to be avoided.

Crossing the threshold of the house in Bedford Street, Christopher saw that his hopes were futile. Henry came bounding along the hall to greet him, embracing him warmly before standing back to look at him.

'Well, Christopher,' he said. 'When am I to see her?'

'I did not come here to talk about Brilliana.'

'What other subject is worthy of a moment's consideration?'

'The death of her father.'

Henry tensed. 'Sir Julius has been killed?'

'No,' said Christopher, 'but his life is in great danger and that means his daughters – both of them – can think of nothing else.'

'Oh, poor Brilliana! I long to comfort her.'

'You can do that best by helping to remove the threat to her father. Until that goes, then her heart is elsewhere.'

'How can I help?' said Henry. 'I've already done what I can.'

'First, let me tell you the news.'

'At least, impart it with some comfort. Follow me.'

As Henry led him towards the parlour, his brother glanced at the painting on the wall of the Roman orgy. Large, colourful and gloriously explicit, it belonged in the home of someone with an unashamed passion for sensuality. The thought that Brilliana

Serle had found it stimulating made Christopher revise his opinion of her completely. It would be wholly out of place in her house in Richmond and was liable to provoke censure among the most open-minded of people. He followed Henry into the room and they sat down.

'Now,' said his brother, 'what tidings have you brought?'

'We tracked down the man who killed Bernard Everett.'

'Bravo!'

'His name was Dan Crothers.'

'I thought it was Field.'

'That was an alias he used to confuse the landlady at the Saracen's Head. He worked as a porter at Smithfield. Separate them out. Smith. Field. He chose the second half of the market as a disguise.'

'Did he resist arrest?'

'No,' said Christopher. 'He was dead when we found him. Someone had cut his throat to stop him from giving anything away.'

'Why employ a meat porter as a killer?'

'Because he was desperate for the money and because he had learned to use firearms as a soldier. Someone knew and trusted him.'

'Then disposed of him when his work was done.'

'But it was *not* done, Henry,' his brother pointed out. 'Sir Julius survived. I think that Crothers was murdered as a punishment.'

'By whom?'

'That's what we have to find out.'

Henry became pensive. Taking off his wig, he laid it aside so that he could scratch his head. Years were suddenly added to his age. A deep chevron of concentration was branded between his eyebrows. His eyes took on a watery look. After a while, he snapped his fingers.

'Were there any clues on the dead body?' he asked.

'Only these,' replied Christopher, taking out the two letters to pass to him. 'These were hidden inside his coat. They are both instructions to kill but, as you see, the calligraphy differs.'

Henry held up one letter. 'This is the work of an educated hand,' he said, 'while the other could have been written by a child that had just mastered his letters. Neither is known to me.'

'The one is on expensive stationery, the other on cheap paper.'

'Was Crothers employed by two separate people?'

'Yes,' said Christopher, 'but to the same end. Both wanted him to shoot Sir Julius Cheever. Luckily, his two attempts were failures.'

'A third ambush might be more successful.'

'That's my fear.' Taking the letters back, he slipped them into his pocket. 'What do you know about a pamphlet called *Observations on the Growth of Popery and Arbitrary Government in England?*'

'Only that its author should be burned at the stake.'

'You've heard of it, then?'

'It was the talk of the coffee houses for weeks. Ninian Teale even got hold of a copy. He said that it was the most treasonable piece of prose he'd ever seen. A scurrilous essay, penned by a frothing dissident.'

'Did he know who wrote it?'

'No,' said Henry, 'and that's what made it so maddening. It was a cruel attack on His Majesty by someone who lacked the courage to put his name to such mutinous opinions.'

'The pamphlet achieved its aim, then. It caused an uproar.'

'Ninian Teale wanted the author to be weighted down with stones and dropped in the deepest part of the Thames. And he was not the only one moved to thoughts of revenge. All civilised men were affronted. Had they caught the wretch, they'd have disembowelled him.'

'Who was most outraged by the pamphlet, Henry?'

'That's difficult to say.'

'Ninian Teale?'

'Oh, no. There were several people more incensed than he.'

'Such as?'

Henry scratched his head again. His lips moved as he mumbled to himself a list of possible names. A light finally came into his eyes and he slapped his thigh with finality.

'Cuthbert!' he declared.

'Cuthbert?'

'The Earl of Stoneleigh,' said Henry. 'I remember the anger with which he spoke about that pamphlet. I shared a box with him at the theatre one day. Cuthbert spent a whole hour, devising horrible deaths for the man who wrote those heretical *Observations*.'

Christopher was curious. 'Did the earl ever see military action?'

'See it? I should think so. Cuthbert had his own regiment. One of the suggestions he made in the theatre that day was to have the author of that pamphlet tied to two stallions so that he'd be torn asunder when they were whipped into gallop.' Henry gave a harsh laugh. 'But on consideration, he thought that too mild a punishment.'

'Too *mild*?'

'Cuthbert has a vengeful streak. But let's put him aside,' said Henry. 'I want to talk about a vision of loveliness. How can you bring me to Brilliana's side?'

'I'll do everything I can to keep you away from it, Henry.'

'What sort of repayment is that?'

'The best kind. I'm saving you from humiliation.'

'I want her, Brilliana wants me. Where's the humiliation in that?'

'You misunderstood the lady.'

'No man could misunderstand the glances she darted at me.'

'Brilliana is married.'

'Her husband is my gateway to ecstasy,' said Henry, rubbing his hands. 'Lancelot Serle has ambitions to enter parliament and to consort with His Majesty. I'm in a position to assist him in both of those endeavours – at a price.'

'To extract it from his wife would be dishonourable.'

'What place has honour in a love affair?'

'Henry!'

'The match is made. Brilliana sealed it with a smile.'

'I know that you've stolen quietly into a marital bed before,' said Christopher, 'and I accept that no amount of finger-wagging from me will ever make you abandon such lascivious escapades, but your interest has alighted on the wrong person this time. Look elsewhere, Henry.'

'How can I when I know that Brilliana is waiting for me?'

'The only thing she is waiting for is the capture of the men who are plotting her father's murder. Once that's been achieved, she will return to domestic harmony in Richmond.'

'Then I'll visit her there.'

'Her husband would not allow it.'

'He'll be too busy in London, distracted by certain friends of mine who'll instruct him in the best way to pursue a political career. While Mr Serle is being educated in the city, I'll tutor Mrs Serle in the country.'

'You'll do nothing of the kind.'

'I will,' said Henry, grinning wolfishly. 'And I have the right to call on you for some brotherly assistance in my wooing.'

'It falls on deaf ears.'

'Will you at least carry a message to Brilliana?'

'Not unless it be a promise to stay out of her way.'

'She pines for me as I pine for her.'

'Henry, you only met her once.'

'Once is enough. Within seconds, I was enraptured.'

'Pure fancy.'

'I was, Christopher. When did you take an interest in her sister? Was it after a week of knowing her, a fortnight, a month, a year? No,' said Henry, confidently, 'I'll wager that it was the *first* time you set eyes on Susan. Am I right?'

'Yes,' admitted Christopher. 'It was.'

'There you are. We were jointly enthralled in an instant.'

'It's a false comparison. Brilliana is married, Susan is not.'

'A trifling detail.'

'It's the one that will keep you at bay, Henry. If you really care for Brilliana, you would not trample on her happiness.'

'I seek only to increase it.'

'By forcing your unsought attentions upon her?'

'By showing her that at least one member of the Redmayne family has the courage to follow his heart. You've been walking in circles around Susan for an eternity without getting any closer to her.'

'We have an understanding.'

'So do Brilliana and I,' said Henry, rolling her name around his mouth as if it were a delicious sweetmeat. 'We understand that love is but a brief prologue to consummation. She will soon be *mine*.'

The evening got off to an uneasy start. Arriving by carriage at the house, the visitors were conducted into the parlour. Dorothy Kitson was wearing a beautiful ruby-coloured dress with a bone-fronted bodice and a looped skirt. Puffed and slashed, the elbow sleeves were finished with a row of ribbon loops. Bows adorned the front of the bodice. Her hair was puffed above the ears and held away from her cheeks by concealed wires. She looked poised and handsome. Her brother, by contrast, wearing a serviceable black suit and sporting the periwig that he used as a justice of the peace, was ill at ease and seemed rather dowdy beside her.

Introductions were made and everyone sat down. Susan Cheever was wearing an elegant new dress but it was her sister who had gone to elaborate lengths with her appearance. Serle, too, in a suit of blue velvet, had taken time with his preparation. Sir Julius was oddly uncomfortable, a nervous host who was desperately hoping that his daughters would approve of Dorothy and, by the same token, that she would like them. The grim, judicial expression on Orlando Golland's face suggested that no approbation would ever come from him.

There was a long and very awkward pause. Even Sir Julius was at a loss for words. Sitting in a circle, they all waited for someone to speak. Into the void stepped Brilliana Serle.

'Have you known Father long, Mrs Kitson?' she asked.

'A matter of weeks, that's all,' replied Dorothy.

'Over a month,' corrected Sir Julius, softly. 'But I feel that I've known you so much longer.'

'Yes, I feel that as well.'

'The acquaintance is still very new,' said Golland, implying that it should proceed at a slow pace. 'I was there when my sister and Sir Julius first met. It was at Newmarket.'

'I understand that you own racehorses,' said Serle.

'It's my one weakness.'

'I don't think that an interest in horses is a sign of weakness, Mr Golland. Horses are the most superb creatures. I've seven in my own stables, though only one competes in races. How many do you have?'

'Three at the moment but I'm negotiating for a fourth.'

'How did you first get involved in the sport?'

Serle's curiosity had two important results. It not only brought a whisper of a smile to Golland's face, it detached him from the general conversation and allowed the other four to begin a separate dialogue. Serle was a keen horseman and a frequent visitor to races. He and the magistrate were soon discussing the finer points of rearing and riding thoroughbreds. Susan, meanwhile, impressed by Dorothy Kitson's demeanour, made an effort to be friendly towards her.

'Father has told us so little about you,' she said. 'He's been hiding you away like a secret horde of gold.'

'That's exactly what she is,' said Sir Julius, stiffly. 'A human treasure chest. Dorothy – Mrs Kitson, that is – has enriched my life in every way and I am deeply grateful.'

'We can understand why now that we've met her.'

'Yes,' said Brilliana. 'You are nothing at all as we pictured you, Mrs Kitson. We expected someone rather older.'

Dorothy smiled. 'I'm not in the first flush of youth, Mrs Serle.'

'Father did not describe you with any accuracy.'

'Really?'

'Words could never do you full justice,' said Sir Julius.

'You are too kind.'

'We look upon you as a benign sorceress,' Brilliana told her.

'A sorceress?'

'You've cast such a wondrous spell upon Father. Instead of ranting and raving at us—'

Sir Julius frowned. 'I never rant and rave.'

'—he's been the soul of affability. Don't you agree, Susan?'

'Your effect on Father has been truly astonishing, Mrs Kitson,' said Susan, looking fondly at Sir Julius. 'He's been transformed. The shame of it is that you've come into his life at such a troublesome moment.'

'Yes,' said Dorothy, sadly. 'I heard about the attack on him. It's a miracle that he survived. You were brave to travel without a bodyguard, Sir Julius, but I hope that you will be not display such bravery again. In the eyes of those that care for you, it's akin to folly.'

'For your sake,' he promised, 'I will exercise the utmost caution.'

'I'll hold you to that.'

'And so will we, Father,' said Susan.

Brilliana nodded. 'We could not bear to lose you.'

'I intend to be here for a long time yet,' he told them. 'When a man has so much to live for, he'll make sure that premature death is kept at arm's length.' He winked at his elder daughter. 'You'll have to continue to endure my ranting and raving, Brilliana.'

'Mrs Kitson has cured you of it.'

'Not when I enter parliament,' he confessed. 'I am as choleric as ever there. I was so sorely pressed today that I could not help but rant and rave at Maurice Farwell.'

'Maurice?' said Dorothy, ears pricking up. 'How did he arouse your ire, Sir Julius?'

'By trouncing me in debate.'

'He rarely loses an argument.'

'That's what I've discovered.'

'Adele, his wife, tells me that he's the most mild-mannered man at home. In the House of Commons, clearly, he's a very different person.'

'He's as slippery as an eel,' snapped Sir Julius. On reflection, he summoned up a forgiving smile. 'No, give the man his due. He's an adroit politician with the gift of rhetoric. I have to be on my mettle to best him in argument. Every blow I try to land seems to miss him.'

'Father, this is hardly the time for political discussion,' warned Susan. 'You are not in the Parliament House now.'

'Yes,' said Dorothy. 'It's a subject about which I know nothing.'

'Then I'll not bore you with it,' vowed Sir Julius, graciously. 'Especially as we have so many other things to talk about.' 'I'd like to know more about your lovely daughters.'

'I'll tell you about Susan,' offered Brilliana, 'then she can tell you about me. Not that you should believe a word she says, mind you. Younger sisters never appreciate the problems and responsibilities that an elder sibling has to face.'

'You talk of nothing else,' said Susan.

'You see? She contradicts me all the time.'

'I deny that, Brilliana. Be more just, please. We don't wish to give Mrs Kitson the wrong impression.'

Dorothy smiled. 'My impression is that your father is blessed in his daughters. He's told me what a comfort you've been at this difficult time. I can see why he's immensely proud of you both.'

Susan and Brilliana were touched. They turned to their father with gratitude but Sir Julius was not even looking at them. A beatific smile covering his face, he was gazing intently at Dorothy Kitson.

Christopher Redmayne was not entirely convinced by the evidence. After studying one of the notes found on the body of the dead man, he shook his head.

'I think it's just a coincidence, Jonathan,' he said.

'But his hands were shaking, Mr Redmayne. He told me that he could not stop them. That letter was written by Erasmus Howlett.'

'He's not the only man to suffer from some kind of palsy. Many people – especially older ones – have hands that tremble badly.'

'I still believe that we should look into it.'

'What is the point? You met Mr Howlett, did you not?'

'Yes, sir.'

'How would you describe him?'

'I found him very personable.'

'And he's one of Francis Polegate's friends. That in itself should be enough to exonerate him.'

Jonathan Bale was abashed. Having walked all the way to Fetter Lane with the information, he had expected it to be received with more interest. Instead, Christopher was inclined to discount it completely. Bale still felt that he had stumbled on something of importance.

'Look at the facts, sir,' he said. 'The killer fired his musket from a window of the Saracen's Head in Knightrider Street. Only days before, Mr Howlett had visited the tavern.'

'He had good reason. His brewery supplied its beer.'

'But he's not involved in its delivery. His draymen take care of that. Mrs McCoy made that very point. She could not understand why he bothered to come in person when he could easily have sent one of his employees.'

'And what's your conclusion?'

'That he came to see if the tavern would provide a good vantage point from which to overlook Mr Polegate's shop.'

'Surely, he'd have known that in advance?'

'I doubt it. The brewery supplies taverns all over London. Mr Howlett could not remember the exact location of each one.'

'So he went there that day to refresh his memory?'

'Yes, Mr Redmayne.'

'But why would he want Sir Julius Cheever killed and how would he know that he would be there on that day?'

'You answered the second half of that question yourself,' Bale reminded him. 'You told me that lots of people were aware that you'd be attending the opening of the shop with Sir Julius and his daughter. In any case, Mr Howlett might have heard it when he dined with the vintner. If he talked about his brother-in-law being there, Mr Polegate would probably have mentioned that you and Sir Julius would also be present. That could have been the origin of the plot.'

'It could,' conceded Christopher, 'but I remain sceptical.'

'As to the first half of your question, I freely admit that I have no idea why the brewer would want Sir Julius to be murdered. But that does not mean a reason does not exist.'

'Quite.'

'We simply have to discover what it was.'

Christopher glanced at the letter again. They were in the parlour and candles had been lighted to dispel the evening shadows. He was on his feet but Bale – always uneasy in a house that was so much bigger and more comfortable than his own – sat on the edge of a chair with his hat in his hand. Christopher could see how disappointed he was at the architect's luke-warm response. He also knew that his years as a parish constable had sharpened Bale's instincts, and that it was unwise to discard any of his suggestions too rashly.

'There's an easy way to discover if Erasmus Howlett wrote this,' he said, holding up the letter. 'We simply compare it with another example of his handwriting. Are there any invoices from him at the Saracen's Head?'

'I thought of that, sir,' said Bale. 'When I asked Mrs McCoy, she showed me all the correspondence she had from the brewery and it had been sent by a clerk.'

'Then we need to look elsewhere.'

'Why not go straight to Mr Howlett?'

'No,' said Christopher, firmly. 'That's the one thing we must not do, Jonathan. If he's innocent – as I suspect – he'll be deeply insulted.'

'Supposing he's guilty?'

'Then we must creep up on him stealthily. He must have no warning that his name has even crossed our minds.' Christopher handed the letter to him. 'Take charge of this in case you can find something else that Mr Howlett has written. And speak to Mr Polegate.'

'I thought that he was away.'

'They return from Cambridge tomorrow. Sound him out gently on the subject of Erasmus Howlett. Say nothing to show that we have any suspicions of his friend but find out if the brewer has any political allegiances,' said Christopher. 'If we can establish a connection between him and parliament, then, in due course, we may think about confronting Mr Howlett.'

'Very well.'

'And it might be worth speaking to Lewis Bircroft again.'

'Why is that?' said Bale.

'I talked to my brother about the pamphlet that caused such an uproar. Henry says that there was an intensive search for the author. Mr Bircroft was one of the suspects.'

'That's why he was set on by bullies.'

'Drop a name into his ear and see how he responds.'

'And what name would that be, Mr Redmayne?'

'One that my brother mentioned. A man who was so infuriated by the pamphlet that he would do absolutely anything to catch and punish the man who wrote it.'

'Who is he?'

'The Earl of Stoneleigh.'

'Is he an acquaintance of your brother?' said Bale, glowering as he thought about Henry Redmayne's irregular private life.

'Yes,' replied Christopher with a laugh, 'but there's no need to look at me like that. The earl does not share Henry's faults. By all accounts, he's a man of many parts.'

'Is he?'

'Soldier, statesman, poet, playwright, favourite at court. The Earl of Stoneleigh has even stolen some of *my* thunder.'

'In what way?'

'He's also a talented architect.'

The evening had been only a moderate success. Too many hidden tensions had surfaced for it to be an occasion when any of them could relax properly and have any real enjoyment. Sir Julius Cheever had tried too hard to win over Orlando Golland, succeeding only in alienating him even more. Brilliana's questioning of Dorothy Kitson had soon evolved into a searching interrogation and the other woman was discomfited. In attempting to rein back her sister, Susan had only made her lose her temper and Brilliana had been unnecessarily spiky thereafter. The only person to get real satisfaction from the evening was Lancelot Serle, glad to have found a fellow connoisseur of horses and to have gleaned such excellent advice from him about how to become a magistrate.

Conscious that the evening had been less than a success, Sir

Julius consoled himself with the thought that Dorothy Kitson had looked so beautiful in the candlelight. He retired to bed early so that the others could conduct a post-mortem.

'I thought that she was delightful,' said Brilliana.

'Then why did you never stop harrying her?' asked Susan.

'I harried nobody.'

'You did hound her a little, my dear,' said Serle.

'I was entitled to search for the truth, Lancelot. If Mrs Kitson is to marry Father, I need to know as much about her as possible. Having done so, I must say that I would have no qualms about her being our stepmother.'

'Nor would I.'

'Then I must disagree with both of you,' said Susan.

'Why? Mrs Kitson is a charming lady.'

'I do not doubt her charm, Lancelot. She could not have been more pleasant. What I could not do was to see her and Father together somehow. They seem so ill-assorted.'

'That's what people said about Lancelot and me,' Brilliana put in. 'And, quite candidly, I could make the same observation about you and Christopher.'

'Our ages are at least fairly similar,' said Susan. 'Father is so much older than Mrs Kitson and his background is so different. Can you imagine her being happy in Northamptonshire?'

'If a wife loves her husband, she will be happy wherever they are.'

'Thank you, Brilliana,' said Serle.

'Differences simply disappear in a close relationship.'

'That was certainly so in our case.'

'I still have reservations about this friendship,' said Susan, 'and I do not wish to see Father getting hurt. Though he's advanced in years, he's very sensitive in some ways. We must protect him from making a mistake by acting too hastily.'

'There's no chance of that with Mr Golland involved,' remarked Serle. 'He wishes to slow everything down to a snail's pace.'

Brilliana sniffed. 'I found him a rather disagreeable fellow.'

'I liked him. He knows so much about horses.'

'He did not come here primarily to talk about those, Lancelot,' said Susan. 'While we were getting acquainted with Mrs Kitson, her brother was subjecting us to scrutiny. And he was very displeased.'

'How could he possibly have found us wanting?' said Brilliana.

'Because he was looking at us through a haze of prejudices. Mr Golland holds one set of values and they are firmly imprinted on his face. Father has strongly differing principles and we, by extension, are tarred with the same brush. He resented us from the start.'

'But I do not share Father's political views,' said Brilliana.

'Neither do I,' added Serle.

'It does not matter,' said Susan. 'We are all one to Mr Golland. He will do everything in his power to dissuade his sister from continuing with this friendship. Put simply, he detests Father.'

'I gave him the benefit of the doubt,' said Orlando Golland. 'I went there, with judicial impartiality, to weigh the evidence as I saw it.'

'Your mind was made up before we even arrived.'

'That's not so, Dorothy.'

'Yes, it is,' she rejoined. 'You are a man of fixed opinions, Orlando. Those opinions were formed when you were an undergraduate at Cambridge and you have not changed any of them since. I knew that it was a mistake to take you.'

'You needed someone there as an objective observer.'

'You were only a hindrance.'

'So much for gratitude!' he said, huffily.

Dorothy put a hand on his arm. 'I did not mean to hurt your feelings. I can see it from your point of view. You feel that I need safeguarding.' She gave a wan smile. 'Not any more, Orlando.'

They had returned to her house in Covent Garden and were seated in the parlour. On the drive back, Golland had not restricted his criticism to Sir Julius. He considered Brilliana Serle to be too garrulous and Susan Cheever to be too quiet and watchful. The one person who had excited his admiration was Lancelot, a son-in-law who clearly had nothing whatsoever in common with Sir Julius and who would therefore suffer at his hands. He decided that the disparity between the two men was as glaring as that between Sir Julius and Dorothy.

'Differences will out, Dorothy,' he warned.

'You do not have to lecture me.'

'But you did not see how out of place you were in that family.'

'I felt it,' she confessed, 'and it made me look at myself afresh.'

'Sanity at last!'

'No, Orlando. Plain commonsense.'

'Sir Julius is a ridiculous suitor for a woman of your quality.'

'I do not want him as a suitor – only as a friend. When I saw him with his daughters this evening, I realised that I could never replace the wife that he lost. I would be like a fish out of water. When we are alone together,' she went on, 'Sir Julius is wonderful company and I'd hate to lose that. Anything else, I've come to see, is out of the question.'

'I told you so.'

'I had to find out for myself.'

'What will you tell, Sir Julius?'

'Nothing,' she said. 'He's an intelligent man. He could sense that we did not belong together in the wider circle of his family.'

'You do not belong together *anywhere*, Dorothy.'

'I'll not let you spoil our friendship.'

'But it's so embarrassing for me. How could I admit to anyone in my circle that my sister has formed an attachment with Sir Julius?'

'That's a problem you must cope with as best you may. I love you as a brother and listen to you as an adviser. But the one thing I will not allow if that you should dictate the terms of my social life.'

'As you wish,' he said, backing off. 'One object has been achieved. I've saved you from even contemplating a third marriage. Well,' he added quickly as she tried to speak, 'if we are being pedantic, you saved yourself from that irredeemable folly. But I do claim credit for moving you in the right direction.'

She kissed him on the forehead. 'It's too late for an argument, Orlando,' she said, wearily, 'and I'm far too tired to engage in one. Though you might not have thought it, this evening was a rather bruising encounter for me.'

'I blame Mrs Serle for acting like a Grand Inquisitor.'

'I did not even mind that. Brilliana was within her rights to question me. No,' she continued with a sigh, 'my pain arose out of a sense of loss. The longer the evening went on, the more convinced I became that hopes I'd once nurtured were silly and inappropriate. I'm too old and contented to consider a third marriage.'

'It would have been a form of suicide.'

'No, Orlando. That's unfair. Sir Julius is a good man and my affection for him remains. But the gap that exists between us could never be bridged,' she concluded. 'I'll cherish his friendship instead.'

'Allow a decent interval to elapse before you see him again.'

'I had already intended to do so. Both he and I need to recover from this evening's setback. It was a salutary lesson for me.' Dorothy pursed her lips in resignation. 'I am simply not ready for a more serious relationship with anybody.'

Christopher Redmayne was thrilled to see her again and pleased that she had travelled to his house by coach this time. Since it was such a glorious morning, he took Susan Cheever out into his garden and they sat in the shade of a pear tree. She was unusually subdued.

'You seem rather sad,' he observed.

'Not on my own behalf,' she said. 'I feel very sorry for Father.'

'Why?'

'He built so much upon his friendship with Mrs Kitson. She brought happiness into his life and nobody could deny him that.'

'What happened, Susan?'

She told him about the visit on the previous evening and how the presence of Orlando Golland had cast a dark shadow over it. Christopher was not surprised to hear that Brilliana had been too enthusiastic with her questioning. She had always lacked her sister's tact and forbearance.

'Your father must have been very disappointed,' he said.

'He put a brave face on it last night, Christopher. This morning, over breakfast, he could not hide his feelings.'

'What did he say?'

'Almost nothing – and that was an indication in itself.'

'Did he accept that the friendship with Mrs Kitson would go no further than it already has?'

'Yes,' she said. 'I think so. He looked exhausted. I suspect that he stayed awake all night, tormenting himself with thoughts of what might have happened. By this morning, Father seemed to have realised that Mrs Kitson would not fit easily into our family any more than he would fit into hers. He's deeply upset.'

'How did your sister respond?'

'Fortunately, Brilliana did not join us for breakfast and Father had left the house before she even got up. I don't think that he could have coped with losing Mrs Kitson as a possible wife *and* facing Brilliana.'

'But you told her how he felt, presumably?'

'Of course. That's what prompted me to come here.'

'I don't follow.'

'It was to issue another warning,' said Susan. 'After protesting for a while, and claiming that she could bring Father and Mrs Kitson back together again, Brilliana finally accepted that it was better to leave things alone. Having failed to engineer Father into a marriage, she's now free to exercise her influence on us again.'

'Not entirely, Susan.'

'What do you mean?'

'It pains me to say this,' he went on, shifting uneasily on the bench, 'but your sister may be distracted by someone else. It's my turn to give you a warning.'

'About whom?'

'My brother, Henry. For reasons that I would not dare to explore, he has conceived a passion for Brilliana and intends to woo her.'

'But she is happily married to Lancelot.'

'Henry sees the bonds of marriage as a challenge to his ingenuity rather than as any safeguard for a wife. In his mind, no woman is beyond his grasp, however unattainable she might seem. And he insists – though I do not believe him for a second – that your sister has given him some encouragement.'

Susan was alarmed. 'Your brother certainly made an impact on her,' she said, 'and she kept praising his taste in art. But that should not have been mistaken for encouragement. Brilliana respects her marriage vows.'

'Henry does not,' cautioned Christopher. 'That's why we must try to put distance between them. When will they return to Richmond?'

'Not until they are convinced that Father's life is out of danger.'

'That can only happen when we have caught those responsible for the attempts at killing him. As you may know, we no longer seek the man who actually fired the shots.'

'Father told me. He was found dead.'

'Silenced before he was able to tell us who his paymaster was. That's the person we must unmask, Susan. The one who is bent on seeing Sir Julius killed.'

'Do you have no notion of whom he might be?'

'One name will bear inspection, Susan.'

'What name is that?'

'The Earl of Stoneleigh.'

'An earl?' She was shocked. 'Could he really be behind all this?'

'Only time will tell. When you arrived, I was just about to go off to make enquiries about him. I can make the first one right now. Did you ever hear your father mention the Earl of Stoneleigh?'

'Not to me. But I did hear it in passing a number of times.'

'When your home was turned into a Parliament House?'

'Yes, Christopher,' she explained. 'I heard Father yelling that name more than once. There was real anger in his voice. And I seem to recall that Mr Bircroft took the earl's name in vain as well.'

'But he sits in the Upper Chamber. Neither Sir Julius nor his supporters will ever have come face to face with the Earl of Stoneleigh.'

'That's where you're wrong.'

'Oh?'

'Father first met him almost twenty years ago,' she said. 'He had not been ennobled then. His name was Cuthbert Woodruffe in those days and he had good cause to remember my father.'

'Why?'

'Because he was captured by Colonel Cheever – as Father then was – at the battle of Worcester. He was not held for long. Mr Woodruffe escaped and fled abroad to join the rest of the scattered Royalists. He was so loyal that, after the Restoration, he was granted an earldom.'

'I see,' said Christopher, thoughtfully. 'So he and Sir Julius faced each other on a battlefield, did they?'

'Yes,' she replied, 'and that is something not easily forgotten. From what I've heard Father say, the earl has ever forgiven him for being on the winning side that day.'

'He's waited a long time to take his revenge – if, indeed, that's what he been trying to take. Thank you, Susan,' he said. 'What you've told me is very helpful. The Earl of Stoneleigh clearly needs close examination.'

Even that late in the day, the Parliament House was reasonably full. As a former chapel, it had no aisle and was an ideal conference chamber. The Members sat in the choir stalls on the north and south walls, crammed in together for important debates. The Speaker's chair was placed where the altar had been, in an elevated position from which he could see and control the entire room. His symbol of office, the Mace, lay on a table where the lectern had once stood. Separated from the main chapel by choir-screen was the ante-chapel that served as a lobby when a vote was taken. Those who wished to register their votes as Ayes filed into the ante-chapel while the Noes were accustomed to remain in the chapel.

Countless decisions of historic significance had been made there over the years. Debates had raged, reputations had been made and lost, impeachments had added to the drama of the place. It was at once a seat of government and a cockpit of robust argument. That evening, however, the mood was almost light-hearted. Though a debate was in progress, it was of little general interest and most of the Members were not even listening to the exchanges. They were waiting for something else before they were ready to leave. Whispers had passed around the whole chamber and there was an atmosphere of high amusement.

Eventually, their patience was rewarded. Sir Julius Cheever, who had been there all day, had spent most of it in an anteroom, serving on various House of Commons committees. As one had completed its business, another had taken its place. Only now could he come into the Parliament House itself to take his seat. The moment he appeared, dead silence fell on the chamber and all eyes turned on him. Sir Julius was used to feeling a tide of hostility rolling in his direction but this reception was unlike any he had ever received before.

'Here he is!' cried someone. 'Hail, Caesar!'

'Hail, Caesar!' chorused the Members, rising to their feet and lifting their arms in a mock gesture of obeisance. 'Hail, Caesar!'

The explosion of mirth started. It was not the affectionate laughter of friends but the harsh, derisive, sustained cachinnation of enemies. It went on for minutes, getting ever louder and building to a crescendo. Sir Julius had been howled down in parliament before but this was a more disturbing experience. Almost everyone there was jeering him. He was the laughing stock of the House of Commons and he felt as if he were being pummelled by the deafening noise. What mystified him – and what made his ordeal even worse – was that he had absolutely no idea why he had been singled out for such collective ridicule.

Chapter Eleven

Henry Redmayne could not miss such a golden opportunity. Though he knew that he should confide in his brother first, he decided to ignore Christopher and deliver his message directly. It would not only earn him certain gratitude, it would give him the chance to get close to Brilliana Serle again. To be in the same city as her was, for him, an exciting experience. To be under the same roof with Brilliana once more would be exhilarating. Accordingly, he ordered his horse to be saddled then rode off towards what he hoped might be Elysium.

When he reached the house in Westminster, he could not believe his good fortune. Sir Julius Cheever had not yet returned but his elder daughter was there with her husband. Henry was shown into the parlour, almost swooning as he caught a whiff of Brilliana's delicate perfume. He also took note of the suspicion in Lancelot Serle's eye and realised that he had to get rid of the husband before he could negotiate with the wife. Dispensing with the social niceties, he came straight to the point.

'I need to speak to Sir Julius at once,' he said.

'Father is still at the Parliament House,' returned Brilliana.

'So I was told by the servant who admitted me. I think that your father should be rescued from there at the earliest opportunity.'

'Rescued?' said Serle. 'Is he in some kind of danger?'

'Grave danger – though not of a physical kind.'

'I do not understand, Mr Redmayne.'

'I'm not able to enlighten you just yet, I fear,' said Henry. 'It's a matter of the utmost discretion. I'm sure that Sir Julius would rather hear my news in confidence. Only he can decide whether it should reach a wider audience.'

'But we are his family,' said Brilliana.

'And how fortunate he is in having such a daughter.'

'Can you not even give us a hint what this news portends?'

'No, Mrs Serle. I simply want to place certain facts at the disposal of your father. It might explain what has probably happened to him at the House of Commons today.'

'And what is that?' asked Serle.

'Only he can tell you.'

'You have me troubled, sir.'

'Mr Serle,' said Henry, trying to manoeuvre time alone with Brilliana, 'if you have your father-in-law's best interests at heart, you would go and fetch him at once.'

'I can hardly drag him out of a debate.'

'Oh, there will be no debate, I assure you. My guess is that Sir Julius will be relieved to see a friendly face. He'll need no persuasion to come home with you.'

'Do as Mr Redmayne suggests,' urged Brilliana.

'Your father will soon return of his own volition.'

'This is a matter of great importance, Lancelot.'

'A true emergency,' insisted Henry.

'Then why not go yourself?' said Serle, unwilling to leave the two of them alone. 'You could have ridden to parliament instead of coming here.'

'What use would that have been? The name of Henry Redmayne carries no weight with Sir Julius. If I were to have a message sent to him in the chamber, he would surely disregard it. If, however,' he went on, pointing at Serle, 'he hears that his son-in-law is without, he will respond immediately.'

'What are you waiting for?' demanded Brilliana, pushing her husband towards the door. 'Away with you.'

'Not until I know what this is all about,' said her husband.

'It's about Father. What else do you need to know?'

'Think of the perils he's come through recently,' added Henry. 'This is the latest of them and, perhaps, the most agonising. It will be a cruel blow to his pride.'

'Lancelot – go!'

With obvious misgivings, Serle left the room. After closing the door behind him, Henry turned to feast his eyes on Brilliana. She was even more gorgeous than he had remembered. Her fragrance was captivating. He took a few steps towards her.

'Mrs Serle, I cannot pretend that concern for your father was the only thing that brought me here this evening. I had hoped – nay, I'd fervently prayed – that I might be rewarded with a glimpse of you as well.'

'Why, thank you,' she said, smiling at the compliment.

'Since our chance meeting the other day, my mind has dwelt constantly upon you. Am I being presumptuous in thinking that you might have entertained pleasant memories of me?'

'Not at all. We enjoyed our visit to your house.'

'No guest was more welcome.'

'You have such an original taste in decoration.'

'I'm known for it.'

'And you are so utterly unlike your brother, Christopher.'

'We are equally talented – but in very different ways.'

'That's what I sensed.'

He took a step closer and beamed at her. Striking a pose, he turned what he believed to be his better profile towards her. Brilliana was struck by the arresting flamboyance of his attire and by his Cavalier elegance. What she found slightly unsettling was the intensity of his manner. When she had met him before, she had her husband beside her, a line of safety behind which she could retreat at any point. Because Serle had been there, she had felt able to be bold and forthcoming with a new acquaintance. Now, however, she had nobody to give her that invisible sense of security. As he stepped even nearer, Brilliana retreated involuntarily.

'Why do you flee from me, Mrs Serle?'

'I was merely adjusting my dress,' she said, playing with the folds of her skirt. 'Pray, do sit down while you are waiting.'

'I'd sooner stand in your presence – stand or kneel.'

'Mr Redmayne, I do believe that you are teasing me.'

'Not at all,' he assured her, producing his most disarming smile. 'I'd never even dream of it. I seek only your happiness. To that end,' he said, 'I will not rest until I have furthered your husband's political ambitions and found a way to introduce him at Court.'

'Lancelot is having second thoughts about that.'

'But you deserve a husband with such achievements to his name.'

'I still hope to have one,' said Brilliana, 'in the fullness of time. Thank you very much for your generous offer. It is much appreciated but Lancelot prefers to forge his own destiny.'

'And so do I.'

Henry took a deep breath. This was his moment. The speech that he had honed to perfection over the years was trembling on the tip of his tongue. It had never failed him, melting the heart of any woman who heard it and sweeping aside any lingering reservations that she might have. Brilliana was there for the taking. He had the familiar sensation of power as the blood coursed through his veins. He was ready to strike. Henry put a hand to his breast in a gesture of love. Before he could ensnare her in the seductive poetry of his declaration, however, the door opened and Susan Cheever entered. She took in the situation at a glance.

'Good evening, Mr Redmayne,' she said, blithely.

'Oh, good evening, Miss Cheever.'

'How nice to see you again! I apologise for this interruption. You don't mind if I spirit my sister away for a moment, do you?' said Susan, crossing the room to take a grateful Brilliana by the arm so that she could lead her out. 'There's something that I *must* show her.'

The pair of them swept out. Henry wilted.

The Polegate family did not return to London until late afternoon, so it was evening by the time that Jonathan Bale called on the vintner. He was invited into the counting house.

'How was your journey, sir?' said Bale.

'Slow and uncomfortable. We left with heavy hearts.'

'Mr Redmayne told me about the funeral. He was very moved by the ceremony. He said that it was conducted with great dignity.'

'That's the least my brother-in-law deserved,' said Polegate. 'We stayed on for a few days to console his wife. I assume that you've come to tell me about the progress of the investigation into Bernard's death? Has anything happened in our absence?'

'Yes, sir. We found the man who shot him.'

'You did? That's cheering news. Has he been imprisoned?'

'Alas, no.'

'Why not?'

'Because he was no longer alive when we caught up with him.'

Bale described their visit to Old Street and told him what conclusions had been drawn from the murder of Dan Crothers. The vintner was disturbed.

'Are you telling me that my brother-in-law was killed by a meat porter?' he said with patent disgust. 'Bernard was a man of great intelligence. He was a politician, a philosopher and a scholar. It's horrifying to think that he was shot by some illiterate labourer from the lower orders.'

'Dan Crothers was not illiterate,' said Bale, recalling the letters they had found upon him. 'And he was only the tool of someone else, sir. His services were bought.'

'By whom, Mr Bale – and for what reason?'

'We will find out in due course.'

'I have every faith in you and Mr Redmayne. I understand that this is not the first time you've been involved together in solving such a heinous crime.'

'No, Mr Polegate. We've joined forces in the past with some success. What we've learned is that nothing can be rushed. Patience is our watchword. Slow, steady steps will eventually get us to the truth.' He changed his tack. 'I spoke to those friends whose names you gave me. They were all full of sympathy.'

'That's good to know.'

'Mr Howlett was particularly upset to hear the sad tidings.'

'He would be. Erasmus has a kind heart – except when it comes to business, that is. There's no room for sentiment in that.'

'It surprised me that the two of you should be on such familiar terms when you must be keen rivals.'

'Not really, Mr Bale.'

'You both sell drink to the public.'

'Yes,' said Polegate, loftily, 'but we reach different markets. Beer is the choice of the majority of the populace. It's cheap and relatively easy to make.'

'I know, sir. My wife, Sarah, brews it at home.'

'Wine is more expensive because it has to be imported and is heavily taxed. In the main, I sell French and Rhenish wines, though

I expect to import from Spain and Portugal as well in future. Customers who drink beer at a tavern like the Saracen's Head would not even consider purchasing my stock.' He gave a dry laugh. 'Here's a paradox for you, Mr Bale. One of the city's leading brewers will not touch a drop of his beer. He prefers my wine.'

'Mr Howlett?'

'He has an educated palate.'

'And he can afford the higher prices.'

'Yes, Erasmus is a wealthy man. A very amiable one, too.'

'So I discovered,' said Bale. 'Though I felt sorry for the way that his hands were constantly trembling. That must be a problem.'

'It does not prevent him from counting the week's takings,' said Polegate, wryly, 'I know that. It's a problem he's had for years and it seems to be beyond cure.'

'Does it prevent him from writing?'

'I don't think so – not that I've had any correspondence from him myself.'

'Is he interested in political affairs?'

'Everyone in business takes a keen interest in that, Mr Bale. Our livelihoods are closely linked to the laws that are passed, and the taxes that are voted in. Why do you ask about Erasmus?'

'He had the air of a politician about him.'

'I've never noticed that. Sir Julius Cheever is my idea of a Member of Parliament – strong, outspoken and committed to his principles. My brother-in-law would have been the same,' he continued with a shrug, 'but it was not to be. Erasmus Howlett is hardly in their mould.'

'He would hardly share their ideals,' said Bale. 'What I meant was that Mr Howlett had unmistakable character. He spoke well and with great confidence. Such men often drift into the political arena.'

'In one sense, you are right about him.'

'Am I?'

'Yes,' said the other, 'Erasmus may have no ambitions to enter the House of Commons but he does have one dream with a political flavour to it – he wishes to be Lord Mayor one day.'

'Really?' said Bale. 'Is there any likelihood of that?'

'A definite likelihood and I would certainly profit from it. What better advertisement could I have than to be known as the vintner who fills the cellars of the Mayor of London?'

'And does Mr Howlett provide you with beer in return?'

'Oh, no, Mr Bale,' replied Polegate. 'Once you have acquired a taste for wine, beer is anathema. At least, it was in my case. As for dear Erasmus,' he went on, 'his desire to become Lord Mayor is no idle dream. It's a project on which he has worked very carefully. He's taken advice on how to achieve his aim from a true politician.'

'And who is that, sir?'

'His cousin – the Earl of Stoneleigh.'

'Stoneleigh!' exclaimed Sir Julius Cheever, cheeks puce with rage. 'I should have known that that wily devil was behind it.'

'I felt it my duty to report to you,' said Henry.

'I'm grateful to you, Mr Redmayne. It solves the mystery.'

'Word of it would have spread quickly. You must have been the subject of considerable mockery in parliament.'

'I was,' admitted the other, shuddering at the memory. 'They laughed at me like so many hyenas. Had I walked stark naked into the chamber, I could not have provoked more ridicule.'

Lancelot Serle had not needed to go to the Parliament House. He had met Sir Julius as his father-in-law was on his way home and told him of his visitor. Throbbing with fury, Sir Julius had refused to confide the cause of his anger to Serle. As soon as he got back to the house, he took Henry into the upstairs room he used as a study and demanded to know why he had come.

'Explain it in full,' he now invited. 'I want to know all the details of this outrage.'

'Earlier today,' Henry explained, 'I was taken by friends to visit the theatre. It's not something that I would ordinarily do, Sir Julius,' he lied, 'for I do not like to have my sensibilities offended by some of the base and slanderous matter that seems to inhabit our stages. I only agreed to go on this occasion because I was acquainted with the author of the play.'

'The Earl of Stoneleigh.'

'I know him as Cuthbert Woodruffe.'

'And I, as an arrant knave,' growled Sir Julius.

'The play was called *The Royal Favourite* and I had, by sheer chance, seen it when it was first performed at the King's Theatre. It's an amusing comedy and free from the kind of salaciousness that seems to infect the work of most dramatists.'

'Yet you say a new scene had been added to the play.'

'A long and very significant new scene, Sir Julius.'

'Portraying me in a very unflattering light.'

'Alas, yes,' said Henry, pretending to a sympathy he did not feel. 'I was so shocked on your behalf that I almost fled the theatre. What kept me there was the fact that you deserved a full account of what took place, so I forced myself to sit through the scene.'

'You deserve my gratitude for that, Mr Redmayne.'

'There could be no doubt that you were being lampooned. The name of the character was Sir Julius Seize-Her, a rapacious country gentleman from Northamptonshire.'

'Now I see why they cried "Hail, Caesar!" at me in parliament.'

'The actor had a clear resemblance to you and dressed in the sort of apparel that you wear. Everyone recognised you instantly.'

'I did not know that I was so famous,' said Sir Julius, grimly. 'Was I shown as a Member of Parliament?'

'Oh, yes,' replied Henry. 'In fact, the whole scene took place in the Parliament House. Sir Julius Seize-Her had inveigled an attractive young woman into the chamber so that he could prey upon her virtue. When she resisted, he pursued her around the stage with gusto.' He gave an admiring smile. 'As a matter of fact, you showed a wonderful turn of foot, Sir Julius.'

'It was not *me*, man – only some crude version of me.'

'Crude and insulting.'

'How did the scene end?'

'Rather painfully,' said Henry. 'When she could not outrun her would-be seducer, the lady used her only means of defence and struck him with the Speaker's mace in a part of the anatomy that caused him to abandon his designs.'

Sir Julius flopped into a chair and brooded on what he had heard. Knowing Henry to be an incorrigible rake, he did not for a second believe that his visit to the theatre had been a rare event. It was a place that Henry and his friends haunted on a regular basis. Nor did Sir Julius accept the claim that Henry had been so scandalised that he had an urge to abandon the play. He was much more likely to have relished the scene with the rest of the audience.

That being said, the fact remained that he had taken the trouble to call at the house and describe what had happened at the King's Theatre that day. It explained everything. Sir Julius was certain that some of his fellow Members of Parliament had also been at the play, more interested in watching the denigration of an enemy than in attending a debate in the chamber. Sir Julius could imagine how quickly they had raced to Westminster to tell their friends what they had witnessed. When he had joined them, Sir Julius had walked into a solid wall of derision and he was still reeling from the impact.

Henry cleared his throat to attract the other man's attention.

'May I have permission to speak to your daughter?' he said.

'What?'

'Mrs Serle was understandably upset when I told her that you might be in danger of some sort. Since I was unable to give her any details, her fears were only intensified. If I could have some time alone with her,' Henry added, tentatively, 'I could explain to Brilliana – to Mrs Serle – why I had to hold the information back.'

'No,' snarled Sir Julius. 'You'll tell her nothing.'

'But she has a right to know.'

'And I have a right to shield her from any unpleasantness. At this stage, neither of my daughters need know the truth so you must not dare to divulge a word.'

'On my honour, I'll divulge nothing.'

'Then I've no need to detain you, Mr Redmayne.'

'If I could speak to Mrs Serle alone for a mere two minutes...'

'No,' said Sir Julius, getting to his feet. 'You'll talk to nobody in this house. Leave any explanations to me. It's no secret to you that I've never held a very high opinion of you and I daresay that you know the reasons why. On the other hand, I can recognise a good deed when I see one and this particular deed has earned my undying thanks.' He offered his hand and Henry shook it. 'You have not merely lifted a veil from my eyes. You have helped to determine what my course of action must be.'

Though he took no active part in debates, Lewis Bircroft was a dutiful man who felt honour bound to represent his constituents on the occasions when parliament met. He had been present during the humiliation of Sir Julius Cheever and was one of the few who had not joined in the raucous laughter. When he got back to his lodging in Coleman Street, he was still wondering why the appearance of his friend had aroused such concerted mockery. Hobbling into the parlour on his walking stick, he learned that he had a visitor. Jonathan Bale rose up out of the half-dark to welcome him.

'Good evening, Mr Bircroft,' he said. 'Forgive the lateness of this call but you've been out of the house all day. I wonder if I might have a small amount of your time?'

'As long as it is only a small amount, Constable. After a full day in the chamber, I'm extremely tired.'

He moved to the nearest seat and lowered himself slowly into it. Bale waited until the other man had settled down before he spoke.

'You remember what we discussed last time we met, sir?'

'I do and I have nothing else to add.'

'What you did not give me was the name of the man who paid those bullies to cudgel you.'

'I cannot give you what I do not know,' said Bircroft.

'Then perhaps I could suggest the man's identity.'

'No, Constable. The incident belongs in the past. As I told you before, even a mention of it causes me great pain and upset.'

'Would you not like to see justice done, Mr Bircroft?'

'I've rather lost my belief in the concept.'

'Well, I haven't,' said Bale, proudly. 'My whole life is dedicated to it, sir. Nobody can right all the wrongs that are committed for they are too many in number. But I like to feel that I've brought justice to bear in many instances – and I would like to do the same here.'

'What can a mere constable do against such people?'

'So you *do* know who ordered that beating.'

'That's not what I said,' retorted the other. 'I was trained as a lawyer, Mr Bale. I choose my words with great care. In the wake of what happened to me, I've exercised even more precision.'

'I do not blame you, Mr Bircroft.'

'Then do not add to my discomfort by harping on the subject.'

'Let me ask but one question,' said Bale.

'The other man sighed. 'Very well – just one.'

'Do you know the Earl of Stoneleigh?'

'Yes.'

'What manner of man is he?'

'I answered your question – now leave me alone.'

'Even if we are able to prove that it was the earl who paid those men to attack you?'

'No,' said Bircroft, crisply.

'You may have no faith in justice, but surely you can take some satisfaction from revenge?' He sat close to him. 'Yes, I am only a parish constable but I can draw on immense resources. I've arrested members of the peerage before, Mr Bircroft. Nobody is above the law.'

'But there are those who can twist it to their advantage.'

'As a lawyer, you should want to stop them doing that.'

'I tried, Mr Bale – and look what happened to me.'

He stretched out both arms. Even in the flickering candlelight, Bale could see how frail he was. All the life seemed to have been knocked out of Lewis Bircroft. He was a hollow shell of a man.

'Are you afraid of the earl?' asked Bale.

Bircoft indicated the door. 'You will have to see yourself out.'

'Who are his friends? What company does he keep?'

'Only he can tell you that, Mr Bale.'

'What will it cost you to give me the truth?'

'*This* is the truth,' said the other, sharply, pointing to his wry neck and injured leg. 'I have to live with it every day. I was suspected of causing offence to someone and I suffered as a result. A man can only take so much truth, Mr Bale. I've already had my fill.'

'So you fear a second beating, is that what troubles you?'

'It would be a death sentence. I could never survive it.'

'You'll not need to if we arrest the man responsible.'

'He's way beyond your reach, Mr Bale. Nobody is above the law, you tell me? You have clearly not been following the activities of the King and his Court. They revel in their lawlessness,' said Bircroft with rancour. 'They commit crimes upon innocent people whenever they choose and an army of constables could not stop them. When you live under such tyranny, you learn to be circumspect.'

'Sir Julius Cheever is not circumspect.'

'His turn will come, alas.'

'Every man is entitled to fight back against his enemies.'

'Not when they hold a power of you.'

'Is that the situation *you* are in, Mr Bircroft? Does someone hold a power of you?'

'I think that I would like you to go, Constable.'

'Is the name of that person the Earl of Stoneleigh?'

Bircroft said nothing but his eyes were pools of eloquence. Bale did not need to stay. He had the answer he sought.

Christopher Redmayne went to open the front door himself. When he saw the coach draw up outside his house, he thought that Susan Cheever had returned and he rushed to greet her. In fact, it was her father who descended from the vehicle. After issuing a gruff apology for the lateness of the hour, Sir Julius followed the architect into the house and they settled down in the parlour. Sensing that it might be needed, Jacob materialised out of his pantry to place a bottle of brandy and two glasses on the table between them. From the eagerness with which his visitor accepted the offer of a drink, Christopher could see that he was thoroughly jangled.

'Has something happened, Sir Julius?' he asked.

'Another attempt has been made to kill me.'

'When? Where?'

'At the King's Theatre,' said Sir Julius, taking a long sip of his brandy. 'Since musket balls will not bring me down, they are trying to murder my reputation.'

'I do not understand.'

'Then let me explain.'

Sir Julius told him about the savage laughter he had endured from his parliamentary colleagues, and how he had been unable to fathom its cause until Henry Redmayne had arrived at his house. When he recalled the scene in the play that traduced him, he was shaking with uncontrollable anger. By the end of his account, he had finished his brandy and requested another.

Christopher was annoyed and troubled. His ire was reserved exclusively for his brother. He could see exactly why Henry had concealed the information from him so that he would have an excuse to visit the house in Westminster in the hope of seeing Brilliana Serle. It made Christopher seethe. At the same time, he was deeply concerned for Sir Julius. He had never seen him in such a ravaged condition. His visitor looked like an old bear that had been chained to a stake then attacked by a pack of hounds.

On any other day, Sir Julius would have beaten them away with a growl of defiance but he was already in a weakened state as the result of a personal setback. Christopher knew how upset he must have been when Sir Julius saw his hopes of a closer relationship with Dorothy Kitson founder on the rocks of a family gathering.

'This is most unfortunate, Sir Julius,' he said.

'It's a foul calumny.'

'Invoke the law and have the scene removed from the play.'

'Oh, I want more than that, Mr Redmayne,' said the other.

'When I discussed the matter with Susan, she told me that you and the Earl of Stoneleigh were sworn enemies. He still nurses a grudge against you from the battle of Worcester.'

'I should have had him hanged when I had the chance!'

'I gather that you've been a thorn in his flesh ever since you entered parliament.'

'I've endeavoured to be. Stoneleigh is in the Upper House so we never actually meet, but he has a large following in the Commons – Ninian Teale, Maurice Farwell, Roland Askray, to name but a few. I abhor everything such men represent. Most of all, I loathe Stoneleigh.'

'Would it surprise you to know that he may have been instrumental in having your friend, Lewis Bircroft, set on by bullies?'

'Not in the least. But we have no proof.'

'We do now,' said Christopher. 'Had you arrived ten minutes earlier, you would have heard Jonathan Bale's account of his visit to Mr Bircroft. It's the second time they've spoken.'

'Then your friend, the constable, has had more conversation with Lewis than I have. Since the beating, he's refused to talk to me and would never name the person who initiated the attack.'

'He did not name him this evening, Sir Julius. He is clearly in a state of fear. Jonathan, however, is very tenacious. He kept waving the Earl of Stoneleigh in front of him until Mr Bircroft eventually gave himself away.'

'Lewis was his first victim,' said Sir Julius. 'I am his second.'

'Except that he used words against you instead of cudgels.'

'They hurt just as much, Mr Redmayne. Every jibe I received in the chamber was like a physical blow. Well, I am not one to turn the other cheek. When someone hits me, I strike back hard.'

'You've every right to do so.'

Sir Julius became conspiratorial. 'I need your help and I must avail myself of your discretion. Before I say another word,' he added, 'I must extract a solemn promise from you. Nothing that passes between us will go any further than this room. Is that agreed?'

'Agreed, Sir Julius.'

'It must *never* reach the ears of my daughters.'

'As you wish,' said Christopher, unhappy at the thought of having to conceal something else from Susan. 'May I ask why?'

'Because they would do everything they could to stop me.'

'Why is that, Sir Julius?'

'I've challenged the Earl of Stoneleigh to a duel.'

Christopher was stunned. 'A duel?'

'It's the only way to answer such vile slander against me.'

'But duelling is against the law.'

'Then the law must be broken on this occasion. Honour demands it. My challenge has already been sent.'

'I wish that you'd consulted me before dispatching it, Sir Julius,' said Christopher, worriedly. 'You should first have asked for a full public apology. If that had not been given, resort to litigation would have achieved your ends.'

'The only way to do that is to kill Stoneleigh.'

'But he's somewhat younger than you, I believe.'

'So?' said the other, indignantly. 'Are you suggesting that I do not know how to handle a sword, Mr Redmayne?'

'Of course not.'

'Then obey my commands. When my challenge is accepted – as it must surely be – I need you to be standing ready.'

'Why?' asked Christopher, increasingly alarmed at what he was hearing. 'What do you require of me, Sir Julius?'

'You will act as one of my seconds.'

Dorothy Kitson was about to retire to bed when she heard the front door being unlocked. Voices rose up from the hall and she recognised one as belonging to her brother. Putting on her dressing gown, she took up her candle and made her way along the landing.'

'Is that you, Orlando?' she said.

'Yes,' he replied, 'and I know that it's an inconvenient time to call but I felt that you should hear the news at once.'

'What news?' She came down the marble staircase and saw the animation in his face. 'Whatever's happened?'

'I'll tell you in a moment.'

Taking a candle from one of the servants, he shepherded her into the parlour and shut the door behind him. Both candles were set on a table so that they cast a glow across the two chairs on which they settled. Dorothy looked bewildered.

'It's unlike you to call at such an hour, Orlando.'

'I felt that the tidings could not wait.'

'What tidings?'

'You have had a narrow escape, Dorothy.'

'From what?'

'The ignominy of having your name linked with that of Sir Julius Cheever. I praise the Lord that I rescued you from that.'

'You are talking in riddles,' she complained.

'I'm sorry,' he said, reaching out to take her hands. 'I only heard about it myself over supper with friends. It's now the talk of the town, it seems, and will certainly feature in tomorrow's newspapers. A play called *The Royal Favourite* was performed today at the King's Theatre. It contained a vicious – if highly comical – satire on your erstwhile friend.'

'Sir Julius Cheever?'

'In the play, I believe, he is Sir Julius Seize-Her.'

He told her what he had heard from someone who had actually witnessed the performance, and Dorothy sat there with an expression of dismay on her face. When he had finished, Orlando Golland was almost giggling with pleasure.

'Well? What do you think of that?'

'I think it very unkind of you to take such satisfaction from someone else's pain,' she reproached. 'It's unworthy of you, Orlando.'

'It was the laughter of relief,' he said, trying to be more serious. 'I was celebrating my sister's escape from her unwise entanglement with Sir Julius. Were you and he about to contemplate marriage, then you would have suffered this public disgrace along with him.'

'I do suffer it. I have the greatest sympathy for him.'

'Sir Julius *deserved* it.'

'I disagree.'

'He's upset too many people – Stoneleigh among them.'

'Cuthbert?' she said. 'This is one of his plays?'

'Yes, Dorothy,' he replied. 'And from what I hear, it's nothing short of a masterpiece. Sir Julius has been well and truly stoned by the Earl of Stoneleigh.'

'How cruel!'

'It will finish him.'

'What do you mean?

'Even someone as obtuse and insensitive as Sir Julius will not be able to shrug this off. Public humiliation will force him to quit London and run all the way back home.'

'You are quite mistaken,' she said. 'Sir Julius is neither obtuse nor insensitive. In some ways, he's one of the most sensitive men I've ever met. This will not simply wound him. It will shake him to the core. But he'll not take flight, Orlando,' she predicted. 'Of that you may be certain. You reckon without his pride.'

'When he reads tomorrow's newspapers, he will have none left.'

'You underrate him badly.'

'My guess is that he may already have left the city.'

'Then you do not know him as well as I. He will stay.'

'As long as he does not turn to you for succour,' said Golland. That would be too much to bear. I'd hoped that Stoneleigh's play would chase the old fool out of the capital, not send him running to your arms.'

'At a time like this,' she said, 'Sir Julius needs friends. He'll find plenty of compassion here. I judge it to be heartless of Cuthbert to indulge in such gratuitous spite, and I shall tell him so if I see him. I feel sorry for anyone who is pilloried on stage like that.'

'So do I,' said Golland, complacently, 'but not in this case. I've never been a theatregoer but, if the play is ever staged again, I will make certain that I'm there to see it.'

Henry Redmayne was still trying to appease his employer by working at the Navy Office in the mornings. It was a torment. Two servants were needed to get him out of bed, the barber was on hand to shave him and a breakfast was prepared for him even though he barely touched it. He was on the point of leaving that morning when his brother presented himself at the door.

'Christopher,' he said. 'What on earth has brought you here?'

'Anger,' replied his brother, using the flat of his hand to push him backwards into the hall. 'Anger, disappointment and disgust.'

'Such emotions can hardly have been engendered by me.'

'All three, Henry, and many more besides. I'm angry because

you hid something important from me that I had a right to be told. I'm disappointed because I did not think you'd go behind my back to consort with a man I regard as a murder suspect. And,' he continued with rising iritation, 'I'm disgusted that a brother of mine should enter a house under false pretences so that he could ogle a married woman under the nose of her husband.'

'Brilliana wants me.'

'Only in the confines of your fevered mind.'

'She does, Christopher. I saw it in her eyes.'

'And what do you see in *my* eyes?'

Henry was frightened by the look of fierce displeasure that his brother shot him. He had never seen Christopher roused to such a pitch of fury before. He tried to mollify him.

'I can explain everything,' he said, palms upraised. 'Yes, I did attend the play yesterday, and it did cross my mind that I should come straight to you afterwards.'

'Why did you not come *before* the play was performed?'

'Before?'

'Yes, Henry,' said his brother. 'If we had known what the play contained, we could have moved to stop it before its poison was displayed on stage. You are a friend of the Earl of Stoneleigh. When you heard that his play was being revived, you must have been aware that new material had been added.'

'I did and I did not.'

'Don't prevaricate!'

'I knew that Cuthbert had introduced a new scene into the play but I swear that I did not know what it contained.'

'But you were told that it related to Sir Julius Cheever?'

'Yes and no.'

'You are doing it again!' protested Christopher.

'Cuthbert hinted that a certain Member of Parliament would find it very uncomfortable if he were seated in the audience. No name was given, I assure you.'

'But one was implied. In short, you *knew*.'

'Let us just say that I had a vague idea.'

'Henry, you appall me sometimes,' said Christopher, barely able to keep his hands off him. 'You are fully cognisant of the situation. A man was murdered in place of Sir Julius. A second attempt was made on his life. Your own brother was involved in tracking down the killer. Yet you say nothing – nothing at all – when you are forewarned by a friend that his play will contain a brutal attack on Sir Julius.'

'It was comical rather than brutal, Christopher.'

'Only to those who enjoy the sport of blood-letting.'

'And I could hardly alert you to something that I had not actually seen. All that you would have had was a rumour. That would not have been enough to halt the performance.'

'It would have prepared Sir Julius for what was to come.'

Henry sniggered. 'It was highly amusing, I must admit.'

'Yes,' said Christopher, vehemently. 'And the moment you stopped laughing, you put on a different face and have the gall to tell Sir Julius that it was a trial to sit through so unjust a lampoon. The only reason you even bothered to tell him was so that you could get within reach of Brilliana Serle.'

'And, by a miracle, I did. But she was snatched away from me at the critical moment. I'll never forgive Susan for doing that.'

'I must remember to congratulate her.'

'A man must follow the dictates of love.'

'I'll not have you dignifying your lust as pure romance.'

'You've never understood the promptings of my heart.'

'I understand them only too well,' said Christopher, 'and I pity the poor wretches who are victims of them. Well, Mrs Serle is not going to be one of them. To sneak into her company on the pretext of helping her father was improper, immoral and ignoble. I've never felt so ashamed of you in all my life.'

Henry yawned. 'Your impersonation of Father is very tiresome.'

'He'd disown you if he knew what you had done – disown you and deprive you of your generous allowance. Where would you be without that?'

'You will surely not tell him of this?' said Henry, suddenly afraid. 'I *need* that money, Christopher.'

'Then do something to earn it or, by this hand, I'll let him know what kind of a son you are. What you did was unpardonable but you can at least try to repair some of the damage. Now,' said Christopher, advancing on him, 'this is what I want you to do.'

Sir Julius Cheever spent the whole day locked in his study. Meals were taken up to him but he was never even seen by his daughters. It increased their concern. Their father was in great distress yet he refused to tell them why. Tiring of being kept ignorant, Brilliana Serle had dispatched her husband to speak to his father-in-law and elicit the truth. Serle was met with such a verbal broadside from Sir Julius that he cut his losses and withdrew. The day wore relentlessly on. By the time they went to bed, Susan and Brilliana were still no nearer to understanding the cause of their father's evident suffering.

Early next morning, they were awakened by the sound of wheels scrunching the gravel outside. Susan was out of bed in a flash and got to the window in time to see Sir Julius getting into his coach and being driven away. It was shortly after dawn. Before Susan could work out where he was going, there was a tap on her door and Brilliana came into the room in her nightgown.

'What's going on, Susan?' she asked in consternation.

'I wish that I knew.'

'Father never gets up at this time of the morning.'

'Well, he did today,' said Susan. 'He has not been the same since we had that visit from Henry Redmayne – though I don't believe that a desire to see Father was what really brought him here.'

Brilliana was rueful. 'You are right,' she said. 'The first time I met Mr Redmayne, I must inadvertently have given him the wrong impression. Now I can see why he was so eager to get Lancelot out of the house. Fortunately, you were still here, Susan.'

'What message did Henry bring for Father that day? That's what I'd like to find out.'

'Christopher might know.'

'Unhappily, no,' said Susan. 'I sent him a note on that very subject. He replied instantly but said that he was unable to help us.'

'Then I must speak to his brother directly.'

'That might not be a sensible idea, Brilliana. Stay clear of Henry Redmayne in future. If he had wanted us to know his secret, he would have divulged it. All will soon become clear.'

'I hope so. Lancelot was most upset yesterday.'

'Why?'

'He asked to see the newspaper. Father had it delivered to his study and it remained there all day. When Lancelot sent a servant upstairs for it, his request was turned down with uncalled-for rudeness.' Brilliana's face puckered. 'Why was my husband prevented from seeing the newspaper?'

'I wish I knew.'

'Oh, I do so hate a mystery, Susan.'

'Especially one of this nature,' said her sister. 'It was bad enough for us to be denied the information that Father's life was in danger. We are his daughters. We should have been told.'

'Christopher let you down badly.'

'I remonstrated with him over that. He'll not fail me again.'

'And if he does?'

Susan let the question hang in the air. She could not believe that Christopher would deceive her twice in a row. He had vowed to be more open with her. She had to trust him.

'Did you see Father leave?' said Brilliana.

'I had a fleeting glimpse of him as he climbed into the coach.'

'Did you notice anything odd about him, Susan?'

'Odd?'

'He was carrying a sword in his hand.'

The duel was to be held in the walled garden of a private house in the Strand. Though it was not far for Christopher Redmayne to ride, he slowed his approach to a gentle trot so that he could reflect on what lay ahead. He had profound misgivings about the whole exercise. His worst fear was that Sir Julius Cheever would be mortally wounded in the duel and that the Earl of Stoneleigh would have accomplished what his hired killer had been unable to do. What exasperated Christopher was the thought that the earl would suffer little punishment beyond a reprimand from the King. It would be a case of sanctioned murder.

It was deliberate. Christopher was certain of that. The offending scene in *The Royal Favourite* had not simply been written to malign Sir Julius. It was there to goad him into a duel and put him at the mercy of his enemy. A good swordsman in his younger days, he had lost all of his speed and dexterity. Sir Julius was travelling to the duel in a spirit of revenge that obscured from him facts that were obvious to others. Stoneleigh was years younger than him. He was slim and lithe whereas his opponent was portly and cumbersome. Since the older man had been lured into a duel, Christopher suspected that the earl would have been practising hard for the contest with his fencing master. Sir Julius had not used a sword for ages.

The potential consequences were too hideous to contemplate. Christopher would first be answerable to Susan, a woman to whom he had pledged his honesty. Yet here he was, conspiring in something that would rob her of her one surviving parent and of any trust she still placed in Christopher. In losing the father, he would surely forfeit the daughter whom he loved. Susan would never forgive him, and there would be recriminations from the other members of the family. Earlier, he had acted as Sir Julius's bodyguard. Now he was assisting him in what might well turn out to be a suicidal encounter.

Then there was Jonathan Bale. He would be horrified that a friend whom he respected so much was implicated in what was, in fact, an illegal act. And the constable would be even more shocked to learn that Christopher condoned a duel in which one man was at such a severe disadvantage. Why spend so much time trying to hunt down the person who had ordered Sir Julius's death and then deliver him up to their prime suspect? It was indefensible. Christopher had toyed with the idea of warning Bale about the duel so that he could interrupt proceedings. He had abandoned the notion because he knew that it would only be arranged on another day at a different venue. Sir Julius would not be baulked.

Arriving at the designated house, Christopher was in a sombre mood. Sir Julius's coach reached the house shortly after him. When he stepped out, he was followed by his other second, Francis Polegate. Christopher caught the vintner's eye and saw that they shared the same reservations. Notwithstanding that, they had both agreed to participate in the event and had to fulfil their duties. Admitted to the garden, they took up their position beneath the boughs of a chestnut tree. It seemed an appropriate place for someone as prickly as Sir Julius Cheever. Christopher found himself praying that, unlike ripe horse chestnuts, the Member of Parliament would not fall.

'I'm not at all sure that this is wise, Sir Julius,' said Polegate.

'I did not ask for your advice, Francis,' said the other, 'only for your assistance. My honour is at stake here. Would you have me walk away?'

'No, but there are other ways to resolve this quarrel.'

'I agree,' said Christopher. 'What appeared on that stage was a dreadful libel. There are countless witnesses, including my own brother. Fight for your honour in a court of law.'

'That would take an eternity,' replied Sir Julius, 'and I do not see it as my mission in life to enrich squabbling lawyers. This matter can be settled within minutes.' He raised his sword. 'Here is the only lawyer that I'll employ.'

Christopher and Polegate continued to try to dissuade him from going ahead but he dismissed their entreaties with scorn. It was too late to withdraw now. Once given, a challenge could not be rescinded. All that his seconds could do was to hold their tongues and hope for a miracle. Their pessimism deepened when

Cuthbert Woodruffe, Earl of Stoneleigh, finally appeared. He had already divested himself of coat and hat. Wearing a pair of breeches and with a crimson waistcoat over his shirt, he entered the garden with a flourish and gave Sir Julius a mocking bow. He was a striking man. Tall, lean and moving with easy grace, he exuded confidence. Stoneleigh was too sharp-featured to be handsome but it was an arresting face with a hooked nose and a pair of gimlet eyes.

'Look at the fellow,' said Sir Julius. 'He's full of himself.'

'Give him the chance to make an apology,' suggested Polegate.

'He can have it engraved on his tomb, Francis.'

'There's still time to abandon this folly.'

'I'd not even consider it.'

Sir Julius turned round so that Polegate could help him off with his coat. Christopher was more interested in the people who had come into the garden with the earl. Like Sir Julius, he had brought a surgeon in case he sustained a wound but it was one of the seconds that made Christopher start. The man was wearing dark apparel and a wide-brimmed black hat pulled down over his face, but his gait was unmistakable. Incredible as it might seem, it was his brother, Henry. Christopher had never felt such a burning sense of betrayal. Knowing that Stoneleigh was under suspicion for instigating a murder, Henry was actually helping the man in his long-standing quarrel with Sir Julius Cheever. The sight of his brother sickened Christopher.

'Let's get on with it,' said Sir Julius, impatiently.

'Ready when you are,' called Stoneleigh with a grin.

'Stand back.'

Christopher and Polegate moved away so that Sir Julius could practise a few lunges in the air. The earl and his supporters gave him an ironic cheer. Christopher was relieved to see that his brother did not join in, but his outrage at Henry remained. The two men were eventually called to the mark and reminded of the strict rules that governed such a duel. They then separated and, on a signal, the bout started. Christopher glanced at his brother but Henry was still hiding beneath his hat, determined not to acknowledge him. Both of them watched the contest with interest.

Sir Julius was the first to attack, circling his man before lungeing at him. Stoneleigh parried the stroke with ease and did exactly the same when his opponent slashed wildly at him. He was in no hurry to attack, content simply to use his superior footwork and his deft control of his blade to ward off any danger. Sir Julius's lunges grew ever more desperate and he was soon starting to pant. The earl, by contrast, was fit and nimble, showing a speed of movement that belied his age. Christopher could see that he was playing with Sir Julius, wearing him down before moving in for the kill. To show that he had the upper hand, Stoneleigh suddenly feinted, went down on one knee and thrust hard. Sir Julius's waistcoat was sliced open and some of the buttons tumbled on to the grass.

There was laughter from the earl's friends but Sir Julius was not deterred and he was still strong. Breathing heavily, he continued to advance and lunge at his opponent. Christopher could hardly bear to look any more. When the earl parried a thrust and flicked his blade with precision, he drew a first spurt of blood from Sir Julius's wrist. Since it was from his sword arm, he was halted in his tracks for a few seconds, using his other hand to wipe away the blood. It was a moment when he was completely off guard but the earl did not seize his advantage. Instead, he raised his sword and stood back.

'Hold there!' cried a voice. 'Stop – in the name of the law!'

A strapping man in uniform was striding across the grass with six officers at his back. He made straight for Sir Julius, bringing the duel to an end by standing between him and the earl. The officers quickly surrounded Sir Julius and he was forced to surrender his weapon. The burly man produced a document from his pocket.

'I am James Beck, sergeant-at-arms at the Tower,' he declared, 'and I have a warrant for the arrest of Sir Julius Cheever.'

'On what charge?' asked Christopher.

'If you arrest Sir Julius,' argued Polegate, 'you must surely take the earl into custody as well.'

'No, sir,' said Beck.

'Both are guilty of taking part in a duel.'

'There's no mention of a duel in this warrant. Sir Julius is being arrested in compliance with a statute that was passed in reign of King Henry VII – to whit, that it is a felony for any to conspire the death of a Privy Councillor.'

'Such as myself,' said the earl, hand to his chest.

'I'll not be held on such a dubious warrant,' roared Sir Julius.

'You have no choice,' said Beck. 'Seize the prisoner.'

Before he could move, Sir Julius was grabbed by the officers and swiftly pinioned. He protested loudly but in vain. Christopher now understood why Stoneleigh had not tried to inflict a mortal wound on his opponent. The earl had obviously known that the interruption would come and that, as a Privy Councillor, he would be exempt from blame. The playwright had stage managed the whole event. Instead of killing his opponent, he was having him immured in the Tower.

'What's the punishment for this offence?' said Christopher.

'The decision lies with His Majesty,' replied Beck.

'And what is the usual sentence?'

'Death.'

Christopher saw all the fight drain out of Sir Julius. Far from wreaking his revenge on a hated enemy, he would be hauled off to face the possibility of a death penalty that was legally enforced. The earl did not need to hire another assassin. Sir Julius Cheever could be dispatched with the aid of a long-forgotten Tudor statute. Beck gave a command and the prisoner was hustled off, much to the amusement of Stoneleigh and his supporters. Things had gone exactly to plan.

Convinced that his friend was going off to certain execution, Francis Polegate was grief-stricken. Christopher was dumbstruck. The outcome could not have been worse had Sir Julius been killed in the duel. If he were sentenced to death, his family would bear the stigma forever. Christopher wondered what he could possibly say to Susan or to her sister and brother-in-law. They would hate him for what he had done. Dorothy Kitson, close friend to Sir Julius, would doubtless add her rebuke, and there would be political allies of Sir Julius to face as well. Christopher was jolted.

Then he remembered that his brother had had a significant role to play that morning and been guilty of the most blatant treachery. Christopher swung round to confront him but to no avail.

Henry Redmayne had vanished from the garden.

When he entered the brewery, Jonathan Bale found the compound of smells quite overwhelming. He could not understand how anyone could work in such a hot, fetid, oppressive atmosphere. Shown into Erasmus Howlett's office, he had a partial escape from the all-pervading odour. The brewer smiled.

'One soon gets used to it,' he said.

'I'm not sure that I would, Mr Howlett.'

'What you think of as a noisome stink is really the pleasing aroma of money. I could inhale it all day.'

'Well, I could not.'

'Then it is as well you do not work in the leather trade or as a butcher, for they have to endure far worse stenches. However,' said Howlett, hands twitching throughout, 'you did not come here simply to catch a whiff of my beer.'

'No, sir. I came out of courtesy.'

'That's something in rather short supply these days.'

'Since I questioned you earlier, I thought you would like to know that the man who shot Bernard Everett has been found.'

'Congratulations, Mr Bale!'

'Unfortunately, we did not take him alive.'

He explained how they had tracked the killer to Smithfield then on to his lodging in Old Street. The brewer was fascinated to hear how they had caught up with the killer and he plied Bale with endless questions. He was particularly interested to hear of the contribution made by Christopher Redmayne.

'He sounds an enterprising young man.'

'He is, Mr Howlett.'

'And a brilliant architect, so Francis Polegate tells me.'

'Well, you've seen the shop yourself,' Bale reminded him. 'It's opposite the Saracen's Head, the tavern you visited some while ago.'

'Yes, but I only saw the building from outside. I'm told that the interior is a minor work of art. Francis was delighted with it.'

Howlett's office was on the upper level of the brewery. It was a small, cluttered room with a desk that was covered with letters, bills and documents of all sorts. In an adjoining office, clerks were at work and Bale could see them through the window that separated the two rooms. Through the main window, he could look down at the brewery itself and see the men toiling in a miasma of steam.

'I helped to design this place myself,' said Howlett, thrusting his hands into the pockets of his waistcoat. 'I made sure that my office overlooked the whole brewing process. Nobody dares to slack when I am up here.'

'I'm sure that you only employ industrious workers, sir.'

'There's no place for any other kind here. Howlett's Brewery has a reputation to maintain. We are famed for our quality.'

'Yet you do not drink the beer yourself, I hear.'

Howlett chortled. 'I see that Francis has been letting you into my little secret. I used to sample my own product in large quantities,' he said, patting his paunch, 'and I have the stomach to prove it. Wine is kinder to my anatomy in many ways.'

'But much more expensive.'

'I allow myself a few luxuries in life. What about you, Mr Bale?'

'One of my luxuries is a tankard of beer, sir.'

'Brewed right here, I hope.'

'No,' said Bale. 'My wife, Sarah, brews it at home and, though there is a smell during the process, it's nothing like as powerful as the one you have to endure. You must use stronger ingredients.'

'Stronger ingredients and greater volume. I doubt if your wife makes anything like the quantities that we produce. Well, you can see how many men I employ. We have many taverns to supply.'

'Is there any advice you could give?'

'About what?'

'How to brew good beer. I could pass it on to my wife. Sarah does her best but her beer always tastes rather weak. It's too thin.'

'Often the case with housewife brewers.'

'I hope that you don't mind me asking, Mr Howlett.'

'Not at all, not at all.'

'At the end of a long day, all that I want is a drink of beer to revive me. I just wish that it would have more body to it.'

'Every brewer has his secrets,' said Howlett, 'and I'd never disclose those to anyone. But I can tell you what the basic ingredients of our beer is and how best to brew it.'

'I'd be greatly obliged to you, sir,' said Bale, deferentially.

'Let me write them down for you.' Howlett sat down at his desk and reached for his quill pen with a trembling hand. 'Since you had the courtesy to come from Baynard's Castle ward to give me your news, the least I can do is to help you to enjoy a stronger drink.'

He began to write. Watching over his shoulder, Bale smiled. He was more than satisfied with his wife's beer and would never dare to suggest that she brewed it a different way. What he really wanted was a sample of Erasmus Howlett's handwriting. To get that, he would gladly endure the pungent reek of the brewery.

'The Tower of London!'

Susan Cheever was mortified. She spoke with a mixture of shame and horror. To have her father imprisoned in the Tower was a mark of ultimate disgrace. Even more appalling was the fact that he might pay with his life for his alleged crime. Brilliana Serle burst into tears and her husband had to comfort her. All three of them glared at Christopher Redmayne as if he were solely responsible for the grim predicament of Sir Julius Cheever. Informing the family of what had happened was a daunting task but he had forced himself to do it. As he sat opposite them in the Westminster House, Christopher felt cruel in having to impart so much pain and suffering. Susan's face was a portrait of anguish, Brilliana could barely speak and Lancelot Serle looked as if he were ready to challenge Christopher to a duel.

'You must take some of the blame for this,' he accused.

'I acknowledge that, Mr Serle,' replied Christopher.

'You should have prevented him from going through with it.'

'Once he has embarked on something, your father-in-law is not an easy man to stop. Had I refused to act as his second, he would simply have found someone else.'

'Not if you had warned us. It was your duty to do so.'

'Sir Julius had sworn me to silence. I gave him my word.'

'I seem to remember that you gave it to me once as well,' said Susan. 'You promised never to conceal from me anything that related to Father's safety. And yet you did *this*, Christopher.'

'Against my will.'

'That's no excuse.'

'None at all,' said Christopher, lowering his head.

'You should be in the Tower with Father,' cried Brilliana, pointing at him, 'and so should that brother of yours. He came to this house in possession of information that should have been passed on to us, and he kept it to himself.'

'No wonder Sir Julius would not let me read the newspaper yesterday,' said Serle. 'It must have contained a report of that play and its attack on him. I agree with my wife. We've been ill-served by the Redmayne family in every way.'

'That's how it appears to me as well,' said Susan, levelly.

'Between the two of you,' said Brilliana, 'you have delivered our father up to complete humiliation. Thanks to you and your brother, he languishes in a cell at the Tower with a possible death sentence hanging over his head. Oh!' she went on as more tears came, 'it's too horrid to contemplate.'

'Come, my dear,' said Serle, easing her to her feet. 'The shock of it is insupportable. You need to lie down.' He led the sobbing Brilliana to the door then stared at Christopher to make a final comment. 'I hope, when I return, sir, that you have left this house.'

Christopher was relieved that they had gone and grateful that they did not realise that his brother had, in fact, acted as one of the seconds for the Earl of Stoneleigh. That would have complicated the situation even more and drawn additional bile from them. It was something that Christopher would admit to nobody. Left alone with Susan, all that he could do was to gesture an apology. He could see from the coldness in her eyes that it was not accepted.

'How *could* you, Christopher?' she asked, quietly.

'I did my best to talk him out of it.'

'That was our duty. We are his daughters. Our task is to look after him. You are not part of the family at all.'

Her tone was ominous. She was telling Christopher that he would never be more closely linked with her family. The stab of rejection was like the thrust of a knife. He winced.

'Susan,' he said, 'please listen to me. All is not yet lost.'

She was sorrowful. 'What else is there to lose?'

'I'll hire the finest lawyer in the city to defend your father. The Earl of Stoneleigh never intended the duel to continue for long. He simply enticed Sir Julius into a trap. That will count against him in a court of law.'

'And if father is found guilty at the trial?'

'Even then, there is still hope,' he told her. 'I will appeal directly to His Majesty. I've been in a position to render him some service in the past and he has been very grateful. A plea to him will surely meet with favour.'

'Only if it is made on your behalf, Christopher.'

'What do you mean?'

'He would hardly lift a hand to help my father. His Majesty once fought at the battle of Worcester – just like the Earl of Stoneleigh. Neither will show any mercy to someone who was in the opposing army. Father is doomed.'

'You must not think that.'

'What else can I think?'

'Look,' he said, moving across to sit beside her, 'there is something you must know. Berate me all you wish but please accept that I have gone to great lengths to protect your father, and to find out who sponsored the attempts on his life.'

'You and Mr Bale have worked hard on his behalf,' she admitted.

'And not without success. We found one killer and we will find a second. More to the point, we will discover who has been paying them. Evidence so far points in the direction of the Earl of Stoneleigh.' She was startled. 'Yes, Susan, if we can *prove* that he is involved then Sir Julius has no case to answer. He may have attacked a Privy Councillor but the earl will lose all protection if arrested on a charge of conspiracy to murder.'

'And what chance is there of that?'

'A slim one at the moment,' he admitted, honestly, 'because he is cunning enough to cover his tracks. But we are making definite headway. Do you recall that I asked about Lewis Bircroft?'

'Yes, he used to come here often at one time.'

'He stopped doing so because he was badly beaten by a gang of ruffians. Jonathan Bale has spoken to him. At first, Mr Bircroft was too frightened to name the man who had ordered the attack but, at a second meeting, Jonathan managed to elicit that name – not in so many words, perhaps, but it was a clear identification.'

'The earl again?'

'Precisely.'

'Why can he not be arrested?'

'Because we need more evidence, Susan. And we'll get it.'

She chewed her lip in despair. 'This is a tragedy,' she said. 'It seems that the Earl of Stoneleigh will do anything to hound Father. Not content with putting a caricature of him on stage, he has now contrived to have him imprisoned in the Tower.'

'We'll get him out,' said Christopher, purposefully.

'How?'

'Wait and see. Meanwhile, think of others who need to be told the news. Sir Julius has friends in the House of Commons. This is a time when they should rally to him.'

'There's someone else who must be told.'

'Who is that?'

'Mrs Kitson,' said Susan. 'She is very fond of my father. This will cause her enormous distress.'

Orlando Golland was reading his newspaper when his sister called at the house. Seeing the disturbed state she was in, he took her into his parlour and invited her to sit down.

'Whatever is the matter, Dorothy?' he asked.

'I came to see if the rumour was true.'

'What rumour?'

'Sir Julius Cheever has been imprisoned in the Tower.'

'Never!' said Golland in surprise. 'On what possible charge?'

'I hoped that you could tell me that, Orlando.'

'This the first I've heard of it. Where did you pick up the news?'

'I was visiting my milliner,' she said, 'and I chanced upon Adele Farwell. She had heard it from her husband. According to Maurice, there was a duel between Sir Julius and Cuthbert, Earl of Stoneleigh.'

'I can guess what provoked that. I saw the report in yesterday's newspaper. One of the earl's plays, *The Royal Favourite,* was revived at the King's Theatre. Apparently, it contained defamatory matter about Sir Julius. He must have issued a challenge.'

'But he would stand no chance against Cuthbert.'

'Are they both locked up in the Tower?'

'No,' said Dorothy. 'Adele did not know all the details but it seems that the duel was interrupted by officers and that they had a warrant for Sir Julius's arrest.'

Golland sniffed. 'In that case, they were warned in advance.'

'It was something to do with Cuthbert being a member of the Privy Council. I was hoping that you could enlighten me.'

'I wish I could,' he said, going through a list of statutes in his mind to find the one that had been invoked. 'If he is being charged with trying to kill a Privy Councillor, it could go hard with Sir Julius. Are you not relieved now that you and he have parted?'

'We did not part,' she corrected. 'We are still friends.'

'Then I'd advise you to distance yourself from that friendship at once, Dorothy. It was an unfortunate relationship from the start. To continue it now may bring opprobrium down upon you.'

'I cannot simply desert Sir Julius.'

'You can and you must.'

'But he will marshal his defence and seek an acquittal.'

'Even if he is released,' he told her, sententiously, 'it would be foolish to allow this attachment to continue. Do you wish to be known as the intimate of a man who was lampooned in a play?'

'It would be cruel to turn my back on him, Orlando.'

'Cruelty to him, kindness to yourself – and to me.'

'Stop thinking of yourself all the time,' she said, reproachfully. 'I came in the hope of learning more details of the situation, not to listen to you telling me what to do.'

'I'm sorry,' he said with an appeasing smile, 'but one must always look at the implications of any action. Let me find out more about the case. If it has reached Maurice's ears, it will be all around the House of Commons by now. Sir Julius will not receive much commiseration from there, I fancy.'

'That's why I must offer him my sympathy.'

'No, Dorothy.'

'It's the least I can do.'

'The gesture would compromise you.'

'Sir Julius lies in the Tower, facing some awful charge. Imagine how he must feel, Orlando.' She reached a decision. 'I think that I should visit him.'

'I forbid it!' he said rising to his feet. 'That was too harsh,' he apologised, waving a hand. 'I've no right to give you any commands, Dorothy. I merely advise you – very strongly – to keep away from Sir Julius Cheever. You'll be contaminated with his crime.'

'But I'm not even sure that he committed one.'

'If a warrant was issued, there is a charge to answer.'

'Discover what it was as soon as you can.'

'I will,' he promised. 'Meanwhile, dismiss all thoughts of Sir Julius from your mind. I insist upon it. I'll not have a sister of mine entering the Tower to visit a felon.'

'Sir Julius is no felon, Orlando.'

'He is in the eyes of the law and that is all that matters.'

Susan Cheever was still trying to cope with the impact of what had happened. It was only when they were being conducted through the Tower that the full seriousness of her father's situation was borne in upon her. Everywhere she looked were high stone walls and armed guards. Feet rasping on the cobbles, they passed tower after tower, each one more sinister and threatening than the one before. She felt oppressed. Built by William the Conqueror six hundred years earlier, the Tower of London had been associated with royalty ever since. It had seen births, weddings, processions, tournaments, banquets, even a royal menagerie and it had hosted many foreign dignitaries for generations.

All that Susan could remember was that it was closely allied to death. Murders and executions had left a trail of blood behind them. Kings, queens and leading statesmen had perished there. Notorious prisoners had endured agonising tortures before being released by a merciful death sentence. The ravens that inhabited the Tower were harbingers of disaster, birds of prey that alighted greedily on every fresh grave, noisy spectators to a long succession of horrors. When she saw them, Susan felt a chill descend upon her. It was as if she were a prisoner herself, stripped of any rights or self-respect. Even on such a warm day, she began to shiver.

Her discomfort was soon intensified. Sir Julius Cheever, it transpired, was being held in an upper room in the Bloody Tower, a place with a bleak and gory history. When they climbed the stairs, Susan was glad that Lancelot Serle had volunteered to accompany her. Sensing her distress, he put out a supportive hand to help her. A guard was standing outside the room. After they had identified themselves, he took a bunch of keys from his belt and unlocked the door. Susan burst in and flung herself into her father's arms. She did not hear the door being locked behind her.

'How are you, Father?' she asked, appraising him.

He forced a smile. 'All the better for seeing you, Susan.'

'Brilliana did not feel well enough to come, Sir Julius,' said Serle. 'She sends her love and asked me to visit in her stead.'

'You are welcome, Lancelot,' said Sir Julius, shaking him warmly by the hand. 'I'm only sorry that you have to see me in this state.' He looked around. 'This is one of the rooms where Sir Walter Raleigh was kept before his execution. His wife and son lived with him. As you see, it is quite comfortable.'

It did not seem so to the visitors. The room was small and bare with oak boards that creaked whenever they were walked upon. There was a table, two chairs and a straw mattress. On the table were a Bible and some writing materials. A jug of water and a cup stood on a shelf. They did not need to be told why a large bucket had been put in a corner and covered with a piece of sacking. It was a prison cell and it degraded any person who occupied it.

'How much do you know?' said Sir Julius.

'Only what Christopher told us,' answered Susan.

'We hold him largely responsible for this,' said Serle, glancing around with disgust. 'He was the one person in a position to stop you and he failed to do so. I find that deplorable.'

'Then you do not appreciate the circumstances,' Sir Julius told him. 'Christopher had no option but to concur with my wishes. Nothing would have stopped me from issuing that challenge. I turned to him because I knew that I could trust him.'

'I thought that I could,' said Susan to herself.

'Just remember this. But for Christopher Redmayne, I would not still be alive. As to this enforced visit to the Tower, it was in no way his fault. I must take all of the blame.'

'Why is that, Father?'

'Because I should have known that Stoneleigh was too crafty to fight a duel to the death. He only agreed to face me so that I could be ensnared by some obscure piece of legislation that makes him look like a victim while showing me up as a would-be assassin.'

'Christopher had never heard of the statute,' said Serle.

'No more had I. Sir John Robinson explained it to me.'

'Who is he?'

'The Lieutenant of the Tower,' said Sir Julius. 'The law reached the statute book in the third year of the reign of King Henry VII. That would put it in 1488. In sending a challenge to the Earl of Stoneleigh, I committed a felony for I had designs on the life of a Privy Councillor. That much I admit,' he went on. 'Had we not been interrupted, I'd have cut the villain down.'

Humouring her father, Susan said nothing. She knew from Christopher's account that the earl was getting the better of the duel when it was stopped but Sir Julius would never concede that. What she wanted to hear was how they could extricate him from the Tower. Without his coat, and weighed down by anxiety, he was a sorry figure. His flashes of fighting spirit seemed incongruous in such a place.

'You do not belong in here, Father,' she said.

'The law says that I do.'

'Then we must hire someone to defend you,' said Serle.

'I'm not sure that I have any defence, Lancelot.'

'The earl maligned you in his play. A writ of libel can be issued against him. No man – aristocrat or commoner – should be allowed to get away with such vilification. Demand redress.'

'I tried to do that with my sword.'

'See him prosecuted.'

'It would never happen,' said Sir Julius, resignedly. 'Libel is a minor offence compared to the one with which I am charged. In truth, we were both liable to arrest when we took part in that duel but there is no way that Stoneleigh will be arraigned.'

'He should be,' said Susan, angrily. 'He fought with you this morning and you have witnesses to prove it. Christopher and Mr Polegate were there.'

'So was my surgeon but what are three voices against the dozen that Stoneleigh will call? He brought a whole entourage with him. They will swear that he was trying to reason with me rather than fight a duel. No, Susan,' he said. 'The earl thought it all out in advance. I was to be arrested while he goes scot-free. There's no help for it.'

'There must be.'

'I fail to see the way out.'

'Then we must rely on Christopher,' she said, surprised at the affection she felt for him again. 'He is the only person who has a means of saving you, Father, and he'll dedicate himself to doing just that. Rely on him.'

'How ever did you get hold of this?' asked Christopher Redmayne, studying the list of ingredients in one hand and comparing it with the letter he held in the other. 'The hand is a perfect match.'

'I called on Mr Howlett at his brewery,' said Jonathan Bale.

'On what pretext?'

'To tell him that we had found Mr Everett's killer. He seemed pleased that I'd taken the trouble to do so.'

'Even though he already knew of our discovery.' Christopher indicated the list. 'These are the constituent elements of beer.'

'I asked him for advice on how best to make it.'

'And you're certain that he wrote this?'

'I stood over him while he did so.'

'Well done, Jonathan. You outwitted him.'

'I had a feeling about Mr Howlett, sir,' said Bale. 'It was that visit he paid to the Saracen's Head. There was no need for him to go there. Now we know why he did it.'

'Thanks to you.'

Christopher was delighted. It was not just the handwriting that matched. The paper was identical as well. He put both examples of Erasmus Howlett's shaky calligraphy down on his desk. They were in the study of his house in Fetter Lane. Having returned there in a mood of dejection, Christopher was now almost elated.

'We have enough to make an arrest now,' said Bale.

'No, Jonathan.'

'But we have written proof that Mr Howlett instructed Dan Crothers to book a room at the tavern that day. And we also know that he's the cousin of the Earl of Stoneleigh. What more do we need?'

'Evidence that the earl wrote this other letter,' said Christopher, taking it up from the desk. 'The one that warned Crothers that Sir Julius was leaving for Cambridge. It will be much more difficult to do that. I don't think that the earl will oblige you so readily with some advice on how to make beer.'

'Then how *do* we get an example of his handwriting?'

Christopher thought about his brother. 'I may have the answer to that, Jonathan. Give me some time.'

'Yes, Mr Redmayne.'

The constable was so happy with what he had discovered at the brewery that Christopher did not want to deprive him of his pleasure. But it was inevitable. Bale simply had to be told about the duel and its unforeseen consequences. Knowing that his tale would be frowned upon, Christopher kept it as short as he could. Bale was astounded. He could understand why Sir Julius had reacted so violently but not why Christopher had agreed to act as a second at the duel. And he was taken aback when he heard that Sir Julius was now in the Tower.

'Had you told me,' he said, 'I could have broken up the duel.'

'That would not have prevented Sir Julius's arrest. It had already been set in train by the earl. That's why we must expose him as the villain he is, Jonathan. Only then can we apprehend Erasmus Howlett.'

'You're forgetting someone else, sir.'

'Am I?'

'The man who was hired to cut Dan Crothers's throat. In fact, you must take especial care when you go abroad in future.'

'Why?'

'Mr Howlett showed too great an interest in you,' said Bale. 'He wanted to know where you lived and why you had involved yourself in the investigation. We may both be in danger now. Since we managed to find Crothers, Mr Howlett will fear that we may one day catch up with him – as, indeed, we have done. Not that I gave him any hint of that.'

'Thank you for the warning. I take is as a good sign.'

Bale scowled. 'I'd not describe being threatened by a proven killer as a good sign.'

'It means that we have frightened Mr Howlett. And frightened men often act too precipitately. They make mistakes.' He pointed to the list of ingredients. 'There's an example.'

'We both need to take greater care, sir.'

'I certainly will,' said Christopher. 'No more duels for me.'

He laughed light-heartedly but Bale's face was impassive. When he heard the doorbell ring, the constable got to his feet immediately.

'If you have a visitor, I'll be off.'

'Stay and talk. You're the only visitor I want to see at the moment.' He heard the front door opening and the sound of voices. Christopher leapt up from his seat. 'With one exception – my brother, Henry. I'm surprised that he has the audacity to show his face.'

Moments later, Jacob appeared to say that he had shown Henry into the parlour. Taking the constable with him, Christopher charged off to challenge him. When his brother saw that Bale was there, he took a step backwards.

'Heavens!' he exclaimed. 'Is he going to arrest me?'

'If deceit and disloyalty were against the law,' said Christopher, bitterly, 'that's exactly what I would ask Jonathan to do.'

'Do not judge me too hastily.'

'You acted as a second to the Earl of Stoneleigh.'

'He asked me to, Christopher.'

'Did you not see that as an act of gross betrayal?'

'Betrayal of whom?'

'Of Sir Julius Cheever and me.'

'You urged me to get close to Cuthbert,' Henry said. 'You told me that I had to find out certain things about him. I could hardly do that if I stayed out of his way.'

'You did not have to support him at a duel.'

'A duel that should never have taken place,' said Bale, darkly.

'There's such a thing as honour, Mr Bale,' said Henry.

'I see no honour in killing a man with a sword. Duelling is a devilish practice and it was rightly abolished. Too many good men died for no reason.'

'That's not the point at issue here,' said Christopher, annoyed that his brother could stand so calmly before him. 'The duel was merely a way of drawing Sir Julius into the open. Once there, he could be trussed hand and foot with this ancient statute.'

'Yes,' said Henry, 'that rather took me by surprise.'

'Are you sure?'

'I'd swear to it, Christopher. What do I know of legal matters? When I was asked by Cuthbert to act as his second, I thought that he meant to proceed with the duel.'

'And kill Sir Julius.'

'He's never killed an opponent before and I've been at his side on three occasions. Cuthbert – the Earl of Stoneleigh to you – has a softer side. He prefers to humiliate an opponent, draw blood then show magnanimity by withdrawing.'

'He showed no magnanimity to Sir Julius.'

'I taxed him about that.'

'And what did he say?'

'That if a man is stupid enough to put his head in a noose, he must not be surprised if someone pulls it tight.'

'I wonder that you can be so blithe about it, sir,' said Bale.

'So blithe and uncaring,' said Christopher. 'Sir Julius is incarcerated in the Tower. Think what that means to a man of his dignity. And spare a thought for his family. I had to tell them what had happened. They were distraught.'

Henry was concerned. 'Was Brilliana upset?'

'She was in floods of tears.'

'I'd not have hurt her for the world. If I'd known what Cuthbert had in mind, I'd never have agreed to act as his second. But you insisted that I court him,' he told Christopher, 'and that's exactly what I did.'

'Even though it meant enraging your brother?'

'I hoped that you'd not recognise me.'

'I'd recognise you *anywhere*, Henry. I was simply grateful that Sir Julius did not realise you were there. He'd have run you through.'

'Then he'd not have heard what I discovered.'

'What do you mean?'

'The duel need never have taken place, Christopher.'

'It should not have taken place,' said Bale, officiously. 'If it were left to me—'

'One moment, Jonathan,' said Christopher. 'I fancy that Henry has something important to tell us. Am I right, Henry?'

'You are,' replied his brother, 'and it will demonstrate which side I am really on. Be prepared for a revelation.'

'Go on.'

'The duel was arranged on false grounds.'

'Sir Julius was goaded into it.'

'That was deliberate, Christopher – but not strictly fair.'

'Nothing about the earl suggests fairness.'

'Do not deride him,' said Henry. 'He's a brave man. When you take part in a duel, you put your life at risk. How was he to know that Sir Julius would not turn out to be an expert swordsman?'

'I saw no bravery in him today – only arrogance.'

'That's because you did not know the circumstances.'

'They seem clear to me, sir,' said Bale. 'A play was performed that held Sir Julius up to ridicule. He was bound to feel the need to strike back at its author.'

'I agree, Mr Bale, but that's not what he did.'

'It's exactly what he did,' argued Christopher. 'He issued a challenge to the Earl of Stoneleigh.'

'Yes, but Cuthbert did not actually write the offending scene.'

'But it was in a play that bore his name.'

'Inserted there by another hand, a very mischievous hand.'

Christopher was bewildered. 'Are you telling us that the man who belittled Sir Julius Cheever in front of a theatre audience was not the earl?' Henry nodded. 'Then who did write that scene?'

'Maurice Farwell.'

Maurice Farwell rolled over in bed and reached for his goblet of wine. He offered it first to the woman who lay beside him and then, when she had taken a sip, he put it to his own lips. Farwell set the goblet back on the bedside table.

'What better way to toast our success?' he said, suavely.

'I knew that we'd bring him down in the end.'

'I'm sorry that it took so long, my love. It meant that you had to endure his attentions far longer than I'd hoped.'

'The most difficult part of it was being compelled to meet his family,' said Dorothy Kitson, purring as he caressed her thigh. 'He had a frightful daughter who badgered me all evening. It was not helped by the fact that Orlando insisted on being present.'

'Your brother is such dull company.'

'No woman could say that of you, Maurice.'

'Orlando still thinks that it was an accident that we met Sir Julius at Newmarket that day. In fact, knowing that he'd be there, you made sure that you introduced me.'

'One glance at you, Dorothy, and he was bewitched.'

'Thank you,' she said, accepting a kiss, 'but there's only one man in whom I have any real interest and he lies beside me now.'

'What would Orlando say if he saw us together?'

She laughed. 'I think that he'd have a fit. My brother knows so little about the ways of the world. He's very gullible. When I told him that I'd heard about the duel from your wife, he believed me implicitly. Poor Orlando!' she sighed. 'He's so blind.'

'Forget about him, my love. Forget about everyone but us.'

'The person I most want to forget is Sir Julius Cheever.'

'Being alone with him must have been a trial for you.'

'It was, Maurice. I'd hoped he'd be shot in Knightrider Street. When he somehow survived, I had to grit my teeth and carry on with the charade. And when he came back alive from Cambridge,' she said, pulling a face, 'I could not believe my misfortune.'

'His luck has finally run out now, Dorothy.'

'What will happen to him?'

'I'll let him rot in the Tower for a few weeks.'

'And then?'

'I'll have him poisoned,' said Farwell, reaching for the goblet again. 'More wine, my love?'

Still at home with his two visitors, Christopher Redmayne needed time to think. Two imperatives were guiding him. He had to rescue Sir Julius Cheever from his perilous situation, and he had to win back Susan's love and trust. The two demands were linked. The only way that he could liberate Sir Julius from the Tower of London and restore his reputation was by unmasking those who had devised the plot against him. That, in turn, would make Susan look on him more favourably again. At least, that is what he hoped. After the way that he had let her down, there was no guarantee that she would ever let him back into her heart. Christopher accepted that.

After what Jonathan Bale had told him, he felt certain that the Earl of Stoneleigh and his cousin, Erasmus Howlett, were implicated in the murder of one man and the attempted murder of another. And it seemed crystal clear that the earl had baited the trap that had left Sir Julius imprisoned on a serious charge. The revelation from Henry Redmayne had forced his brother to question his assumptions. It had been Maurice Farwell who had penned the defamatory scene in *The Royal Favourite* and not the play's author. Were the two men working in concert with Howlett, or had Farwell and the brewer hatched the plot between them? An already complex situation had suddenly become even more confusing.

While his visitors waited in silence, Christopher pondered for a long time. Eventually, he turned to Henry.

'What do you know of Maurice Farwell?' he asked.

'Nothing to his disadvantage,' said Henry, peevishly. 'Every man should have at least one vice in his life but Farwell seems to have none. While others scheme, he has risen by sheer merit. Now Cuthbert is cut from a very different cloth,' he added with a grin of approval. 'He knows how to carouse the night away with a pretty actress on each arm. Cuthbert is able to enjoy himself.'

'That's not my idea of enjoyment, sir,' said Bale.

'Then your life is too circumscribed.'

'My enjoyment comes from my wife and family.'

'It's the same with Cuthbert,' said Henry. 'He delights in his wife and children as well. But he keeps them in their place so that they do not interfere with his work.'

'Carousing with actresses is hardly work,' noted Bale.

'It's one of the privileges of being a celebrated playwright and Cuthbert is like me. He's not a man to neglect any of his privileges.'

'What about Mr Farwell?' said Christopher. 'Is he a good friend of the earl's?'

'I've never seen them together. On the other hand, they must be well-acquainted if he was allowed to write a scene in one of Cuthbert's plays. And what a hilarious scene it was! I laughed for an hour.'

'Did you admit that to Sir Julius?'

'Of course not,' said Henry. 'I'm not that stupid. And his daughter must never find out the truth either. Jeering at her father is not the best way to endear myself to Brilliana.'

'I think that she already has your measure,' said Christopher.

'What can I do next?' asked Bale. 'We know that Mr Howlett is related to the earl. Do you want me to find out how well the brewer knows this Mr Farwell?'

'My brother is the best person to do that,' said Christopher. 'We need him to obtain a copy of their handwriting.'

'Whatever for?' asked Henry.

'Because we have that unsigned letter, instructing a man to kill Sir Julius on his way to Cambridge. The person who wrote it was either the Earl of Stoneleigh or Maurice Farwell.'

'It was certainly not Cuthbert.'

'How can you be so sure?'

'Because I know his hand well,' said Henry, reaching into his pocket. 'In fact, I have an example of it right here.' He produced a piece of paper and gave it to Christopher. 'It was my summons to act as his second. You showed me the two letters you found. As you see, Cuthbert's hand bears no resemblance to either of them.'

'None at all,' said Christopher. 'Look, Jonathan.'

Bale glanced at the letter and shook his head solemnly. 'It's not him, Mr Redmayne. The earl did not send that letter to Crothers.'

'Then only one person could have done so.'

'Maurice Farwell.'

'Get us a copy of his handwriting, Henry.'

'I'm not on those terms with him,' said his brother.

'Then find someone who is,' said Christopher. 'And do so as a matter of urgency. We're trying to solve one murder and prevent another one.'

'Another one?'

'You don't suppose that they will let Sir Julius escape now, do you? They have him exactly where they want him.'

'The law must take its course,' said Bale.

'I don't think that it will be allowed to, Jonathan. These men are devious. Why wait for a trial when they can have him removed any day they wish? No,' decided Christopher, 'my guess is that they had Sir Julius imprisoned in the Tower so that he would be at their mercy. Act swiftly, Henry,' he instructed. 'We simply must find out the truth about Maurice Farwell.'

'I thought that I might catch you, Maurice,' said Orlando Golland. 'You always dine here when parliament is in session.'

'I'm a creature of habit,' said Farwell.

'You are like me. Work comes before everything.'

'But I do like to eat well while I'm doing it.'

Maurice Farwell had just left the tavern in Westminster when Golland intercepted him. The lawyer was itching to learn more about the rumour that his sister had passed on to him.

'I can guess why you came, Orlando,' said Farwell, tolerantly.

'Dorothy gave me the most remarkable tidings.'

'She had them from my wife, I believe.'

'Is it true? Sir Julius has been arrested?'

'Arrested and clapped into the Tower. He challenged Cuthbert to a duel and committed a crime in doing so by seeking the life of a Privy Councillor.'

'I had a feeling that might be the offence.'

'It all arose out of a scene in one of Cuthbert's plays,' said

Farwell, blandly. 'You may have seen mention of the performance in the newspaper. Sir Julius was attacked with unabated savagery, I hear, and several Members were there to witness the wicked satire. When they reported what they had seen to the rest of us, we could not help laughing at Sir Julius Seize-Her – his name in the play, apparently – as he entered the chamber. The whole place was consumed with mirth.'

'That must have made him smoulder.'

'He turned bright red and stormed out of the House.'

'I can picture it well, Maurice,' said Golland, 'and I have no pity for him. He's brought all his troubles upon himself.'

'This may be the last time he does that.'

'What does the law dictate?'

'A death penalty has been imposed in the past.'

'His Majesty could show leniency.'

'Yes,' said Farwell, 'he could, and I hope, for my part, that he does. We need one or two politicians like Sir Julius Cheever. His chances, however, are not good.'

'He has too many enemies on the Privy Council.'

'When all is said and done, Orlando, we hold the major offices of state. We advise His Majesty and we make all the decisions affecting the people of this country. To threaten one of us is a rash thing to do,' he said. 'To challenge a Privy Councillor to a duel and thereby seek his life is even more impulsive. In pleading for clemency, I suspect that I may well be a lone voice.'

'If he came up in front of me, I'd pronounce him guilty.'

'Is that a judicial or a personal opinion?'

'I never let my personal opinions influence me,' said Golland, pompously. 'I assess each case on its merits then make an objective judgement. In this instance – though I would have to study the relevant statute beforehand, naturally – the outcome is unavoidable. Sir Julius was bent on taking the life of Cuthbert, Earl of Stoneleigh.'

'He was provoked, Orlando.'

'He should not have yielded to provocation.'

'Sir Julius is hot-blooded,' said Farwell. 'You must make some allowance for that.'

'None at all,' said Golland, dogmatically. 'A man should learn to control himself at all times. It's what I do. I never lose my temper.'

'You must have solid ice in your veins. Unless one of your horses is running in a race, of course. Then you can actually show passion. Disciplined passion, Orlando.'

'As you wish.'

Farwell touched Golland on the arm by way of a farewell. 'It's good to talk to you, Orlando, but I must get back. We have a committee meeting in half-an-hour. By the way,' he said, casually, 'how is Dorothy? This news must have shaken her.'

'It did. In time, she'll come to perceive that it was good news for her. At the moment, however, she still has emotional ties to Sir Julius. For that reason, Dorothy is suffering.'

'Your sister was always soft-hearted.'

'It's a weakness I've pointed out on many occasions.'

'An attractive weakness,' said Farwell with affection. 'I've not seen Dorothy for ages, not since our visit to Newmarket, in fact. You and she must call on us some time.'

'Thank you, Maurice. We'll take up that invitation. When this whole business is settled.'

'Yes, it might be sensible to wait.'

'The fate of Sir Julius Cheever weighs down on her. Until he is dispatched, Dorothy will pine for him. She is not good company at the moment. It would be wrong of me to inflict her upon you.'

'Pass on my warmest regards.'

'I will, Maurice.'

'And assure her that at least one member of the Privy Council will be speaking up for her friend. Sir Julius can count on my vote.'

It was Jacob who saw him first. Old as he was, his eyes remained sharp and his instincts keen. Since his income was more regular now, Christopher also employed a youth to do all the menial chores but it was Jacob who still ran the house and watched over his master with paternal care. He raised the alarm at once.

'There's someone outside, Mr Redmayne,' he said.

'There are hundreds of people outside, Jacob. Fetter Lane is always busy. People come and go all day.'

'But they do not stand still in the same place.'

'What do you mean?' asked Christopher.

'I noticed him when I showed your brother in, and again when I showed him out. He was still there when Mr Bale left.'

'So?'

'He's keeping the house under surveillance.'

'Surely not.'

'See for yourself, Mr Redmayne,' advised the servant.

Christopher went over to the front window and, standing well back so that he would not be observed from the street, he peered out. Two coaches were passing in opposite directions to obscure his view. When they had vanished, he saw a figure lurking in a doorway that was diagonally opposite. The man was pretending to show no particular interest in Christopher's house but, every so often, he tossed it a look. Jacob stood at his master's shoulder.

'Well, sir?'

'As always, Jacob, you are right.'

'Would you like me to scare him away?' offered the other.

'No,' said Christopher. 'I want to know who he is and why he's there. Jonathan warned me that this might happen.'

'What, sir?'

'Never you mind.'

Christopher did not want to alarm Jacob. If he confided his fears, the old man would worry. He hated the thought that his master could be in any danger. Christopher welcomed the appearance of the stranger. If someone was concerned about the way that the murder investigation was going, it showed how much he and Bale had achieved. Since he was taking the leading role, Christopher was almost more likely to be a target. He recalled what Bale had said about Erasmus Howlett. The brewer had taken an unduly close interest in the architect. The man outside might well be the result.

'Fetch my hat, Jacob,' he said. 'I think that I'll take a stroll.'

'When that fellow is still watching the house?'

'He'll lose interest in that when he sees me.'

'That's what I'm afraid of, sir. Let me come with you.'

'There's no need.'

'I could ensure your safety,' said Jacob.

'You'd also frighten the man away,' said Christopher. 'If I'm on my own, he may follow me. With you at my side, he'll be more circumspect and I'll never get to know his business.'

While Jacob went for his hat, he strapped on his sword belt and slipped his dagger into its sheath. He took another look at the man who was keeping a vigil outside. Wearing nondescript clothes, he was a relatively short individual of stocky build. He wore a dark beard so Christopher could see little of his face beneath the hat. At that distance, it was difficult to put an age on him. Christopher could see that he wore a dagger but there was no sign of a musket or pistol.

'Goodbye, Jacob,' he said. 'I'll not be long.'

'Take care, sir.'

'I always do.'

Opening the front door, Christopher stepped out and walked towards High Holborn. He did not look in the direction of the man as he passed and gave no indication that he knew he was being followed. He turned the corner and joined the many pedestrians heading east towards Shoe Lane. Strolling along, he sensed that his shadow was not far behind him. He felt safe. An attack was unlikely in such a crowded thoroughfare. To tempt him to make his move, Christopher had to go somewhere more private.

He soon saw his opportunity. An alleyway zigzagged off to the left, too narrow for coaches, too dark and uninviting for most passers-by. Crossing the road, Christopher turned into the alleyway and lengthened his stride. He was going around the first bend when he heard footsteps scurrying behind him. The ruse had worked. Following the next twist in the lane, he stopped abruptly and flattened himself against the wall. Hurried footsteps now broke into a run.

Sword drawn, Christopher was ready for him. As the man came running around the bend, the architect stuck out a leg and tripped him up, sending him headfirst into the accumulated refuse on the ground. The man let out a roar of anger and tried to reach for the dagger that had been dashed from his grasp as he hit the hard stone. Christopher's foot jabbed down on his wrist and he used his sword to flick the dagger out of reach. The point of his weapon also deprived the fallen man of his hat so that he could have a proper look at him. When his would-be attacker attempted to get up, Christopher held his sword at the man's throat.

'Who sent you?' he demanded.

'Nobody, sir,' replied the man, feigning innocence.

'Then why were you watching my house?'

'What house?'

'You were hired to kill me,' said Christopher, pricking his neck so that blood trickled down. 'I've every right to kill you in self-defence and that's exactly what I will do if I do not get honest answers.'

'I'm a thief,' pleaded the other. 'I was only after your purse.'

'Yes – when you'd slit my throat. Were you the villain who murdered Dan Crothers?' The man started guiltily. 'Yes, I thought that you might be. So you have two crimes to answer at least.'

Close to desperation, the man began to burble excuses. His eyes darted everywhere. He was about Christopher's own age with a craggy face and long curly hair. Seeing that there was no escape, he appeared to give in. His head hung in shame.

'I do confess it, sir. I did cut the meat porter's throat.'

'Who paid you?'

'A certain lord, sir. He did not give his name.'

'I think he did,' said Christopher, 'but you are obviously not going to give it to me. I'll take you somewhere where you can be interrogated by people who know how to get the truth out of criminals.' The man glanced downwards. 'Leave the dagger here.'

'All I want is my hat, sir,' said the other. 'May I?'

Christopher relented. Standing back, he allowed him to stoop down to retrieve his hat. Instead of putting it on his head, however, the man put his hand around the crown and squeezed it tight so that he could grab Christopher's blade without risking injury. At the same time, he leapt up and swung a vicious kick at his groin. Had it connected, Christopher would have been badly hurt but he managed to jump back in time. It was all the leeway that his prisoner needed. Leaving go of the sword, he dropped the hat to the ground and sprinted off down the alleyway. Christopher went after him but he soon abandoned the pursuit. The man had outrun him.

'How did you find him, Susan?' asked her sister.

'Very low.'

'Did you apologise on my behalf?'

'Lancelot did that,' said Susan. 'Father understood. He was very embarrassed that we should see him in such a condition. To have you there would only have added to his grief.'

'What did he say? How can we help him?'

When they returned from their visit to the Tower, Susan and her brother-in-law were disconsolate. Brilliana was desperate for hopeful news but there was none to give her.

'Under the circumstances,' said Serle, 'your father is bearing up remarkably well but, then, Sir Julius has always been resilient.'

'Were you able to offer him any succour?' said his wife.

'Very little beyond a promise to engage a shrewd lawyer to plead his case. His defence will be that was deliberately incited by that lampoon. The Earl of Stoneleigh tricked him into it.'

'Why?'

'Father is a stern critic of all that he stands for,' said Susan. 'The earl is in the Upper House but he has a large following in the Commons. They would all be happy to intrigue against Father.'

'That's outrageous!' said Brilliana.

'That's political life, my dear,' her husband pointed out.

'Then I'm not at all sure that you should enter it, Lancelot. You have too much integrity for such a world. I could not bear the thought that you would be a party to such conspiracies.'

'Treachery is foreign to my character.'

'Then you are too good for parliament.'

'I disagree,' said Susan. 'Goodness is exactly what the place needs. That's why Father was such a breath of fresh air in the chamber and why others flocked to him. He was seen as a good man.'

'And reviled by the bad ones.'

'They hold the reins of power, Brilliana, and some of them have been determined to bring Father down. They finally succeeded.'

'Yes, Susan.'

'Do not admit defeat yet,' said Serle, firmly. 'If the plot is fully uncovered, Sir Julius will have to be set free. Christopher will be working hard to effect that.'

'Yet it was he who acted as a second at the duel,' recalled Susan, bitterly. 'He took part in the event that landed Father in the Tower. And he was not the only member of his family to do so.'

'What do you mean?' asked Brilliana.

'Sir Julius could not be certain,' said Serle, 'but he had a strong impression that one of the earl's seconds at the duel was none other than Henry Redmayne. I find that astonishing. The man who came here to warn your father about that disgraceful play then turns up to assist its author. It's beyond belief.'

Brilliana was simmering. 'It's a betrayal,' she said, mind racing. 'A vile and unforgivable betrayal.'

After his confrontation with the man sent to kill him, Christopher went back to Fetter Lane to collect his horse, then he rode to Addle Hill to see Jonathan Bale. The constable was alarmed by the report.

'You took too great a risk, Mr Redmayne,' he said.

'I was determined to find out who he was.'

'Yes, but he may not have been acting alone. Granted, he kept watch on your house. But, for all you knew, he might have had a confederate loitering nearby. Two attackers would have given you much more of a problem.'

'I agree,' said Christopher. 'I could not even hold on to one.'

'You disarmed him, that was the main thing.'

'Could we trace the owner of the dagger somehow?'

They were in the kitchen of Bale's house and the constable was holding the weapon that Christopher had recovered from the alleyway. It was a long-bladed dagger with a carved handle.

'There's nothing distinctive about this, sir,' said Bale. 'I've seen a dozen that are identical.'

'Not quite, Jonathan. In one respect, that dagger is unique.'

'Unique?'

'It slit the throat of Dan Crothers.'

'Did he confess that?'

'Loud and clear.'

'And he intended to do the same to you.'

'I did not give him the opportunity,' said Christopher. 'Is it worth trying to find out where that dagger was made and sold?'

Bale returned it to him. 'It would take far too long,' he said, 'and we might never get the name that we seek. The weapon could have been stolen, or passed on to him by someone else. No, the dagger will not help us, alas. It's a pity he left no other clue behind.'

'But he did.'

'And what was that?'

'His hat,' explained Christopher. 'I'd hoped the dagger might help us but maybe the hat will do so instead. Perhaps we can find out who made it and to whom it was sold. A dagger is the same size for everyone but a hat has to fit an individual head. It's outside, in my saddlebag.'

'Then let me see it,' said Bale.

The horse was tethered to a post near the house and someone was stroking its flank. It was Patrick McCoy and he stood to attention as the two men came out of the house. There was still bruising on his face but the black eye was now a faint yellowish colour.

'I'd still like to help you, Mr Bale,' he volunteered.

'You did your share earlier on, Patrick.'

'I enjoyed being a constable.'

'Even though you were beaten as a result?' said Bale.

'He took me unawares.'

While the two of them were talking, Christopher extracted the crumpled hat from his saddlebag and straightened it out. It was wide-brimmed and high-crowned. It had a black hatband around it. Before giving it to Bale, he tried to remove some of the filth it had acquired in the alleyway.

'What's that?' asked Patrick, fascinated.

'It might be a clue,' said Bale.

'How do you know?'

'Here you are, Jonathan,' said Christopher, handing it over. 'I'm sorry about the dirty marks and the creases. It was twisted out of shape when he grabbed my sword.'

Bale examined the hat, turning it over so that he could look inside it. Then he did something that had never even occurred to Christopher. He held it to his nose and sniffed it.

'What are you doing, Mr Bale?' said Patrick.

'Trying to find out where someone worked,' said Bale with a grin of pleasure. 'In this case, it's quite easy.'

'Why?'

'Because that smell clings to your clothes, your face and, most of all, to your hair. I had some of it on myself after I'd been there.'

'Where?' asked Christopher.

'The brewery,' said Bale. 'This hat stinks of it. I suspect the man who tried to kill you is employed by Erasmus Howlett.'

After the exigencies of the morning, Henry Redmayne felt the need to return home to change out of the dull apparel he had worn to the duel into something more ostentatious. He felt restored. When he glanced out of the window of his bedchamber, he saw a coach draw up outside his house and he was thrilled when its passenger turned out to be none other than Brilliana Serle. Completing his joy was the fact that she seemed to be alone. He grabbed his periwig, thrust it upon his head, spent only seconds in front of a mirror to adjust it then fled down the stairs so that he could open the front door himself.

His prayers had been answered. Instead of rebuffing him, as he had feared, Brilliana had simply waited until a more suitable time to declare her love. When a beautiful woman came alone to the house of a man who adored her, it could have only one meaning. He flung the door wide then spread his arms in a welcome.

'I need to speak to you, Mr Redmayne,' she said, calmly.

'Then step inside, Mrs Serle.'

'Thank you.'

He stood aside so that she could pass and was rewarded with another whiff of her exquisite perfume. Closing the front door, he led her into the parlour and indicated a seat.

'I prefer to stand,' said Brilliana.

'As you wish, dear heart.'

'Are you an honest man, Mr Redmayne?'

'I am renowned for my truthfulness.'

'Then I expect an honest reply from you. Did you or did you not act a second to the Earl of Stoneleigh this morning?'

'Ah,' said Henry, sensing from her tone that the wrong answer could ruin all his hopes. 'I was forced into a situation that was not of my own choosing.'

'One word is all I require – yes or no?'

'My brother needed intelligence about Cuthbert – about the earl, that is – and the only way that I could obtain it was by posing as a friend of his. Indirectly, it was in your father's interests.'

'Yes or no?' demanded Brilliana.

'A qualified yes.'

'You viper, sir!'

'But I was trying to help Sir Julius.'

'By assisting a man who had him consigned to the Tower? I fail to see how that helps my father. You were part of the conspiracy against him and I despise you for it.'

'Do not say that!' he implored.

'When you came to our house, you deceived us all.'

'I would never deceive you, Brilliana.'

'Under the guise of supporting Father, you tried to practise your wiles upon me. That was shameless enough. Even more shameless was the way that you told Father about a play you professed to loathe when you are a good friend of the villain who wrote it.'

'Cuthbert did write the play,' he told her, 'but someone else inserted the scene in which Sir Julius was mocked.'

'That does not matter now. The fact is that you were complicit in the whole plot. You sniggered at my father in the theatre then claimed to be appalled at what you saw. And, even though you knew that he would have been roundly abused in the House of Commons as a result of the play, you did not have the grace to confide in Susan or myself. You are a fiend, Mr Redmayne.'

'But I love you!'

'A cruel, uncaring, unprincipled, odious fiend.'

'Brilliana!'

'Do not dare to speak my name, sir. I spurn you.'

'Could we not discuss this more amicably over a glass of my finest wine?' he suggested, quivering with contrition.

'I'd sooner take poison than accept a drink from you.'

'You cannot mean that.'

'Be grateful that I came alone, Mr Redmayne,' she said with blistering anger. 'And be thankful that I am but a woman.'

'A princess among women!'

'Were I a man, I'd have challenged you to a duel and sent you to the grave that is your rightful home. Good day to you, sir. I'll not soil myself with your company any longer.' Henry followed her as she went out into the hall. Brilliana paused in front the painting of the Roman orgy. 'My husband was right. This is an abomination. I cannot believe that it amused me even for a second. It is like its owner,' she went on. 'Indecent, unchristian and utterly corrupt.'

Opening the front door, she sailed out with great dignity. Henry was distraught. His romance with her was unequivocally over.

They first called at his house in Aldermanbury Street but, when they learned that Erasmus Howlett was at work, they walked on to the brewery. Jonathan Bale had the privilege of bearing the warrant. Tom Warburton accompanied him and Bale had taken the precaution of recruiting two constables from Cripplegate ward as well. Since he also had Christopher Redmayne in support, he felt as if he had adequate numbers to apprehend the two men.

'Will you recognise him if you see him, sir?' asked Bale.

'Yes,' replied Christopher. 'With or without his hat.'

'Are you going to return it to him?'

'Of course – though I might think twice about his dagger.'

'Mr Howlett should give us no trouble. He does not have the look of a fighting man to me.'

'He pays others to fight and murder on his behalf.'

'Those days are over,' said Bale, happily, 'and so is his ambition to be Lord Mayor of the city.' Two drays, loaded with full barrels, were driven past them. Bale took note. 'When they learn what Mr Howlett had been involved in, a lot of taverns may choose to buy their beer elsewhere.'

'I suspect that the Saracen's Head will be among them.'

They reached the brewery and went in. Christopher reacted to the insidious aroma. He could understand how it would penetrate the clothes and hair of anyone who worked in it, and why Bale had been able to identify it so easily. It made Christopher grimace. Having seen them from his office, Erasmus Howlett came down the steps to meet them. He seemed unperturbed by the appearance of four constables. When Christopher was introduced, however, a ripple of alarm went across the brewer's face. Bale took out the list of ingredients that Howlett had given him earlier. He held it out.

'We came about this, sir,' he said.

'A complaint about my beer?' Howlett gave a nervous laugh. 'I've never had that before.'

'It's not the beer we complain about,' said Christopher, taking a piece of paper from his pocket. 'It's the handwriting.' He thrust the paper under Howlett's nose. 'It matches *this* exactly.'

'I never wrote that!' exclaimed the other.

'Yes, you did. They were your instructions to Dan Crothers and they sent him off on a murderous mission. When he failed to kill Sir Julius Cheever, you had his throat cut in Old Street.' Christopher took out the dagger he had taken from his attacker. 'We even have the weapon that committed the crime. It belongs to one of your men, Mr Howlett. Perhaps you'd be kind enough to point him out.'

'I've no idea what you are talking about, Mr Redmayne,' said Howlett, indignantly. 'You are trespassing on my property and I must ask you to leave at once.'

'We will, sir,' said Bale. 'When I've served you with this warrant for your arrest. First, however, oblige Mr Redmayne, if you will.'

'Pick out the man you sent to kill me today,' said Christopher, taking out his sword. 'I'd like to renew my acquaintance with him.'

Howlett gave up all pretence of innocence. He knew that he was trapped but his accomplice might yet escape. Cupping his hands to his mouth, he yelled at the top of his voice.

'Run, Sam!' he called. 'Get away while you can!'

A figure emerged from behind one of the huge vats and raced off through the brewery. Seeing that it was his attacker, Christopher went after him, dodging round the various people and obstacles in his way. As before, the man had too much of a start and a far greater knowledge of the geography of the place. After leading his pursuer on a circuitous route, he darted through a door at the rear of the building and slammed it shut behind him. Christopher feared that he had lost him for the second time. When he opened the door, however, he had a most pleasant surprise.

The man he had chased was lying flat on his back with blood gushing from his nose. Standing over him with a grin of triumph was Patrick McCoy.

'I knew you'd come to the brewery, sir,' he said. 'I waited here because I thought someone might try to escape through the back.' He grabbed the fallen man by the collar and lifted him without effort to his feet. 'Here he is, sir. I just wanted to help.'

Susan Cheever was both disturbed and impressed with what her sister had done. When she came back to the house, Brilliana was glowing with satisfaction. Her husband was aghast but Susan had a grudging admiration.

'You scolded Henry to his face?' she said.

'I told him exactly what I thought of him, Susan.'

'Why did you not tell me you were going there?' asked Serle. 'The very least I could have done was to accompany you.'

'It was something I needed to do alone, Lancelot, and it was all the more effective as a result. I accused him of betraying our family in the most atrocious way and told him how much I despised him.'

'That will have curbed his amorous intentions,' said Susan under her breath. She spoke up. 'What did Henry say?'

'I gave him no chance to say anything.'

'Not even an apology?'

'What use is an apology that was bound to be insincere?'

'The strange thing is that you liked him at first, Brilliana.'

'I did,' said her sister. 'I was taken in by his dazzling manner. Then I learned the truth. Henry Redmayne is like that painting he has hanging in his hall – arresting at first sight but, when you look more closely, ineffably sordid.'

'Oh, I'm so glad that you say that, my dear,' said Serle. 'You have described him perfectly. There's a lesson in this for you, Susan. Having seen how both brothers have let us down, I hope you'll no longer seek a closer relationship with the Redmayne family.'

'I'll oppose it with every fibre of my being,' affirmed Brilliana.

'It's highly unlikely that there is anything to oppose,' said Susan with regret. 'Christopher and I have drifted apart. However,' she continued, remembering his vow to her, 'we must not lose all our faith in him. Nobody will try harder to save Father's life.'

'What can he possibly do?'

'You'll be able to ask him,' said Serle, looking through the window as a horseman approached the house. 'Unless my eyesight deceives me, Christopher is outside.'

Susan rushed to the window. 'Where?' She saw him dismount. 'Yes, that's him. He must have news.'

She went into the hall and opened the front door to greet him. Susan was unable to disguise her pleasure in seeing him again.

When she brought him into the parlour, Christopher was smiling.

'I don't know what *you* have to smile about,' said Brilliana, tartly. 'As far as I'm concerned, you are little better than your snake of a brother.'

'I'm sorry you think that, Mrs Serle,' he said. 'I've just come from Henry. You were too severe on him. He deserves rebuke, of course, and I've administered it in full. At the same time, he has earned praise. But for the information he supplied about the certain political figures, we would have made little progress. Only today, he has performed another valuable service.'

'Acting as second to the Earl of Stoneleigh.'

'Discovering that the earl did not write that lampoon of your father at all. It was the work of Maurice Farwell, a Member of Parliament with his own reasons for disparaging Sir Julius. But I run before myself,' he said, indicating that they should all sit. 'I've much to tell you, beginning with the arrest of two men. One helped to devise the plot against your father, the other attempted to murder me.'

'When?' cried Susan.

'I'll explain.'

When they were all seated, Christopher gave them a brisk account of events, taking care to point out that his brother had actually been helpful to them. They were delighted to hear that a warrant had be issued for the arrest of the Earl of Stoneleigh and wondered why Maurice Farwell had not been taken into custody as well. Christopher took out one of the letters found on Crothers's body.

'I was certain that he had written this,' he said, 'and my brother managed to get hold of an example of his hand this very day.' He looked at Brilliana. 'Another reason to moderate your censure of him, Mrs Serle.'

'Does the calligraphy match?' said Susan.

'Unhappily, it does not.'

'So who *did* send the information about Father's attendance at the funeral? Somebody must have done so, Christopher.'

'They did, and I have a vague suspicion of who it might be. In order to secure confirmation, I must ask you a favour.'

'What can I do?' said Susan.

'Give me permission to search your father's study. That's where I'll find the evidence we need. May I?'

'No, you may not,' returned Brilliana. 'It would be a flagrant breach of Father's privacy. He would never allow it.'

'If he knew that it might save his life, I believe that he would.'

'So do I,' agreed Susan. 'I'll show you where it is.'

Brilliana rose to her feet. 'I object strongly.'

'Then you are overruled, my dear,' said Serle, restraining her with a hand. 'Susan and I are both ready to authorise a search. You may proceed, Mr Redmayne.'

'Thank you,' said Christopher.

He went out with Susan, ascending the stairs beside her. Much of her old warmth towards him had returned, and he had been touched by her response to the news that his own life had been threatened. She had been able to see the risks he was prepared to take on her father's behalf. The study was unlocked but she rarely went into it. It was the secret domain of Sir Julius Cheever and she looked at it through Christopher's eyes, as if for the first time. It was scrupulously tidy and lined with books that were neatly stacked on their shelves. On the desk were neat piles of correspondence and notes for various speeches that he had given in parliament.

Christopher sifted through the letters but found none that caught his eye. A thorough search of the drawers of the desk also failed to yield up the confirmation that he sought. What he did unearth – carefully hidden at the back of one drawer – was a copy of the *Observations of the Growth of Popery and Arbitrary Government in England*. Flicking through it, he saw that both Maurice Farwell and the Earl of Stoneleigh were mentioned by name several times. Their influence over the Privy Council was deplored.

'What exactly are you looking for?' said Susan.

'I'll tell you when I find it.'

'But we've looked everywhere.'

'Not quite,' he said, scanning the bookshelves carefully. One title aroused his curiosity. 'I'd not have taken Sir Julius as a lover of poetry. I know that he has a great respect for Mr Milton but I've never heard him speak with enthusiasm about any other poet.'

'Neither have I, Christopher.'

'Then why does he have a copy of Shakespeare's Sonnets?'

He reached up to take it from the shelf and felt a thrill of discovery when he saw that something was pressed between the pages. Opening the book, he extracted a short letter, written in a graceful hand on expensive stationery. Holding it one hand, he took out the letter he had brought with him. Every detail matched.

Susan was wounded. 'Mrs Kitson!'

'Where else would he hide a letter from her but in book of love poetry? It's as I suspected, Susan. On our way back from Cambridge, your father told me that he had dashed off a note to Mrs Kitson before he left London, so she would have known his movements. I never for a moment had any doubts about her,' admitted Christopher, 'but this evidence is conclusive. She probably sent this note to Maurice Farwell and he passed it on at once to Crothers. It's the only way that it could have happened.'

'But she adored Father. She told us so.'

'She was used to win his confidence. Sir Julius would have told her about his visit to Knightrider Street, and that seemed like the ideal opportunity to strike.'

'He loved her. He even thought of marrying her.'

'Dorothy Kitson would never have let it reach that stage.'

'Father will be heartbroken when he finds out.'

'This letter gave him intense pleasure when he received it,' surmised Christopher. 'That's why he treasured it so.'

'He will wish it was never sent now,' she said.

'No, Susan. He will be glad. It was written to deceive him, to let him think that he was loved. When she sent this, Mrs Kitson could not have realised that she was doing him a favour.'

'That was no favour – it was a piece of cunning.'

'But it's worked to our advantage.'

'How?'

'What we have here,' he said, waving the cherished letter in front of her, 'is the key to your father's cell in the Tower.'

Maurice Farwell poured wine into both Venetian glasses then handed one of them to Dorothy Kitson. Caught up in a mood of celebration, they were alone in the parlour of her house. They clinked their glasses gently before sampling the wine.

'Excellent!' he said, licking his lips. 'But, then, everything in this house in an example of excellence – beginning with you, my love.'

'Will you be able to stay the night?'

'Of course. On such a day as this, I'd never desert you.'

'What about Adele?'

'I've told her that I'm staying in London.'

'Strictly speaking, that's quite true,' she said. 'What she does not know – and must never find out – is that you always spend the night with me when here.'

'Who would be the more surprised if they learned the truth?' said Farwell, sitting beside her. 'My wife or your brother?'

'Oh, it would be Orlando without a doubt.'

'Does he think you lead a life of celibacy?'

'My brother thinks that widowhood is a form of virginity,' she said. 'When my first husband died, he could not believe that I should want to take another.'

'And now you have a third husband.'

'Albeit married to another wife. I prefer it that way.'

'Pleasure without responsibility. A love that remains fresh because we spend so much time apart.' He lifted his glass. 'To Sir Julius Cheever for making this evening possible!'

'Sir Julius!'

They clinked their glasses again. The doorbell rang.

'That's not Orlando, I hope?'

'If it is, he'll be sent away,' she said, easily. 'Anyone who calls will be told that I'm not at home. Nothing is going to interrupt this moment, Maurice. We have earned it.'

She leaned forward to kiss him on the lips. They soon sprang apart. Raised voices could be heard in the hall then the door of the parlour was flung open. Christopher Redmayne entered with Jonathan Bale at his heels. Farwell jumped to his feet.

'What's the meaning of this?' he demanded.

'We have a warrant for your arrest, sir,' said Bale, holding it up.

'How dare you burst in here!' exclaimed Dorothy, taking a step towards them. 'Remove yourself at once, do you hear me? Mr Farwell is a guest of mine. I'll not have him insulted under my roof.'

'I'm afraid that we'll have to insult you as well, Mrs Kitson,' said Christopher, 'because there is a second warrant in your name. And before we go any further, you should know that Erasmus Howlett is in custody with a man called Samuel Greene whom he paid to commit murder on your behalf.'

'Those names are unknown to me,' she said.

'And to me,' added Farwell, maintaining his composure.

'I'm surprised that you do not know Mr Howlett, sir,' said Bale. 'He's a brewer and cousin to the Earl of Stoneleigh. I had the honour of arresting the earl as well.'

Farwell shrugged. 'We have no connection with him.'

'Then why did he include a scene that you wrote in his play, *The Royal Favourite*? Mr Howlett attended the performance. You may well have seen him there.'

Dorothy glowered. 'You must be Christopher Redmayne.'

'The very same,' he said, politely. 'I'm a friend of Sir Julius Cheever and I dislike the way that you have maltreated him. Here is a letter you once sent him, Mrs Kitson,' he went on, taking it from his pocket. 'The handwriting is identical to that in a note that we found on the corpse of Dan Crothers, another hired assassin.'

She clenched her teeth and turned to look at Farwell.

'They are bluffing, Dorothy,' he said. 'They know nothing.'

'You must come with us, sir,' said Bale.

'Of course, officer.' He offered his arm to Dorothy. 'We'll come together gladly. My lawyer will soon sort out this horrific mistake.'

'The mistakes were all made by you, Mr Farwell.'

'We shall see. Let's go with these gentlemen, Dorothy.'

'If you wish,' she said, visibly unnerved.

He squeezed her arm. 'Do not lose heart. Trust me.'

Walking past the visitors, he took her out of the room. As soon as they entered the hall, however, Farwell released her and rushed across to the suit of armour that stood in an alcove. He grabbed one of the two swords that hung on the wall beside the armour then he turned to confront the two men.

'Do not be foolish, sir,' advised Bale, holding up a hand. 'There's no escape. We have other officers outside.'

'Then we will have to leave by another means – without you.'

Holding the heavy sword in both hands, he swung it at Bale who stepped quickly back out of reach. The hall was large but it suddenly seemed very small to Bale, Dorothy and the watching servant. It was no place for a duel. Christopher had drawn his own sword but his rapier was no match for the other weapon. As soon as the blades clashed, a shudder went up his arm. Farwell swung the sword again and Christopher ducked beneath it.

'Grab what you need and leave by the back door,' Farwell called to Dorothy, circling his opponent. 'Please hurry.'

She moved to the stairs but Bale got there first, seizing her by both arms and keeping her in front of him as a shield. Christopher tried to distract Farwell by thrusting at him but it was no time for the finer points of swordsmanship. Swishing his weapon in the air, Farwell brought it down so hard that it knocked the rapier from Christopher's grasp. Bale acted promptly, shoving Dorothy towards Farwell before he could strike again. It gave Christopher the moment he needed to snatch the other sword from the wall. They were now fighting on equal terms.

Sparks flew as the blades clashed but it was Farwell's arm that now trembled on impact. Time was against him. Christopher was younger, stronger and more agile. Farwell was bound to tire first. He therefore summoned up all of his remaining energy and hurled himself at his opponent, flailing away with his sword as if intending to hack him to pieces. Christopher ducked, dodged, prodded, parried and retreated. The sleeve of his coat was ripped apart but he sustained no injury. He knew that he was winning. As Farwell's attack weakened, Christopher was able to hit back, swinging the heavy sword at his adversary.

He backed him against a wall then feinted cleverly before thrusting his sword point at Farwell's arm. With a yell of pain, Maurice Farwell dropped his weapon to the floor with a clatter. He put his other hand up to the wound. Christopher relaxed. Pouring with sweat and panting from the effort he had made, he stepped away and lowered his sword. Farwell was not finished yet. Seizing the other weapon, he used it like a lance and hurled it hard at Christopher. It missed its target. Christopher stooped low, the sword shot over his head and it was Dorothy Kitson who was struck by its sharp point. Hit in the chest, she staggered back, uttered a cry of disbelief then collapsed on the marble floor with blood streaming down her dress. Maurice Farwell dropped his sword and darted across to hold her.

His resistance was over.

When he was released from the Tower of London, Sir Julius Cheever found that his younger daughter had come to take him home. Christopher Redmayne was with her but he left one piece of information to Susan. They were in the coach before she told her father about Dorothy Kitson's involvement in the conspiracy against him. He was pole-axed by the news and dazed even more when he heard of the accident with the sword.

'Will she live?' he asked.

'Yes,' said Christopher. 'A surgeon was able to save her though she may not thank him for doing so when she faces her trial. Maurice Farwell was inconsolable. He feared that he had killed her.'

'Dorothy and Maurice Farwell,' said Sir Julius, incredulously. 'I would never have linked their names together. I always thought that Farwell was happily married.'

'That was the impression he strove hard to give in public,' said Christopher. 'It acted as a screen for his private life.'

'But what could possibly have brought them together?'

'Religion, Sir Julius.'

'Roman Catholics?'

'Both of them were devout. Their faith was like their friendship – something deep and lasting that had to be kept secret. Though I doubt if any pope would have blessed their union.'

'They were sinners,' said Susan. 'Capable of any crime.'

'All this makes me feel very foolish,' confessed Sir Julius on the verge of tears. 'I was taken in completely. How ridiculous I must look now. Just think. I wanted that woman to be your stepmother, Susan.'

'Try to forget her, Father.'

'I can never do that.'

She gave him more details of the investigation that had finally led to his release, explaining the vital importance of the letter found in his book of sonnets, and stressing the crucial part that Christopher had played throughout.

'God bless you, Christopher,' said Sir Julius, taking his hand between both palms. 'I owe you everything. A thousand thanks.'

'Save some of those for Jonathan Bale,' said the other. 'It was his sensitive nose that led us to the brewery. Oh, and Patrick McCoy must not be forgotten either.'

'Who is he?'

'The landlady's son from the Saracen's Head. He helped to capture Samuel Greene, the man who was sent after me.'

'You should not have gone down that alleyway,' chided Susan.

'I had to tempt him somehow.'

'Not with your life, Christopher.'

She spoke with such love and concern that he knew she had forgiven him his earlier mistakes. Christopher was reminded that someone else deserved a degree of gratitude.

'My brother made his contribution,' he said. 'Henry not only educated me in the black arts of political life, he discovered that it was Maurice Farwell who penned that callous attack on you in the play, and who led the laughter when you entered parliament.'

'Brilliana scourged him unfairly,' observed Susan.

'I would not go that far. Henry did go astray at times. Your sister's harsh words were a sobering experience for him in a number of ways. But I must add one more thing in his favour,' Christopher told them. 'I needed an example of Farwell's hand to compare it with that in the letter sent about your visit to Cambridge. Within the hour, Henry had answered my plea.'

'How?'

'By going to the Navy Office. He reasoned that someone as important as a Privy Councillor must have had correspondence with the Surveyor at some time or another, so he went through the boxes of letters like a whirlwind.' He laughed. 'He not only found what he was after. Henry was so zealous at his task that his superior was very impressed. He actually commended my brother.'

'Then I shall do so as well,' said Sir Julius.

'Look for no commendation from Brilliana,' warned Susan.

'Henry will not seek it,' said Christopher. 'He's content simply to share in the joy of your father's escape, and in the arrest of those who plotted against him.'

'But why? That's what I never understood. Why did they conspire against him like that?'

'I had to be silenced,' said Sir Julius. 'My voice was getting too loud in the Parliament House.'

'That was not the reason, Sir Julius.'

'What else?'

'They thought you were the author of that pamphlet that created such a scandal. It attacked popery and unfettered power. When we discovered that copy in your study, I was convinced that you had actually written it. Is that correct, Sir Julius?'

'Unfortunately, it's not,' replied the other. 'I'd have been proud to claim it as my work because I shared so many of its sentiments. But I've neither the wit nor the scholarship to produce something like that.' He smiled at Christopher. 'Since you have fought so bravely on my behalf, you deserve to know the truth.'

'Lewis Bircroft? Was he the author?'

'No – and neither was Arthur Manville.'

'Then who was, Sir Julius?'

'Bernard Everett.'

Christopher gaped. 'Are you sure?'

'He let me read it before it went to the printer.'

'But do you see what this means?'

'I think so,' said Sir Julius.

'Well, I do not,' said Susan. 'What is its significance?'

'A man was sent to shoot your father in Knightrider Street,' said Christopher, 'because it was supposed that he was the author of the pamphlet. It was Mrs Kitson who discovered that Sir Julius would be there that day and Erasmus Howlett who put an assassin in position at the Saracen's Head.'

'Then Mr Everett was killed by mistake.'

'But it was *not* a mistake,' said Sir Julius.

'We know that now,' Christopher said, 'but they did not. How ironic! In hindsight, all the efforts they took to kill Sir Julius were quite unnecessary. Without realising it, they had already killed the right man.'